# THRUST

TO: Rhonda

Ken Champion

13-11-'17

# THRUST

## KEN CHAMPION

*First published October 2017*

ISBN  978-0-244-62099-8

PENNILESS PRESS PUBLICATIONS
Website :www.pennilesspress.co.uk/books

For
Toby, Tim, Steve.

*Also by the same author:*

*Fiction*

Urban Narratives
Keefie
Noir
The Dramaturgical Metaphor
The Beat Years

*Poetry*

But Black & White is better
Cameo Metro
African Time
Cameo Poly

*Urban Narratives*

'I thank him for gracing us with his literature. His realism is enriched with imagination, the most real of all qualities.'

*Meredith Sue Willis, Hamilton Stone Review (2014)*

*The Dramaturgical Metaphor*

'An existential thriller which sees psychoanalyst James Kent embark on a disturbing European journey, capturing a sense of time and place that transport us to his host locations whilst also slightly dislocating our commonsensical assumptions. Think Jean Paul Sartre reimagining Alastair Maclean.'

*Chris Connelley, Hastings Independent (2014)*

*The Beat Years*
'I found some beautiful writing here.'

*Susie Reynolds, Chimera (2015)*

*Noir*

'This is probably Ken Champion's best novel to date, a book of great depth, tightly written and with a surprise - and so much life - on almost every page. It's an unusual, gripping book.'

*Meredith Sue Willis, Hamilton Stone Review, USA (2016)*

'These are vast, topical themes, edging Champion closer to explicitly political discussion than in any of his previous work, ensuring NOIR enjoys deep currency in a year that has seen alienation and anger on the part of disconnected publics generate upset on both the domestic and international stage. NOIR is very much of its time, combining social realism with a dreamlike intensity as a man out of his depth tries to make sense of a world out of control.''

*Chris Connelley, Hastings Independent (2016)*

*Keefie*

'This is a splendid novel of the London Blitz that captures life mostly through the eyes of a bright and creative working class boy whose knowledge of what is happening is limited, but whose experience leads us deep into a time and place – and the lives of ordinary people – with more power than any history book can convey.'

*Meredith Sue Willis, Hamilton Stone Review, USA (2015)*

'I really enjoyed Ken Champion's latest novel and am still thinking about its characters. Cultural influences, particularly cinematic scenes, are used imaginatively as themes, while class divisions, diversity, and the use of language are sharply observed. Acute insights into the demands and freedom of city life and of academia further make this novel an absorbing read. This is a writer who pays intense attention to the extraordinary details of ordinary life.'

*Joanna Ezekiel (2016)*

# CHAPTER 1

He was rolling a ceiling in vinyl silk - one of the older painters kidding him that it was cheating because he wasn't using a six-inch brush - musing on how the roller's invention seventy five years ago, taking thirty years to reach this country, had, like the invention of emulsion, deskilled the trade. He could almost hear his old tradesman uncle telling him that 'a granmuvver could put it on wiv a toofbrush.'

Aware that a matt finish would be better, he knew through experience that architects weren't very good at choosing paint finishes. He didn't think they were much good at designing modern buildings either.

He'd briefly met an architect who'd had something to do with this building, a tight-suited hipster with a clipboard, pen and an app-laden phone who had probably designed the toilets. He hadn't known the difference between water-based paint and enamel, nor, Liam Brett suspected, between Art Deco and Algerian wine.

Breaking away from artisanship a few years ago to do a degree in political science but not knowing what to do with it and perhaps preferring the devil you know, he had gone back 'on the brush' - or in the present case, the roller - thus returning to the trade in which he'd been apprenticed, mostly to help out an old friend and then working for himself.

He had, soon after graduating, given teaching a brief try having been invited to take seminars for a term in an annexe of a local poly-soon-to-be-university. He had done it merely to see if he was interested enough in teaching to do it as a job. He'd realised he wasn't.

It had been his old junior school. Sitting in the main hall and looking up at the oriole window of the headmaster's office was a disquieting experience, as had been the voices of schoolboy friends and foes he thought he could hear swirling around the staircases when, as an ineffectual monitor and telling the noise-makers to be quiet, he'd be answered with, 'You ain't nuffin,' geez.' ''ere, 'e's tryin' to tell us wot to do.' 'Teacher's pet, an' 'e.' Looking out of a first floor window, he thought he could see the girls doing handstands against the carpentry shop wall, skirts falling over their faces and knowingly showing their knickers.

He'd been working with and taking charge of a small gang of sub-contracting painters and second-fixing chippies for just three days, previously working at the Swedish Embassy pick-ing out in various colours the details of swags and embossed figures on its staircase. Regretting a refused opportunity to go to an Art College when young, he'd signed up to a well-known builders in the City hoping it could bring out his natural skills and offer the satisfaction of an occasional artistic complete-ness. It had rarely happened.

The building he was in now was rather different. It was a concrete-faced construction of exaggerated, fake perspective with windows at angles dictated by impossible vanishing points. It could well have been the result of the architect going to lunch and leaving his computer on.

He'd seen it first when leaving a Tube station and had stopped onto the pavement, feeling annoyance at this gim-micky, pretentious structure. It was still being completed. A little later, by coincidence, he was asked to work on it; he hadn't wanted to but couldn't afford to turn the job down.

He looked at the windows running at an obtuse angle to-wards the floor and doubted if he could ever get used to the misguided discordance of his surroundings. He'd had a little fun, though, with the site agent, the role recently being substi-tuted by 'project manager.'

There were quite a few extras he'd had to do that hadn't been allowed for in the original estimate and which he'd put on a daywork sheet. This particular agent, being of mediocre intelligence and surrounded by the smell of alcohol wherever in the building he was, would, Liam thought, have signed for anything and had had a bet with one of his gang to that effect. He included items such as 'Paint two coats on sixth floor radiators installed after job was priced: 3 hours,' and 'Make good and repaint north wall of sixth floor after damage by other trades: 14 hours,' 'Egg, bacon and two slices: 7 hours.' It had duly been signed.

He wondered what architects were taught in their initial training. His own simplistic, but he thought significant maxim, was, 'If in doubt go back to the Victorian terrace, the square, or the moderne.'

He'd increasingly mused on this, and not just when seeing a thrusting high-rise starkly brooding over the end of a street of Georgian houses - that almost perfect relationship of window space and London brick mass - creating a jagged dissonance to their decorative pragmatism, but seeing yet another terracotta block of flats and blue-painted balconies and girders which would be more in keeping with a Mediterranean country, not one in the northern hemisphere. Blue was wrong for London, especially a pale one, particularly for Victorian bridges which should surely be Buckingham Green.

He finished the ceiling - still hearing his old governor asking whether he'd 'knocked that lid out yet' - told the lads it was time to knock off, wondering where the phrase came from, deciding to Google it later, and went into the nearby café where they usually had their tea breaks.

He was still trying to make up his mind about doing an evening class in literature or maybe social studies. The former had always interested him - still feeling hurt when recalling a new English teacher at school accusing him of copying his essay from a book - the latter he knew a little of and was cognisant of it crystallizing many of his thoughts about his own class heritage: a small house in a street in Bow, a shop assistant mother and bus driver father seemed to him to be a requisite background for an informative but detached view of social class.

The cafe, smelling like a battle between grease, ketchup and bleach, had large, framed prints of the Temple of Khonsu with thirties ziggurat mouldings between picture rail and dado while, incongruously, inside the plate glass window was a garish, unwelcoming collage of large, coloured photos of burgers, chicken drums and kebabs. His tea was served by the Turkish manager, responding to his usual *'Merhaba,'* with her own, more correct interpretation of the greeting. She had a small tattoo of Che Guevara's profile above, appropriately, her left breast.

He looked out of a side window. He was seeing small rear gardens with long established trees, the back of a corner off-licence, Victorian brickwork, chimney pots and the ever-present hovering cranes emblematic of the area's 'regeneration.' It reminded him of an area near his birth place where he could take neither 'Stratford Village' nor 'Stratford City' seriously.

He knew the former was a sought-after destination and had noticed a tendency for people to claim village status in areas of more modest housing which allowed them - priced out of places they would prefer to live and forced into second choice locations - the fall-back position of claiming to inhabit a semi-rural idyll, even if it was called Tottenham or Walthamstow or one of the other latest hotspots according to the property porn pages of the mid-week's Standard.

Up to his mid-teens he and his parents had shared a house with his mother's sister and her husband while grandparents lived six doors away - 'doors' more appropriate for terraces than 'houses' - but since the rise of the privatised worker it seemed that it was now the higher earners that were, or at least perceived to be, the more community-minded. Such, however, was the hegemony of the public sector salariat that less and less working class families seemed to be left in the area, those still around usually living in housing association conversions.

There were, he knew, characteristics of manual workers that were shared with the rich: self-recruitment; dockers, when they were extant, getting their sons-in-law on the payroll, bankers doing likewise, even the upper class 'gels' was similar to the cockney pronunciation. Perhaps, he thought, he should have done something with his degree: proselytize on Marx perhaps, or atheism, he wasn't sure. But at the moment, he felt like going on a rabble-rousing mission against the world's architects.

Not feeling like returning home straight away, he took a ride on the DLR - he'd gone with his father in his teens from Bow Road to Island Gardens when it had first opened - and was able to get a seat at the front of a train and, as if he was a child, pretend to drive it.

He enjoyed the ride: Canada Square tower's shallow obelisk-shaped top similar to its designer's buildings in Manhattan Liam had looked up at and admired a few years before, the nautical style of the brick and wood residences past Canary Wharf and the pleasant symmetry and realistic imitation of the Art Deco flats between Pontoon Dock and the Thames, though these were gradually being overshadowed by the dark, shapeless lumps of mediocrity being built behind them.

He was looking out at an old Victorian print works when he passed an almost completed monolithic block of flats of deep red brick which was relatively pleasing until the abruptly curved yellow brick end of it. He wondered why the change of colour. He passed a newly built medium-height tower - pleasing, with its ziggurat top and faux Thirties simplicity - yet the architect had added horizontal lines of coloured tiles, suggesting that he had little confidence in its vintage shape and had pandered to the dictates of current fashion and 'livened it up' to take attention away from its perceived plainness.

Again he wondered what aspiring architects were taught in their primary grounding in the subject, what its ideologies, dictates and fashions were. He had a flyer at home somewhere with information about this.

He found it when he returned and noticed that one of the Architectural Association's introductory days was being held in Fitzrovia the following day.

Not being required in the building he was working on because it was being shut down for security reasons due to a long-planned demo - apparently taking place outside a building opposite to protest against government plans to allow a greater reduction in corporation tax and make a post-Brexit Britain even more of a tax haven - he had free day. He was tempted to join he demonstration, but decided to satisfy his urge to find out a little more about the creation of his urban environment.

There were a lot of people there, mostly young, reminding him of when he'd been a commercial artist for a few years until CGI had come crashing in and he'd become surrounded by eighteen-year olds who were, with the new technology, becoming increasingly successful without being able to draw a straight line. He 'd found himself more than ever sketching and painting for himself - he'd occasionally rented nearby studio space in an unused school - because his skills weren't needed in the job any more.

The teenagers here would have to pay for their degree, something he'd never had to do. Education was a public service before the conglomerate, free market deluge committed itself to privatizing everything public and commercialising everything private.

There were photographs around the walls, mainly large: The Walkie Talkie, a looming, asymmetrical waste of air hanging over the City, the Tower of Babel Shard, the snail shell of County Hall, the Lincoln Plaza 'with its fabulous array of life-style choice facilities' printed underneath it, the Strata's three eyes of Sauron at the Elephant and Castle, the giant slug of Oxford Street's Park House ... He looked away from them and walked through the gallery feeling bemused that people were talking about the buildings to each other not dismissively but as if there were something dramatic, intriguing, perhaps beauteous to behold.

After hearing 'iconic building' three times, he went through to a smaller room where, amongst more photographs was a painting or two, one of them of the Empire State where a few years before he'd been on its eightieth floor viewing platform trying to see the very building he was looking from, it was such an integral part of the Manhattan skyline he'd forgotten for a few seconds he was actually in it.

There was also a black-and-white shot looking down at the top of the Chrysler building showing the elegant curves of its radiator top. If this pictorial collection had initially been mounted to inspire contemporary architects and would-be ones it had miserably failed.

He returned to the main room and noticed, past the huddles of tight-suited Jesus lookalikes, a man with long black-grey hair and pale blue linen jacket leaning nonchalantly on a wall in the far corner of the room. He was displaying a mere nuance of a smile as he disinterestedly looked around him and occasionally glanced down at his deep red shoes as if he was making sure they were still on his feet.

Two or three times, people - members of the university staff, Liam assumed - came to have a quick word with him, nod thanks to him and return from where they'd come. Though he couldn't hear the conversations, he noticed deference in their voices. Behind the man was a poster with the Architectural Association's logo. Liam went towards it. It read: 'We emphasise technical knowledge to channel creativity' - the former, he thought, didn't channel so much as largely determine it - 'and the role of technological innovation in contributing to a responsible and resource-efficient built environment.' It continued: 'We have an obligation to students in the idea and practice of making an architect aware of their professional duty of care and social and environmental responsibility.'

He thought of the bulging pint glass of 20 Fenchurch Street. Responsible?

Wondering what to do next, to go or stay and become increasingly annoyed, he turned away and nudged into the tall man still standing there, moving his head slowly up and down as if in approval, even the back of it having a sort of imperiousness. Not wishing to say anything to him, Liam mumbled an 'excuse me,' but briefly glanced at him anyway.

He seemed much taller close up and the shape of his lips appeared to hover subtly between a smile and a faint sneer as he lightly touched the cravat around his tanned neck and looked slightly down at the speaker.

In that second, he seemed to become, for Liam, the stereotype of an architect. He'd occasionally and idly toyed with the pointless idea of what he disliked the most: lawyers - What's the connection between two million spermatozoa and a lawyer? Only one has a chance of becoming a human being - avaricious developers, or architects.

He had never met members of these professions, this seemingly hubris-laden triumvirate, but this man, along with pictures in his head of the Vauxhall tower - a piece of Beijing that had lost its way - and the proposed phallus of the Beacon Tower in Vauxhall, helped solve his conundrum; it was architects.

Leaving the room, he went down to the ground floor café, sat and looked at the waitresses. Dependant on his mood he tended to dramatise them, fantasise them. Sometimes he saw them as legions of mothers offering surrogate suckling - the sweet froth gulp of cappuccino as a breast in a tender universe, the baby in him smiling up at them - even on occasions as lovers, and as a shaft of sun came through a window, pleasantly sensed them surrounding him, greeting him; the Lithuania girls, *labas, prasau, aciu,* Polish girls, *tsech, prosze…* There was, though, something about the girl who served him, the way she worked that was reminiscent of something he liked, but wasn't sure what.

After this brief, rather consoling hiatus and while digesting a baguette and brioche, he tried to mentally gather a pictorial landscape of historical London. He knew little of it really, though was aware that tall structures began with the White Tower of the Tower of London at the end of the eleventh century, with the old St. Paul's the first to surpass a height of hundred metres in the early fourteenth.

Then of course, in the Sixties with the Post Office Tower and the building boom of the Nineties, there was the foundation for the chaotic bling and aesthetic toxicity of the city's current skyline, a horizon that, compared with the rest of Europe looked like a third world city craving for  entry in the Guinness Book of Records.

London, he knew, had almost as many trees as it had residents; never had he seen a city so transformed by the summer. For him, it was a predominantly flat city of Victorian villages, of Georgian and Edwardian streets, of London  brick, of pavement trees and, further out, of stuccoed Thirties avenues and orchard gardens. If developers were given their philistine way it would be turned into an amorphous mass of incongruent, narcissistic edifices that celebrated architects, not people.

For a brief second he saw London as a giant builders' yard of scattered, randomly shaped structures, or even a cage-less zoo of lumpy mastodons.

He thought of his past and present meanderings around the metropolis, walking past high-gabled Edwardian houses, Victorian ones with chimneys like snooker cue tips, the curved bays and scrolled balconies of Regency houses and, always looking up to spot the good bits picked out by a low evening sun; the odd castellations on top of an Edwardian hotel, a white pediment above high Victorian keystones or the set-back top of a Thirties block like the bridge of a liner sailing out of an Art Deco poster heralding the rise of a new aesthetic with its pastel facades, green pantiles, ziggurats, chevrons and stylised shells - the mosaics of urban architecture, the streetscapes of an endless city.

# CHAPTER 2

He had another night dreaming of being lost, this time amongst buildings that seemed to scream in a Gothic bewilderment under huge wrought iron mediaeval bridges leading to nowhere. When he awoke, he rang one of the lads at work and told him he wouldn't be in - he wasn't needed, the job was going okay.

Making himself breakfast, he thought about builders, crane drivers, scaffolders and bricklayers as akin to heroes of the built world, yet having to work from blueprints created by architects producing angles, curves, heights that affect feelings; of excitement, peace, foreboding, pleasure, sometimes of a nihilism … the physical affecting the psychological.

By chance, he'd met someone in New York whose family were from the Appalachians and who had told him that the people there were prone to two basic reactions: to feel the mountains as almost tomb-like and protective, cloistering its inhabitants, and that when such people leave the region they often felt intensely unsettled. When his grandmother, an Appalachian woman, moved to Detroit as an adult she described the city as 'where the mountains are not.' If they moved away to places like Florida or Kansas they couldn't get used to the long gaze of the ocean and prairie, they felt vulnerable, watched.

Yet the same mountains could be a more oppressive presence, they could instil a sense of insignificance, a powerlessness which, the man said, could become a dark fatalism.

Liam saw the analogy with cities, the latter as cloisters, yet the monolithic buildings sharing a similar mountain-like presence. In cities, buildings were the mountains, the ridges, hills of a country wilderness, and if urban populations were to move to the Yorkshire moors or Fenland marshes they would feel disorientated, lonely. They were 'where the buildings are not.'

He would have liked this man to share his knowledge with a mass ensemble of London architects, chaining them to their seats or bolting them to the floor of the aisles if necessary, to destroy their unawareness, instil in them the significance of what they were doing.

He smiled inwardly at himself, it was a little fantasy; some sort of wish-fulfilment that he supposed had been with him for a while, even if unconsciously. It had been with him when walking the Thames Path and looking across to the tree-lined banks at Richmond and walking streets with bits of cemetery and parkland touching back gardens, and following streams, narrow boat canals and gazing at cranes and chimneys, all re-minding him of his childhood escapes.

The city's disfiguring buildings he couldn't prevent; could do little about, and was aware, like a few million other citizens, that he'd been fatalistically accepting it all; capitalism and its edifices moved on relentlessly, he could do nothing.

But maybe, just maybe, he could start in a minor key the next day. He was going to a meeting against plans to destroy a local church. It was an Edwardian redbrick with an unusual spire and, despite its coloured leaded windows, had little more than a rather stately sparseness to recommend it. But it was over a hundred years old and though aware of his views about organised religion which made his attendance a blatant double standard - preferring 'strategic hypocrisy' - he would be loathe to see the building, its tradition, its Englishness disappear.

The meeting was at eight in the evening and he was late. There were over a hundred people sitting on long, curved lines of pews like a flat, mini-amphitheatre. He sat at the end of the first row.

A minister was addressing them. He talked of the cost of the building's upkeep in some detail; that he was the steward of God's money, how small the congregation usually was and that the proposal for fifty apartments, a small prayer room and a café would create yet another 'iconic building.' He used 'needs of the modern age' twice, 'move forward' three times and was visibly annoyed when someone mentioned that the proposal for demolition had been with the council for four years without local residents being informed.

A man, introducing himself as the vicar of a nearby parish, then stepped forward and in a soft, persuasive voice, rhetorically asked, 'How many of you still have your first car? Of course you haven't, it got old didn't it, and you got a newer one didn't you. It's the same with the church, we have - '

Liam stood, walked towards the speaker, gently took the mike from him with a polite 'Excuse me,' looked at the congregation and said, 'This is such a vapid presentation. Look, I'm an atheist, but the one thing I'm interested in is this building.'

He paused for a few seconds, his younger self surprised at the part of him that was now speaking so firmly.

'Look around you, look at the windows, their colours are falling on you, on your faces, shoulders; look up, look at the vaulted ceiling, the symmetry, the proportions, and the oak dado, the mahogany organ, the elegant size of it. Just look.'

He swept his arm expansively around as if he'd built the place himself and was giving it to the people.

'This is a developer's wet dream. These unimaginative apologists for faith leaders who conceive of barrack social housing as an acceptable trade-off are deluding themselves that their well-meaning intent justifies their vandalism.'

While he was talking, rarely hesitating, his face seemed to take on a gloss of enamel, his eyes almost darting.

'It's as if churches weren't built for rich men's social standing; 'I've got a bigger penis than you.' And what sort of analogy is the car one? Are we to destroy St Paul's because it's old? London is still, essentially, a Victorian city; do we raze it because it's ancient? This man has the brain of an amoeba.'

He was feeling solid, stronger, his gestures becoming more precise.

There was a suited man sitting directly in front of him who said quietly as he looked up at him, 'Who's going to pay for it then?'

Liam bent forward a little, frowned down and courteously said, 'Please be quiet, I haven't finished.'

'Well, the fact is; the money's got to come from somewhere.'

The man looked around and behind him, appealing to the obviousness of it all.

'Ask God for it,' Liam shouted.

Such was the incongruity of his anger in a house of worship that the face of the man in the front row blurred into an expressionless splodge.

Liam looked behind him to the corner of the nave where there was a life-size statue of Mary, her face looking modestly down. She was holding in one hand what could have been a star. He took a step towards it then halted. He wanted to clasp his hands behind the neck and pull it towards him, breaking it from its plinth, it falling forward, face down, cracking open with a clattering explosion on the parquet floor.

He stood motionless, picturing the segmented statue; the cracked head, face untouched, part of a finger, a wrist still rolling to and fro against a skirting board. The object in the other hand now looked like a torch, as if the Madonna was a destroyed, useless usherette.

He took a deep breath, said quietly to the people staring at him, frowning, some bemused, 'I've had my say,' then turned towards the heavy church door and as he pulled it open, looked briefly behind him.

The sun seemed to have gone, no coloured light anymore, just the brown-grey of a forlorn, dead space. Perhaps he shouldn't have come, been more cognisant of the size of his resentment.

As he got into his car, feeling a little guilty for not staying and listening to the other speakers supposedly on his side, he realised he was still holding a scrunched-up brochure he'd picked up from a table as he'd come into the church. He absently smoothed it.

There was a photo of the people who were proposing the development, though no details of it except that it would be for 'affordable housing with recreational facilities.' There were three of them; one had been at the meeting. The one in the centre, a tall man wearing a linen jacket, looked familiar.

# CHAPTER 3

This certainly wasn't the University Of Notre Dame in Rome. The building design course there had been more attuned to the classical periods, had to be, it was in the city of pediments, decorative arches, domed villas, of Doric columns, capitals; details etched into Piero Ronzi's mind as a child born in the city.

He'd enjoyed some of the things he'd been involved in: the parties, drinking, the banter; the casual *'Li mortacci tua'* if someone didn't like someone else a great deal, maybe followed by *'Ma che cazo stai facendo?'* even a perverse liking of the cultural separation of Roman students like himself and those from the rest of the country, and of course, the girls. Though there had been none in his first year, in his second, among fleeting relationships, there had been one who actually looked like Loren and around the campus he'd noticed one or two Sylvana Mangano look-alikes.

He'd also enjoyed the drawing and watercolouring course and the general emphasis on urbanism, but not the ultra concern with the traditional city, its architecture and the design of contemporary buildings in the classical manner. He wasn't interested in Palladio and Berini.

The field trips to Tuscany, Campania and Sicily he'd found pleasurable, but not the historic sites themselves. He sometimes felt his views isolated him from some of his fellow students; even, perhaps, most of the academics; a kind of aesthetic isolation.

He'd felt inhibited by the school's unchallenged enthusiasm for the architecture of the past and paucity of interest in the contemporary, also the lack of scope there had been for any of his burgeoning ideas, ill-formed maybe, but they were his. He felt stifled at times and there was also a lack of encouragement and understanding from the tutors.

He was aware of the architecture of the Futurists like Sant'Elia, Mannetti and Michelucci, of Terragni and the Gruppo 7, of the Italian Architectural Association that collaborated on the official projects of Mussolini, but these were given little space in the university's programme. The voguish movement for Swedish brutalism in England - Trellick Tower, a university in East Anglia and the recently completed Royal National Theatre, and which was also alive in Germany - warranted little more than a footnote n the university's literature and only a single lecture.

To come to England six months after finishing his courses was to make a new start, to break free. He decided that it was almost an attempt to flee the womb. Perhaps an extra zing was added by its current Prime Minister's media-popular phrase 'The white heat of technology.' He wanted to crash through the constraining, drooping, spiritual tarpaulin of what he was being taught.

He had done it, but it hadn't felt like he had. Here, there still was an emphasis on classical forms and he was often asked questions not only by the English students - other than an Iranian he was the only foreign one in his school - but also his lecturers about the city of his birth, its architecture, the feel, the spirit of the place. But fortunately there were one or two teachers that appeared to share his architectural *weltanschauung*.

His beginning at this west London University hadn't been particularly encouraging. Situated in an old junior school where the oriole window in the main hall had undoubtedly been used by the head teacher to spy on the pupils, the archaic concern of the introductory lectures, cramped halls of residence, the seemingly ever-present drizzly rain and lack of sun made him miss his Mediterranean country.

As the only one in his seminar group to have done any serious architectural study, the spouting of its terminology in discussions of European design wasn't always received kindly; the only female lecturer there would receive his orations with upraised eyes and rather hostile stares. Thinking her teaching pragmatically unrelated to his interests, he requested, after a few weeks, to join another seminar group.

She responded by inviting him to the staff room, plying him with academia's favourite sherry tipple, raising her skirt very slightly above a knee as if unintentional, and smiling winningly in an attempt to dissuade him from such action knowing it would look bad for a mature student to want to leave her class. He was dissuaded.

He mused on whether his liking for contemporary, innovative architectural movements and his dislike, sometimes intense, of the ornate, the Gothic, Roman, Greek, the archaic styles, was a reaction against his parents; he wasn't sure. They had been, bless them, rather ordinary, unquestioningly catholic and equally unsurprisingly, bringing him up, or attempting to, in the same manner. They had unthinkingly focussed their social relations upwards, to classes above them, having, he supposed, notions that the Italian aristocracy, landowners, businessmen - 'uomini d'affari' they'd say with smug nods of respect - were somehow born to rule.

Although they both held semi-skilled jobs, he as a ticket inspector on the Trenitalia, often working at Rome's Statzione Termini, she, when not fixed into domesticity, a laundress, they were almost, he thought, like rural peasants in their attitude towards the establishment, as if they hadn't been born in a city. And in Rome.

His grandparents - his father's father working in the freight yards, his wife in the Wuehrer Brewery, both in San Lorenzo - raised their child until the bombing of the yards during the Second World War where they then left for Testaccio.

Piero remembered as a boy visiting his grandfather when he lived at the seaside in Nettuno after his grandma had died. He'd walked along criss-crossing canals smelling their vapid water, noticing despite the bright sun that there was a darkness, and not just in the canals, the streets also. They were narrow, the buildings not high enough to block the light, but somehow the walls and the small, iron grilled windows, narrow pavements and cobbles were in shadow. He hadn't liked being there.

He'd liked the house, though, with its terra cotta colour, red flowers on the window sills and in large pots at the side of a red door. His mother had whispered to him before they went in that her father-in-law was a communist, hence the colour of the flowers. He remembered the polished brass knocker making a ringing thud and an elderly, lined face appearing as the door opened and feeling pleased and grown up when he'd been greeted with, 'Piero, *Ciao giovane.'*

Inside was a room with black and white photos spread over the walls where his grandpa proudly pointed to those of himself with folded arms, Zapata moustache and looking tough. It wasn't until he'd grown up that Piero could see the disparity between the political position of his grandfather and that of his son, though the latter wouldn't have seen his conservatism as political, for him it was the natural order and always had been. He'd never asked his parents about it, but could imagine the tensions between the two; it must have been worse than his own, often tense family domicile.

His parents had tried to settle in Testaccio and had mostly succeeded, but when the immigrants came, their long-set prejudicial foundations and the relatively sudden change the *immigrati* bought about meant they felt lost and unsettled; it wasn't for them anymore the country they knew, it had become a cultural melange.

It was, however, a diaspora that Piero relished: Chinese, Koreans, Filipinos, Moroccans... It used to be said, 'Pick a bench in Piazza Vittoria and start up a conversation in whatever language you choose.' His parents were rigidly mono-lingual, like the English, he discovered later. He liked the refurbished piazza with its basketball area, an alien concept to his father as it seemed to represent the beginning of the Americanisation of the world, a colonisation from which his country would never recover.

Piero hoped, still, that he would have been pleased at what his son was doing, what he was trying to become.

The day he arrived in the United States, a month after finishing his courses in England, was both exciting and scary - he was still taking long, deep breaths as he'd got off the plane at Kennedy Airport. It felt so American even before they'd touched down. It was like a scene from a Fifties musical when the captain of the aircraft had sung a chorus of 'New York, New York' as they'd glided onto the runway.

He was here because the skyscrapers were here, a different classical; the Thirties, the moderne. But he wanted to go further, higher - if he could - more glass, metal, the new construction techniques, computer technologies.

In London he'd been interviewed by a man representing a medium-sized practice based in New York seemingly offering both sympathy for and empathy with his views on the built environment. He told his interviewee he would contact his office and let him know. He had, within hours.

There was little pain in leaving the university. He hadn't seen much of the country - though his English, which was good anyway, had improved - for he'd spent a lot of his time working academically and, to get by financially, at a bar in the west end and then at two fast-food outlets, rarely liking his time spent in them, especially having to be nice, even appear subservient to customers. He d spent a month only at each place.

He found an apartment near the centre of Brooklyn and though initially glad to have it - soon wearying of its fluting, finials, elaborate friezes and cornices - desired more typical New York experiences before starting work. He wanted to go to a bar with screens showing baseball and serving manhattans to Manhattans, a delicatessen for brunch, with eggs over, rye, easy on the cheese, wished to ride the Subway to Brooklyn and for somebody to tell him he 'shoulda taken the A train.'

He managed to satisfy a few of his desires. He had coffee at 'Juniors' amongst the bow-tie waiters and photos of Hayworth and Gable, walked over Brooklyn Bridge, imagining Brando toughing it on Pier 17, almost hearing the New Jersey accent of a Cagney cop, and stopped at Grand Central and its sunbeams. It was eighty and humid, the Chrysler seemed to glisten.

He had a quick look in Saks on Fifth Avenue and glanced around Tiffany's, finding that the natives - with lots of Hispanics and Afro-Americans but few white manual workers, fewer Asians and spotting only one jilbab wearer and a mere handful of African women in traditional dress - were civilised, courteous and well-mannered. He felt it a sophisticated city and, with its grid-patterned streets, a commonsensical one.

There were screaming subways, clichéd hydrants - the Upper Eastside ones showing more brass - sidewalk grills and steam. He walked through Harlem, where jeans crotched at the knees and there were high fives on sidewalks, insults mocking across streets, then coffee with the old guy coughing on about sickness and soccer - he, too, was a Roma fan, a *curva sud* - who'd squeezed his arm when Piero left him for the Upper East Side. Here, he enjoyed cappuccinos, ice-packed fruit and rainbow- filled wraps amongst middle-aged professionals wearing Barbours and Abercrombie & Fitch, and browsed with undergrad kids in baseball caps and girls in orange high heels in Barnes and Noble.

Looking across the Bay to Staten Island as he headed Downtown, he thought of his parents and their annual holiday in Ostia with his father wearing a knotted handkerchief on his head and paddling with a cigarette dangling from his lip while his mother lay square-jawed in a deckchair. And images from his home: the brass stair rods, the silent meals, dad sliding the knife into his mouth, the *purili la piastra* response to his wife's accusation of bad manners, and the tassled table cloth, echo of a key in the cheaply grained door, the grim mat-stamping and the shaking of his wet raincoat.

But they weren't alive, and he was in America and about to begin work, real work, to make his ideas concrete, literally, and in glass and chrome and steel.

Mid-sized Company or not, Piero could see from his first day that there was ambition. He was shown some largish projects on the drawing board, mostly condominiums in Syracuse, a low-rise housing estate outside Tarrytown, and an invitation to submit designs for a new theatre in Harlem.

There was a moderne feel to the latter's projected white concrete, its flat, horizontal forms and fake Art Deco frontage. But as far removed as it was from his childhood surroundings and their academic force-feeding a few years later, for him it wasn't enough, was still derivative, wasn't exploratory, innovative; experimental.

They'd shown him some work they had completed recently in Albany with its Romanesque capitol building, its cookie-cutter - the direct, visual interpretation of things unencumbered by historically learned images was something he was beginning to like about America - and its tall glass and concrete towers all in a row. The latter, though liking them, he felt were too symmetrical, too... easy.

Other than where he was living, the two things that bothered him most were the rules and regulations enmeshed in his job, the unnecessary safety requirements and arbitrary aesthetic codes which were open to a variety of interpretations, though the latter were plastic, shifting grounds for discourse and argument which could suit him.

He was aware of his charm, it had worked on women and occasionally lecturers, so why not, when necessary, use it on bureaucratic stimulus-response carriers of a prescriptive correctness, of a kind of would-be architectural morality? He briefly wondered if Wren or Hawksmoor had had to undergo such constraints.

The other problem was one of the partners, 'Signor Falso,' as Piero had named him, who would come into the design office, bend his slick-haired, bright-tied, middle- aged body over him and say, 'How's our graduate then?' in what he was fast recognising as a New England accent and which appeared to give its speaker a culturally-given right to patronise.

He felt at times, when with him, as if he was an early Italian immigrant. He wondered why the man wanted to delineate, to confirm some sort of social divide between them. He used the arts to do it; galleries, theatres, movies and opera, he was a regular at the Met.

'Did you see it then?' he would ask. 'What a superb performance.'

Piero had seen the film being referred to, the actress had overacted, but his colleague had been so enamoured of the broadsheet reviews that whether she had forgotten half her lines his perceptions would have been the same. Piero would make some negative comment hoping he wouldn't hear him.

'Oh, come now,' he'd say, looking at him as if he were a naughty boy trying to worm his way out of being caught in a particularly mischievous deed, 'she was stirring, magnificent, exquisitely delicious. She has that quality of almost disdainfully creating a mood within a mood, she… she… '

He stopped for a while, not because he was delving for suitable phrases, but for those he was supposed to say. Piero could have eased the man's pain by obtaining a copy of yesterday's New York Times. He knew he wasn't making a good impression on him, he couldn't just respond amiably, he tried and succeeded most of the time, but his attempts were getting more reluctant and he could feel the man gradually seeing him as an irritant. This wasn't good, the man was a partner.

He was working as an assistant to one of the designers on a new commission for a site in Queens; ordinary, run-of-the-mill apartments which he'd decided a more extended, curved roof-line would reduce its stodginess and have a little more appeal.

He took it upon himself to make the alteration. Being quite engrossed in it, he forgot that the blueprint was already finished and approved and that he was supposed to be drawing details to order. The Connecticut partner happened to see it and asked what he was doing. Piero told him, explaining his reasons.

'I don't agree with them,' said the man. 'You are here to help, to do as instructed. You cannot do just what you want; you're not a fuckin' bird that can fly off in all directions and shit anywhere it likes. You'll be paid till the end of the month. Go.'

He'd been there only six months.

Not wanting to admit some kind of defeat, he began planning a move elsewhere in the States. He was getting used to the place, to New York. He had hardly begun thinking it through when he received a phone call from one of his few sympathetic lecturers in London telling him of an opportunity in Chicago in an architects practice recently begun by two American friends.

They - Justin and Peter - were looking for a like-minded partner. His tutor thought he'd be an appropriate fit, unless, of course, he was happy where he was. After explaining what had happened, it didn't take him long to decide. Perhaps here he could be a round peg in an appropriately shaped hole.

A day before he left he was sitting alone in a bar, of late a relatively rare occurrence but a girl he'd had a brief relationship with had decided they weren't compatible. He was 'too Italian' apparently, too passionate about his profession, talked about it too much. She was, she said, a woman who wanted different things, his interests were 'part of a man's world' that didn't seem to include her. 'I'm sorry,' she'd said and had walked away.

He felt a little like crooning 'One For My Baby' to himself,
but then his eye rested on the girder men photo oh the wall behind the counter. It was the first time he'd seen a copy since
he'd been in the city. It was as if the workers in their cloth caps
and boots atop the girder, with the East River beyond and
Manhattan below, were in the bleachers waiting for a game to
start while the one on the end cadged a light from his buddy
and another took a peek at a workmate's lunch. He imagined
the man at the side of the cable playing pool next day with Ed
and the boys downtown, the hatless one with his dark-haired
Sue at Coney Island, elbows jutting in *contrapposte* burlesque
giggling into a Kodak, and the man with the vest and the take-
my-wife jokes, 'She's so fat wherever she sits she's always
next to me,' drinking at a bar in Hoboken.

Perhaps the rest of them would be in a theatre on Times
Square or a fight at Madison. Then it would be back to the
metal, chains, the rivets, the heaving and pushing, perhaps
grappling with memories they couldn't hold, which float away,
snatched by the wind below the steel.

He left the bar and looked around a little more of the city
and its neon-edged night, wandered around a couple of mar-
bled foyers which now seemed flashy, not grand, nor did Central station without the sunbeams. He went into a deli just before it closed, watching brown-uniformed, moustachio'd Mex-
icans tidying up and getting ready for home, and not enjoying
his curled cheesecake. Getting a bus downtown, he looked
across at Liberty Island's statue - 'taking liberties' he smiled to
himself, having learnt the phrase in England.

He thought of home: the ancient ruins, the Colosseum - even
the thought of a Roman capital or two seemed to have a reas-
suring feel, though not for long - the trees, the stone pine,
plane, the hornbeam. Trees, he thought, had an almost mythi-
cal quality, but secondary to the constructs he had visualised.

He'd been intrigued by the parks in London, not seeing them
so much as spaces to breathe and walk in but as a potential for

buildings of glass, of light. Le Corbusier's definition of architecture came to mind: 'The magnificent interplay of masses brought together in light.' He would see what happened in Chicago.

Sitting in an airport cafe at Kennedy he heard from somewhere to his right, 'Hey, you've got a great face.'

A teenager came around in front of him and handed him a sketch: the lean profile, dark eyes, long nose like his mother's, clean shaven, black hair. His gut response was one of mild rejection; no, he didn't look like this, but having once attended a life- drawing class he knew he did.

'Yeh, you look a bit like a young Mastroianni, I guess.' It had been said before. 'I love drawing people,' said the young man.

Piero told him it was okay by him and went to Departures.

Failing to conceptually validate 'curry and mushroom croissant' or 'marinated pecans and balsamic reduction' - it was hardly bruschetta of carbonara - at one of the coffee shops, he went to the gate where a fourteen stone female Customs Officer told him to remove his footwear and belt, 'No shoes, no go.' followed by a security guard, hands cocked at his hips, who ordered him to 'Step back sir, take yer hands outta your pockets.'

Piero wanted to tell him he'd seen the movies. All of them.

His excitement building as he arrived at O'Hare he went through the covered walkway after landing and mentioned to a flight attendant how surprised he was that an aircraft that large had only two engines. She pointed to her braided, peak-capped companion.

'Ask him, he knows about planes, he's the captain.'

'I know,' the pilot said, with wide eyes and limp wrist, 'they make them so *big* these days.'

After staying overnight at a nearby hotel - politely refusing to be met at the airport by one of the partners, wishing to make an early statement of independence - he went straight Downtown to get the feel of the Windy City. He wanted to look at the unglamorously named Board of Trade Building, the Home Insurance Building and maybe the Merchandise Mart, seen, as short and stubby as it was by the day's increasingly commonplace heights, as the first modern skyscraper.

And the obligatory Willis Tower of course. He saw these - keeping away from the pediments and columns of the Capitol building - and also enjoyed a cruise around the canals, looking up at some clearly Bauhaus-influenced Twenties and Thirties buildings. But he wasn't satisfied by any and only a little by the Wills, or as he'd always known it, the Sears Tower. They were, for him, too ordinary, there was a kind of uniformity with other constructions he'd looked around and seen photos and illustrations of.

He often had the urge to argue that a building doesn't have to actually look like a building, it could look like so many things; he wondered if it had to actually look like a recognisable object. But humans instantly sought a likeness, a comparison with something they had seen, knew; a comfort in the familiar.

He knew now he'd have to play the game, keep his nose clean, *mantarere pulito il naso,* though maybe not quite as much with his new employers, but he'd have to ask permission to do things, or at least to implement them. He'd have to be patient. He took a bus to Lake Shore Drive and stood looking out across Lake Michigan. He felt as if he was standing on the edge of the sea.

# CHAPTER 4

It was the sort of opening act dining room scene popular with playwrights. Set in County Durham, at least in the North East, a big man, son of a long-dead miner, quickly and noisily finishes his breakfast, looks at the wall clock, shouts to his unseen wife in the kitchen that he'll be late if he doesn't hurry and picks up his jacket from the back of a chair and puts it on in virtually one movement. He then takes a stride towards the kitchen as the woman comes out of it, gives her a kiss on the cheek and a brief hug before he walks to the door and out, the door banging shut behind him. The woman would then sigh at the ritualistic ordinariness of it all and return to the kitchen where, a few seconds afterwards, the sounds of washing up are heard.

Jim Salmon had thought occasionally of writing a play himself with such a setting - the man even asking his wife if she was 'alreet  pet' and maybe her telling him to 'put kittle on grate' - but wasn't sure where to go from there. He fancied a family drama, but had no kids and wasn't sure how to write about them and would have desisted from calling them 'bairns' anyway, though he had begun to write a few poems lately, not that he'd mentioned this to his workmates.

He shut the front door of his back-to-back terrace home in Chester-Le-Street which he'd grown up in and had inherited from his parents and went off to work in Newcastle, only a dozen or so miles away - a picture of him trying to teach the bemused Polish lads that to ascertain whether someone was from that city was to get them to say 'conjunctivitis' came to mind. He usually worked there, but this job was a little different, not so much where he was doing it, but what.

He'd been bricklaying for years, picking up his skills from a couple of young, early Polish immigrants he'd laboured for as a teenager. He'd even learnt a few words of their language: *czesc, prosze, dziekuje, do widzenia,* and particularly liked the sound of their words for brick and trowel, *cegta* and *kielni,* and in turn, he'd improved their English, the Durham version at least.

They knew the English words for the various brick formations and which initially they'd taught him: English bond, alternate rows of headers and stretchers, Flemish bond, the most commonplace, nearly all stretchers, even English garden wall bond. He still thought of them and had kept in touch with one, Thomasz, who was working in London, the other, Jakub, had returned home. He wondered what they'd say about this particular job.

The site was just inland from the quayside. He had rarely started a job so late, the exterior had been virtually finished except for his bit - compared with the size of the building it was little more than that. The whole thing looked like a huge, menacing flying saucer. It was made of dark purple-finished steel and he was bricking an inset on its top floor. He had rarely worked so high.

From a distance, he supposed it looked like two conjoined capital letters, a 'P' and an 'R', though others thought perhaps it was a pair of flags or balloons, or even two toffee apples, nobody was really sure. It seemed ridiculous, so much metal, tons of it in great elliptical shapes one upon the other, each succeeding one bigger than the one below; and then this relatively tiny area of fired clay and cement. Perhaps the architect folks had wanted it to look ambiguous or mysterious or something.

He couldn't quite understand how so much weight could be held by so few slim, shiny, almost glistening vertical struts at its base. He'd been inside on the floors a couple of times, mostly to talk to the project managers and tradesmen - there were carpenters in now, electricians, partition fixers, the painters had begun work, too - anyone really, to see if they knew why he was using such an incongruous material as brick on such a building.

Nobody knew, they seemed to accept it all, their curiosity, he supposed, becoming deadened by the building's familiarity. Hundreds of square metres of metal with hardly a window and yet here he was laying good old-fashioned bricks, even older fashioned for they were London stocks, which he even knew the names of, learning from his old East European mates. There were the yellow stocks, red rubbers, white suffolks and the burnt looking ones, grey gaults. They were wasted up here at this height.

There were more and more buildings now where bricks weren't used, it seemed to be all concrete and steel, especially of course for the higher ones. But there was still a fair bit of work for brickies, even on new-builds, and better to be one here than over in America.

One of his old mates who had recently returned from there had noticed that it was nearly all plastic weather boarding in the suburbs and he hadn't seen any brick terraces even in the cities, though he once thought he had in Aurora, Illinois, but then saw that there was a twelve-inch gap between each house. An American he'd met who'd never been to the UK before told him that he had initially thought that a terrace in Newcastle was really two long houses, one on either side of the road, with lots of front doors.

Thomasz had told him that bricks were making a come-back in London. There was some Peabody type housing which was sticking to the Peabody tradition of both smooth and glazed bricks; he'd also been working with Staffordshire blues. Jim was feeling a little envious.

'When you comin' down to the smoke and earn some good *zloty*?' he would ask him, sounding a little more London each time.

'You could go back to your trouble and strife at weekends, you could afford it. How is the *zlona,* anyway?'

Connie was okay, caring as ever, loving, tolerant, but he wasn't quite sure how tolerant or how forgiving she would be when he told her what he intended to do and where he was going to do it over the next few months.

When he had told her, her response had been an incredulous 'Yer ganna do what, mun? Go doon to Loondon?'

He'd waited till they'd finished a Sunday lunch, knowing she was generally full of amiability when replete, and had cleared the table for her and begun washing up. It was a Sunday ritual.

'I cun mek a fair bit, lass, the money's good, it's good quality weark, new-build stooff, there's less and less of it oop here, I've told yer thut, they want cruftsmen on this particular job. 'er can get tired o' steel and gluss bloody towers, maybe its a kind of... renaissance or summat.

'You and yer words.'

'Thomasz sends his regards. It's good mooney Con, I cun be back weekends.'

'Good cluss weark? Soomtimes I think I married a brick.'

He turned to her, plate and cloth in hand.

'Yer like cookin' don't yer? Yer turn it into an art form, you do. You've won local prizes at it. yer loov doin it, well, maybe not fer me all the time, but it's a big part o' yer, you're creative, and I'm same wi' laying bricks, you've always known this. Aye, and it's not joost the old bricks that have names yer know, there's smoked patra, there's - '

'I know, that's why we've got a fancy gazebo thing at back where a garden should be. You'd get lost. When were you lust in Loondon?

'I went there once as a teenager, you know that, too. It were muckle and reet noisy, I told yer about it. All the sites, Big Ben, St. Paul's, and the way they speak, most of 'em. Couldn't oonderstund mooch of it mesel'.'

'Well, I've never been.'

'I know, but if yer wanna coom doon yer can stay with me for a while then, a weekend at least.'

'That's nice of yer, I'm sure.'

'Yer brother can look after yer mam, it's about time 'e took a turn.'

She got up and took a few steps, shaking her head.

'I dunno.' He woan't like it, but he should have a turn I reckon.'

'Course 'e should. You've doon more than enough. Look, I'm not being cruel, but no one's sure whether it's dementia and she's got a nurse seein' 'er now and there's a social worker promised, you said. Think about it lass. And sit doon. Coom 'ere.'

He went to her, pulled her to him and hugged her.

'You'll be able to afford a few extra things fer yersel', yer deserve it.'

'Why is it we always have to deserve soomthin'? Why do we always think we 'ave to earn' it? Soom people joost 'ave it.'

'Probably don't appreciate it though, lass. The protestant ethic I think it's called. We're brainwashed, lass. I'll probably go next week.'

He disappeared into the small back room. Maybe there was something on telly.

He travelled to King's Cross from Newcastle Central, admiring the Romano-Italian design and Doric ornamental work of its frontage and wondering again what it would have been like to have worked on it a hundred years ago; the curved train shed roof the first, along with Liverpool's Lime Street, to use curved wrought iron ribs to support it. Knowing it was Victorian, he mused, along his journey south, on precisely when different architectural periods actually began and ended.

He imagined a group of people outside a house arguing whether it was Victorian or Edwardian. One of them points out the former's yellow stocks, slate roof and cannon-head chimneys; the other, the latter's multi-paned sashes, veranda and fish scale hanging tiles.

As if there's a moment when a house must change from one style to another, that the foreman, learning of a Queen's death, would carry on helping a mason lift a gargoyle and tell labourers to continue mixing cement or shout for them to cease, and tell a carpenter to lay down his saw and bricklayers their trowels and carry them home along with bossing mallets and hammers, and then ask them to wait till a decision be made, perhaps, even, to start again.

He pictured a young architect, cravatted and elegant, strolling around with blueprints under his arm then the foreman calling at cottages, rounding up his men ready to return to build again. He could see the people outside the house continuing on, laughing at their pedantry. He smiled at his own.

He then thought of Connie and her holding back the tears when she hugged him goodbye inside the front door then stepping outside to give him another squeeze on the step. She was a smasher.

As the train slowed, single faces passed the windows and then groups of faces taking longer to travel across and, just before the last juddering, the profiles moving faster than the train. Jim picked up his backpack with its treasured trowels, spirit level, lump hammer, cold chisel and tingle plate, which had been as comforting a companion as it was pragmatic lying beside him on the seat. He then reached up for his case and went onto the platform.

At the ticket barrier he saw Thomasz reclining comfortably on a bench a few yards from the platform entrance with a raincoat slung over his shoulder and which looked more unwearable than ever. If he had known him for fifty years he was sure he'd still have greeted him with that slow, almost embarrassed grin. He made rapid scooping movements from the region of his waist to his mouth and looked at Jim inquiringly. The latter nodded vigorously; there'd been nothing to eat on the train. They found a café at the station where Thomas asked his friend if it had been hard to leave.

'Aye,' 'it were a bit, long while since I've been wi'out Connie, but too good a chunce to pass oop, really.'

They tucked into their favourite sausage and mash, Thomasz almost wailing that he wanted a Polish version of the latter. Jim asked him about the job.

'You'll love it, it's a housing estate, like I said, actual streets man, only three of 'em, but we've been using reclaimed bricks, dark ones that go great with the old houses we're carryin' on from the ends of, and there's dark, almost black bricks in a saw-tooth shape and... you'll see for yourself. And Mike, the subbie guy we're workin' for is a good 'un.'

'Ah loov bricks, mun, Fired clay, eh?' Jim enthused. 'And not joost because they look great and last for centuries, but they're cheap, cun be made into any shape really, and they keep a house warm. I mean, they cun be made be 'und, by machine, there's reclaimed ones and - '

'What is your saying, 'Preaching to the converted? I know, we're building some of the houses with them on the site.'

'And they cun be in all colours, as yer know, but fook orange and blue.'

Out on the pavement, walking to the lodgings which were only half a mile away, the city was all around them. The American-Afro-Caribbean cockney inflections like a staccato swirl of water surrounding them. 'Wha' yer doin, bruv?' ' 'Wot yew lahk, mun?'' 'But it don't ma'ah, innit.'

'Oi, move yerself mate.' a large, cropped-haired man said to Jim as he slammed his knee into his case. Jim turned to him but he'd gone. He hadn't understood all that was being said around him, it felt the same but different to when he'd first come here. He pointed this out to Thomas.

'It was worse for me when I first came to Britain, I could hardly speak English.'

'Nor can this lot, mun.'

As they laughed, people bumped and shoved, the case twisting around, knocking people's legs.

'Is it always like this?'

'At rush hour, yeh, but not always as busy.'

Crossing a road, making his backpack comfortable, Jim noticed that his old mentor's Polish-Novocastrian accent was being diluted by this place.

They filed slowly through the crowd. On the wide pavement were the railings of a public convenience and across the road a man grabbing newspapers from the back of a van, curling them effortlessly over his shoulder and, cradling more under his arm, waddling across to a news stand, scuttling through traffic as if the weight of a life carrying wars, blood, rapes and tabloid puns had bowed his legs. He then dished out his evening newspapers, weather-beaten hands performing their journalistic sleight of hand. This combination of toilet and typography strangely stayed with Jim as a strong, early image, a sort of visual shorthand of the city.

As they entered the dingy hallway of the house, Jim wondered if the landlady would be the type to say 'I can't shake hands, I've just finished putting lard on the cat's boil.' He hoped not.

It was a largish place with a room on the first floor for him, and Thomasz's on the top. It felt okay. He'd be alright here.

It was a pretty big site. It was off Pentonville Road, so not far from the mainline station. There were not only the newly built  streets and a few separate buildings, but two blocks of five-storey flats, just the right height for apartments he thought, reminding him of Paris where he'd taken Con for their honeymoon a long time ago. He remembered pavement grills gushing water along culverts and washing cobbles all day, yet still surprising him as it trickled around a corner, and on boulevards chestnut and plain trees seemed to fill the city, almost touching eaves and scrolled verandas, yet weren't quite tall enough to see from the Sacre-Coeur.

On his first morning, Thomasz showed him around. There were pale, almost creamy bricks used for several artisan work-shops and homes, and laid as perforated screens for privacy and the shifting light. Thomasz had obviously picked up some of the current developers jargon, but it didn't matter, it was good to see so many sorts of bricks and the variations in their laying: Blockleys smooth blacks, Michelmersh, textured and hand-made bricks in plain and saw-tooth which were angled along the side of an end house.

The names of bricks held a fascination for him, gave him a sense almost of calm when he bent them around his tongue. He felt somehow more... solid when working with them, using his rather scarred, hardened hands to lay the various bonds, almost flippantly wiping up the mortar with his trowel and flicking it into the valley of a brick already laid then placing another on top then a light tapping with the trowel handle to get it level with his line. Then another and another and the almost delicate placing and smoothing of the pointing. He thought of Connie's remark. Perhaps, in another life, he actually had been a brick.

He wasn't working directly with Thomasz, he was going to do a special - *specjalny* as his friend called it - on his own. A life-size brick relief of a mother and child was to go on the outside of the second floor between two windows, which re-quired him to cut bricks to shape, not just in half or making queen or king closures, but cutting them, smoothing them into curves.

The foreman had shown him the drawing, it was detailed enough to show virtually all of the bricks, then had asked him if he could do the work. He hadn't done anything quite like this before but knew he could. The craftsman in him felt pleas-antly excited.

He felt creative when working with bricks; fired ones, he knew, had been used for thousands of years, they could last that long too, and they could be cleaned like new. Concrete couldn't, not satisfactorily. He'd seen it himself; the dark, permanent stains caused by pollution, rain and the old coal fires.

It was more a sculptor's work really, he supposed, as he climbed the scaffolding to begin his task. Although he wasn't carving out full figures - the drawing looked as if they'd been sliced exactly halfway through their centre from top to bottom - the basic details of faces, clothes and toecaps of shoes, even a curved suggestion of hair under a headscarf had to be created.

Ideally, bricks shouldn't have been laid on the area behind he figures, so to give his work a chance to hold he quickly drew the outline shapes on them and began chipping the bricks with his cold chisel. This took less time than he thought and, knocking up his own compo, he started with a few bricks he'd prepared in a quiet corner of the site the day before; some shapes for footwear and the bottom of a gown.

'Gonna do some pretty stuff up there are yer?'

Below him were two plumbers he'd spoken to earlier.

'Lay off the ale then, can't do it if yer Brahms can yer. See yer mate.'

They briefly waved at him as they went off for a bite to eat.

He wasn't sure why they'd referred to a classical composer but they were good cockney lads, and it was better working here than on the pointless, annoying, 'PR' conundrum he'd worked on back home.

# CHAPTER 5

It was a Saturday. Liam had decided to go to Duxford, a museum now but once a Second World War operational aerodrome. The first thing he saw inside the hangar's entrance was a large black and white photo showing, from the foreground to the background of a high, stylized column façade, a sea of helmeted soldiers sitting backs to camera. In front of them, mounted centre- top, was a huge concrete swastika - all reeking of the moderne, of fascism, of a deep, controlled mass hysteria. He felt a childlike awe, also a momentary guilt as his aesthetic sense and the appreciation of the shot pushed out the emotional meaning. It was a willing seduction, burying the repugnance of death.

He was here partly because he'd overheard an enthusiastic train conversation about the place and because he had time on his hands. Inside the building were small and medium-sized aircraft hanging from the ceiling, a few larger ones on the floor, and a jeep. A couple of the staff were walking disinterestedly around, others talking in a corner.

He imagined them when the last visitor had gone opening the showcases and putting on uniforms - the women dressing as WAAFS - then running to the unloaded bombs stacked at the side of the aircraft, others sliding down cables into the cockpits of a hanging Heinkel and Spitfire, and the one with the headphones who tears the tickets at the entrance tapping a dit-dit-dah as the jeep with a chewing gum colonel cruised around the hall. The battle is left to a Sopwith chasing a Focker across the ceiling, and as a caretaker sits astride a silent doodlebug a guide in a medic's coat bears the cleaner away, a mop still clenched in his fist.

Losing himself in his reverie, Liam pictured a shell piercing the tank and making pink spawn of the archivist as it ricochets for ever until dawn lights the windows, planes stop circling and medals and uniforms are returned, and with hair quickly brushed the receptionist welcomes the morning's first visitors.

He left the hangar and went to the parked civilian airplanes on the edge of the runway: the Ambassador, Britannia, the VC 10 and, wandering into a second hangar - the sight making him feel less sombre - the elegant lines of the Comet.

After waking around it he needed a coffee. It was a choice between 'Wingco Joe's' - a strained alliance of transatlantic nomenclature - and 'The Mess,' a tidy, characterless space serving little but tea and buns. He chose neither.

On the train home he recalled another photo in one of the hangars of a Lady Bountiful frowning down at a bedridden airman and amused himself by hearing, 'Rectum?' 'Well, it didn't do 'em much good, ma'am.'

It was still light and warm and although walking around Hollow Pond in Whipps Cross would have been a more appropriate summer evening experience he wanted a little urban stimulus, so broke his journey and wandered around Dalston and Hoxton, the latter, when he was a child, seen as an inner city slum even by people living in Bow, and the image over-rode what he saw as he looked around him.

He remembered there was a roof garden café on top of the Reeves building. He turned back to it, climbed the stairs, opened the door at the top and saw it with a chimney stack nestled against one end of it. Sitting outside, he sipped his drink and took deep, refreshing breaths. On the slate roofs around him were chimneys everywhere. He had a minor flash of interest in what the psychology of chimneys were, representing something or other, possibly a penis.

He could also see a new building standing alone a few miles away in east London suburbia whose top was sloped at an acute angle like a spire that had gone wrong. It was a waste of space, in the idiomatic sense also. Perhaps it was that height because the developers needed to optimise its square metres to offset the cost of the land, but if so, why not go even higher? In fact, the design wasn't doing many favours to any idea of max-imisation, nor to the ease of an eye.

Maybe the driving ethos of construction technology meant that it was that way because it *could* be that way. He had re-cently read that the city's current mayor had just found for the developers for the eleventh consecutive time in appeals against their planned projects.

As he was thinking this, he realised he was gazing at a girl behind the counter, one of the staff, a waitress probably. He then recognized her from the café at the Architectural Associa-tion. It was her brisk and curvy competence, the slightly plump upper arms, the full face with tied-back hair that interested him, recognising that she reminded him of one of his homely, attractive aunts who used to visit his mother.

She came over to a nearby table and wiped it with a cloth. He smiled at her and told her he'd seen her before, and where.

'Yes, I have two jobs; I'm trying to get by without a student grant.'

There was a slight, attractive accent that he couldn't place. He asked her what and where she was studying. It was social psychology at a north London university.

'Number crunching?'

'A bit, I'm more interested in theory. I was hooked as soon as I started, I guess, though I'm sure the application of it is dif-ferent. I should have gone there a dozen years ago.'

He asked her about her job. She shrugged.

'It's a source of income; you meet people.' She finished wiping the table. 'Though some of the people I meet are not worth meeting; the language, the way they eat. And they try to hit on me sometimes. I get tired of it. I dunno why they do.'

'Because you're attractive?'

'I don't think I am.'

'But you are.'

She shrugged. 'If you say so.' and with a pleasant, but fake smile, greeted another customer.

Picking up a newspaper from a shelf, he read an article informing him that the English had invented the garden square. He wondered when the last one was built in London.

He was about to leave when he noticed her wearing non-work clothes. He asked if she was going home. She was. He suggested that maybe he could walk along with her for a while if she didn't mind. She nodded and casually smiled. He couldn't remember asking a woman he hadn't really met something like this before.

They went down the stairs and out of the building. As they walked she asked him what he did. He told her and enquired about her course. It seemed a rather pragmatic one and she hadn't as yet touched on Freud or Fechner and others who'd created the foundations of what, he supposed, she hoped to do for a career.

She talked; he listened, until she halted. It was outside an Overground station; he hadn't really noticed his surroundings.

'I go in here now. It was nice talking to you.'

'You, too. Want to give me your number? I could see you again.'

She hesitated a little. He offered his pen and a scrap of paper. She quickly wrote a number.

'It could be a made-up one couldn't it,' she said mischievously. 'Bye.' and went into the station.

He watched her go through the ticket barrier. She had a surprisingly small waist.

Having nothing to do, he went to a nearby café and sat inside the door. He saw what could have been a playpen pushed against the window, inside it a yashmak'd matriarch was rolling *gozlemes* to a floating thinness, her hands flicking the folded pancakes onto a cloth. There was the clutter of diners; he noticed a wall print of a foam-battered lighthouse, and a yellow cab in a black and white shot of New York. His tea was bought.

Outside were buses, Romanies, an Edwardian Broadway, Hindus, terraced roads, distance; continents. He looked up from the tea and watched a fist squeezing dough and dribbling water over flour; she wasn't seeing anything beyond her movements, the glass pane. She had yet to speak a word.

He went back inside the station and travelled eastwards, getting off near the old sugar factory, lines of terraced roads pointing towards the cliff wall of its front. He went and stood at the edge of a nearby go-kart track, its puddles of tyres flooding over the old railway line and softening the hard chicane as matchstick kids with helmets like smoked glass planets skidded around like their big brothers did in twilight car parks.

It was real, a space utilised by children, casually competitive, relating to each other in fun, but how long, he wondered, would it be here; there was quite a bit of land. How many 'stunning apartments' would sooner or later be provided - he pushed away the politico and developer speak of 'delivered' - by the increasingly used euphemism of 'regeneration,' invariably meaning the loss of community ethos and large monetary gains by developers and, possibly, the bulging of a few local councillors back pockets?

He rang her the following day, the thought of game-playing, of not wishing to appear too keen, didn't bother him, though it wouldn't have been a surprise if it had been a made-up number. It wasn't, but she couldn't see him for a week. He thought of asking her a little more about what she was doing academically but didn't. Her name was Mary. She said she would ring him.

The next day it was work. He'd got friendly with a couple of Irish carpenters and sometimes stood around reluctantly pretending to be working as he listened to them repeating Wilde's epigrams or reciting lines from 'The Ballard of Reading Gaol' as they sawed pieces of four-by-two or tacked plaster boarding.

It was pleasant and unusual, though as a teenager he had gone to an opera with a plasterer who still had bits of plaster on the back of a hand and splashes of cement on a shoe, and once he'd worked with an electrician who had shown him a play he' just finished writing. Liam had unsuccessfully tried to get it into a fringe theatre.

These workers were few and far between. It was nice to know they existed and to be with them, he'd been largely deprived of face-to-face intellectual stimulus for some while.

When she did ring him she suggested a restaurant that was near where she was living. He met her in there. They shared a similar taste in food; and he was right in thinking that analysis was what she eventually wished to do. Going Dutch at her insistence before saying that she had an early class the next day, she got up to go, he in turn insisting he accompany her to her bus stop. The conventional and often empty 'Thanks for a lovely evening,' was transformed by her smile.

Returning home, he was aware that he hadn't really noticed the evening's environment, his usually precise visual recall pleasantly impaired by her presence and what seemed to be a slight non-English accent which intrigued him, but he hadn't as yet asked where it came from.

He saw her again a few days later. This time it was in her local pub. As they sat in its oak-panelled restaurant he noticed, as she turned to attract the waiter, the angle of her neck, the nape, her dark, tight-fitting shirt and was attracted to her again, this time a little more strongly. He felt he didn't have to try to impress; once more it felt easy, as if they were riding a gentle swell. There was no probing from either of them.

This relationship would, he hoped, be very different from his experience with Beryl. He laughed at himself. Of course it would.

He occasionally wrote poetry and had been invited through a chance meeting with its regular mentor to take over from him

for a one-off poetry workshop in a local library as part of a poetry festival. Beryl was one of ten people who'd attended and
whose work he'd quickly photocopied for them to read to each
other and comment upon; the obligatory intro of attempting to
define poetry he'd reduced to 'the best words in the best order.'

She sat at the end of the long table. She was almost skinny,
with dark auburn hair and an adjectival surfeit in her verses
that made him bite his lip so as not to be unkind to her. She
was dyslexic, but had a hard worked for articulacy which partly compensated and a way of intensely gesticulating that conveyed ideas and meanings convincingly.

There was a little strangeness about her: she would drift
away for a few seconds as if she didn't know she was being
spoken to or, sometimes, speaking herself. As the group left
he'd heard one of them say quietly to another that she seemed
'a bit of a nutter.' It was a term he disliked.

He met her again a few days later when she was driving
slowly past his home. He was going out and had just closed the
door. She was looking at him through the side window, smiling. She stopped. He went across to her. She had to see her ex
for something; apparently he lived in the street that ran off his.

'Now I know where you live,' she said, laughing, and drove
off.

Soon afterwards he saw her when meeting a friend who was
lecturing on a Fine Arts course at a college in Canning Town.
She was being taught by him and was with him in the pub. She
merely said hello to Liam and left. His friend got a little drunk
and told him about her.

She was a good student who he found hard to believe was
forty eight, as did Liam, it surprised him; she had a skin of a
thirty-year-old. His friend had once slept with her, literally, she
telling him she had a nineteen year old boyfriend who wanted
sex all the time and she needed a rest. He'd reluctantly given it
her.

The next evening there was a knock on Liam's door and she was on the step looking down at a piece of paper she was writing on.

'I've come to give you my mobile number.' she said, not looking up. She wore large sun glasses, a black, lacy shawl and sandals. He asked where she was going.

'Nowhere.' she answered, still looking down, and gave him the number. She went back to her car and drove off.

He saw his teacher friend on a local train a week afterwards. He told Liam she'd been behaving erratically; working intently for hours in the studio then sitting and staring at her work, unmoving, for long periods. She'd then miss a couple of days and the next be standing outside the college an hour before it opened. He'd tried to get her to tell him what was wrong. She wouldn't. Liam had suggested an analyst friend of his may be able to help.

He'd first got to know Clive Jelien when overseeing some work at the British Psychological Society's headquarters in Wimpole Street. He had asked Liam what colours they were going to use in the refurbishment and was pleased that the theme would be largely dominated by green which, he'd said, was the most psychologically restful colour.

He was there for a conference, remembering such gatherings usually solely in terms of the food that had been served. 'Ah yes, that was the smoked trout one' or the 'chicken l'orange' conference.' They'd chatted about psychology generally and the man asked him to have a coffee with him after work. He did. Since then they had seen each other regularly and enjoyably.

A week later, Liam was asked to do one more workshop. There were the same people as last time. She came in late and sat familiarly next to him. She was fiddling around inside her bag. He imagined her not looking up from it since he'd last seen her. Then she did, with large eyes and a wide, red lipstick'd smile. He asked them to read any new poems they may have written since the week before, if not, any of their work would do.

'I've written two new poems and, before you say it, I've cut the adjectives down,' she said, looking directly at him. Without waiting for his permission she began reading. After readings from the others and their discussions with him and amongst themselves which they all seemed to enjoy, she not joining in, they left, leaving him with Beryl.

He told her he was going and she followed him out of the library then put her arm in his - the reflex action initially being acceptance, not pushing away - and they went out of the library as if old friends, or more.

Easing himself away from her he told her that he had some errands to do and wasn't going home directly. She looked disappointed then brightly said, 'I'll come with you.'

'No, its okay, really.'

It was mildly embarrassing to move a few metres away from her watching the disapproving look then the sudden, beaming grin as she went towards the car park. He was annoyed at himself for lying; most people tell the truth most of the time; as well as the social taboo against not doing so, it's easier. Driving home he thought of her poems and her raw but interesting treatment of primitive subjects, and made up some loose stanzas in his head which he thought captured the feel of hers.

Two days later, placing a book mark in Laing's 'The Divided Self,' he glanced disinterestedly out of the window and again saw her car outside. As he moved to get a better view around the hedge she turned her head to grin at him and drove away.

He began to accept the idea that she was - he wasn't sure how to express it, 'following' was inaccurate, as was 'harassing' - stalking him. He knew the concept referred to a spectrum of behaviours and an even wider continuum of motivations. He didn't care, he was tired. He was sure there was little more involved than a somewhat skewed curiosity.

The following weekend his analyst friend called him. She'd been to see him.

'I don't know how much you know about her, but she's obviously very insecure and perhaps this is manifested in her work. She's shown me some of her paintings, they're rather second-rate, but I don't think that's important. One moment she's all excitement and energy, seeing them vividly, explaining them, objects of worship if you like, then the next... Well, she said she slashed one. There's hatred there, maybe fear. I feel there's obsession, too. Anyway, thought you should know. Pity, she's an attractive woman. So, how's your world, Liam?'

While trying to answer the question he was thinking of her: the dark, auburn hair, giving him her number, her instant mood changes, a slashed painting, wondering what or whom it was of.

Then she rang his home number. He'd given this to the students at the workshop in case they'd wanted to talk about their work.

'Do you want to come to my birthday party tomorrow? It's just a little one, you'll enjoy it.' He didn't answer.

'Please.'

She gave him her address and, having no plans for the next evening and thinking that there just may be some interesting people there, he went, though his instincts were telling him not to.

She lived nearer than he thought. It was a ground floor flat in a Fifties block. She was dressed for a party.

'Come and sit down, have a drink.'

He went into a music-filled room. No one else was there.

'Am I the first? I'm usually last; I like to make an entrance.'

'No, it's just you and me. It *is* my birthday, though.'

It was the last sentence that got to him, he could feel the loneliness. She gave him a glass of wine, changed the music and sat opposite him. He asked her about her work. She talked of Hockney, Bellini; a Turner exhibition.

'Let's dance,' she said, pulling him up and pressing into him. He went through the motions, sat down and mentioned Turner again. 'You know more about him than me.'

In phrases which he assumed were straight from her course book she unenthusiastically told him a little more. He was feeling uncomfortable. He told her he needed to go.

'Why?'

He hesitated. She came right up to him, her face inches from his.

'Don't go.'

He kissed her forehead as if he was kissing someone who he was fond of, perhaps a sister or a child, and turned to leave.

'I hate the way you do that.'

He was thrown; the implication was that he'd done it to her before.

'Look… I'm going.'

'Really?'

Then she slapped him. As he twisted away he was caught on the side of the neck. He could feel her breath.

When film noir heroes hit women there was seemingly something deserved and satisfying about it. He couldn't do it to her. He opened the door, went to his car and drove away.

He was shaken, but what was bothering him was whether he should tell his analyst friend what had happened. He decided not to and guessed she wouldn't either.

She came around next day. He could see who it was through his patterned glass door panes. He opened the door quickly and asked her firmly what she wanted.

'I'm sorry, so sorry. Please let me come in. I want to apologise.'

She was crying.

He let her go before him into the front room. She looked briefly around then stopped, grimacing at a shelf holding a framed sepia shot of two of his great-aunts, one who'd died at ninety nine. It seemed to have been taken during the Twenties; both wore peacock feather hats and flapper skirts.

'Who are they? What are they doing here?'

Putting her hand on her head she clawed at her hair and stepped over to the bookshelf and swept the photo off the shelf along with books and a small urn holding his mother's ashes which for years he'd intended to scatter somewhere she had particularly enjoyed; under a tree in their old local park where she'd taken him numerous times as a child could have been one such place.

He looked at the floor, the books, and the urn, lid still tightly on, rolling slowly to a stop.

She began to stride to another shelf, arm and hand outstretched, but he grabbed her shoulder, pulled her backwards out of the room and along the passage and, opening the front door with his other hand, turned her towards the path. She frantically opened the garden gate and ran across the road to her car. He slammed the door.

He'd never done this to a woman before. He was scared. He'd sat down and tried to calm himself. He attempted to rationalise it all. He couldn't. 'Obsession.' His friend seemed to have been correct. He knew he would soon begin to feel sorry for her, and also that he wouldn't be seeing her again.

No. Mary was much more stable, she was solid. He doubted if there had been many, if any, traumas in her life. He liked her. He was getting increasingly fond of her. She made him feel a little more temperate. When with her, even thoughts of random skylines, inimical, distorted towers and self-congratulatory architectural triumphalism were held in abeyance.

# CHAPTER 6

Piero Ronzi had just arrived back at his apartment from an Architects Awards ceremony in Chicago's John Hancock's building. After it had finished, the audience had quickly gone to its top floor Thirties bar with the fake palms and Lempicka prints and bearing only a slight similarity to his ground floor apartment two miles away.

He was contented enough with its French window leading onto a small garden at the back and the curved suntrap window in the front; not many of the latter were left in residential Chicago. He would have preferred one in the block he had helped design and which was the reason for the evening's occasion.

It was Justin and Peter who had, as Miles & Mycroft, received the prize - a rather elegant statuette that looked a little like New York's Woolworth building - and who, amidst the applause, had invited him on to the stage. He had, although rising from one of the large circular tables filling the floor and bowing slightly towards the partners, declined. Although not formulating exactly why he had, he knew it wasn't just a perverse reaction to other people being given formal recognition; he had, after all, assisted them diligently and skilfully, but wanted it to be him only that was granted the accolade.

He'd been working in the practice for nearly two years and had enjoyed it, except for the hard, frustrating effort needed to subjugate his creative impatience, though it had been let loose a little in that period.

The first time had been on a canal-side house whose new owner had wanted merely a refurbishment of what was there plus a few alterations. Piero had little interest in studying the relevant period for details and had designed a new frontage and roof; both made of purposely discordantly coloured material.

He had, keeping it as cheap as possible, persuaded the man that he would gradually come to like it and it would increase his image, his standing in the neighbourhood. He wasn't sure how the partners perceived it but thought they may, despite their lukewarm response to the acceptance of his plan, have held a rather grudging admiration.

The building which had won - a Downtown office block for an insurance company - was, as far as Piero could see, initially derived from a late Edwin Lutyens building he'd seen photos of near Bank Station in London and a Mies van der Rohe work. That's what did it for them, the judges seduced by their love of the Chicago renaissance of the Twenties and Thirties, and which the building was a forceful reminder of. Most of the jury seemed to be old men who Piero wanted to physically shake and inform them of other buildings, different buildings that were being built in the world, and a few in this very city.

He felt that while they were winning prizes for this sort of work, which he had rather reluctantly agreed was exciting for the firm, they wouldn't really change, it was in effect falling back on the tried and tested. He wanted the untried, and not tested by criteria that seemed to be so deep-seated, so dominant in architectural design in the city.

It was he that wanted to do the trying, to fully design his ideas, often hastily sketched on scraps of paper or, when feeling organized, in notebooks wherever he happened to be: sitting in a delicatessen, waiting for a theatre to open its doors or, one of his favourite pursuits, when walking through Lincoln Park; twice he'd hiked its seven mile length.

He hadn't stayed long after the ceremony; he'd had a drink with Justin and Peter and obligatorily talked to a few people, but felt a little empty and not really a part of it, though pleased on a personal level for his employers. And tomorrow it was back to the drawing board, working a little grudgingly on a new school building the firm and its developers were cooperating on, a rather turgid, hotchpotch of established shapes and details in sandstone which he knew would, over the years, age and turn almost black.

It was soon after this particular work was completed that he was head-hunted. He didn't realise it at first, but when the second man on the same day had strolled into his favourite bar at the corner of State Street and Madison and started talking to him about architecture - this one more directly than the first - it dawned on him that maybe he'd become a wanted man.

He had recently sat in on an informal meeting with a developer and the partners and found himself, uninvited, making comments and counter-suggestions about a proposed site; simple things like lowering ceiling heights to put on another storey, and wider widows - to the visible vexation of Justin who had enjoyed creating his own almost baroque details on the outside of the panes. The building then wouldn't be seen as so skinny, which seemed to please the prospective client. It was someone who worked for the developer who had casually asked him whether he was happy in his job. He'd told him he wasn't fully contented then the man left.

The second approach was also from somebody in the developer's office, a little more senior than the first, who had told him that his employers had been quite impressed with his performance at the meeting. He was being offered a job which, if he accepted, held the prospect of more autonomy; a little more say in what he would be allowed to contribute. And the money was better.

He decided quite quickly. The partners told him they were sorry to see him leave, but had, in retrospect, realised that he wasn't very happy there - 'fidgety' - was how Peter had described his behaviour during the time he was there; Justin's description of 'constrained' and 'kinda holdin' yourself in' was a more accurate comment.

The first project he worked on at Klengle Associates, an architectural firm allied with and situated in the same offices as a development company they did most of their work for, was one in which he could incorporate a few ideas he'd sketched previously though not been allowed to use: a steeply curved roofline and wide, rounded corners ascending the whole of a twenty-storey building which was a change from conventional hard edges. It had been accepted.

The second was a hotly debated - he had more freedom to be himself here and became less inhibited in his opinions - reconfiguration of a junior partner's design for the front of a forty-storey building in Elgin that was a rather ordinary rectangle jutting out thirty feet to half the building's height. He turned it into a triangle built from the ground floor length of the construction rising to the top and containing roughly the same amount of rentable space.

Raul, the junior designer of the building and only a little older than himself, walked around the office for a few days after the senior partners had passed Piero's idea, occasionally mumbling discontentedly to himself in his native tongue *'No est justo,'* or *'Es mi edificio,'* even more so when it was enthusiastically welcomed by the developers.

The partners also commented on his freehand drawing ability. He'd told them that as a young child he'd always been able to draw well and that once, in a school exam when he was thirteen, he had, the night before, found a copy of a pen and ink sketch of a tomb in Florence and copied it. It took three hours. Next day he'd remembered every line and scroll of it and drew it in the exam. He was top of his class.

He was pleased by his employers' interest and that they seemed pleased with him, and felt somewhat satisfied as he returned to his flat in Adele Street, a place he'd hardly touched since moving in, being too busy working and thinking of work. He looked through a drawer in which, when moving in, he'd hurriedly thrown a selected few of his old drawings and looked with a smile at a design he'd thought up a few years previously.

It was a little more detailed than the others. It was of a large house shaped like a grand piano with a violin appearing to lean on the larger instrument. The violin, the top of its handle higher than the house and made almost completely out of glass served as the entry linking the elevated piano to the ground. The piano portion of the house stood on three concrete legs and featured a roof terrace beneath a canopy shaped like the piano's open top.

One day perhaps; though it would be a copy of things already extant, well known objects, clever perhaps, and if it was ever built would be striking, but for him - the word 'gimmicky' came to the fore - it wasn't original, the shapes weren't what he wanted, and there were so many that he wished to create; in cities, towns; fields would do.

He put the sketch away, closed the drawer and, other than thinking that he'd probably sit in a bar alone again that evening thinking as ever about his job, of buildings, concepts, contours, heights, thought once more of his curving, twisting tower that he wanted to lean more than the famous one in Pisa that had fascinated him when seeing it as a boy.

He wasn't sure how high it could go, but knew that it could be done by making the central core of the building slant in the opposite direction to the lean of the structure and would straighten as it grew higher. He'd mentioned it to a contractor on one of Miles & Mycroft's designs who, after initially being amused by the idea, had thought about it and reckoned that with a deep concrete base and a mesh of reinforced steel and many piles drilled far underground - the amount depending on its height - it could be done.

Meanwhile, still feeling pretty good after moving up from his usual modest creative contributions since being in the US, he carried on working assiduously however reluctant he felt at often being restricted, as before, to the 'acceptable' shapes, materials and functions of the buildings of the time and which the partners seemed to be creating an increasing number of, and hoping that he would be put on something more adventurous. The Hancock Center had been up a dozen years, the Willis Tower wasn't that much younger; it seemed time for something else.

The firm seemed to think so, too. After having for months to almost sneak in a few ideas and details of his own as additions or alterations to the work he was given, the partners were commissioned by the City to build an office block on West Washington Street which was to house dozens of State agencies along with the Illinois governor's Chicago office.

Part of Klengle Associates' description of the finished project was:

'... its circular atrium will give visitors a stimulating view of glass-walled elevators, floating staircases and floor plates stacked up to seventeen storeys. The space will be illuminated by a massive canted oculus.'

It was the oculus he liked, he'd even suggested that it be more curved than the original design and, after being told that if it could be done without cutting out any of the square footage of office space, to go ahead and do it.

As computers were increasingly being used to aid design, not just in mechanics and electronics but also in architecture, he had diplomatically but repeatedly suggested to the partners they make more use of them and had purchased his own CAD as well as some of the new programmes to complete the greater curvature. He'd worked on it at home till the early morning of the same night.

While waiting for the erection of this building to begin, a developer they had worked for intermittently asked them to design a medium-sized housing scheme. It may have been that the main partners were very busy or they now had enough confidence in him, but after some discussions on the form it would take allowed him his head, though keeping a close eye on what he was planning.

It wasn't really original, he'd seen a photo of the shapes in a development in East Germany, and at first his employers weren't that keen, but his enthusiasm seemed to wear them down and they relented. It was a radical building.

The exterior shapes were of two cast concrete, serpentine, snake-like shapes with a tall atrium; his employers, though initially doubtful, agreed when he did a watercolour impression for them.

The design didn't win any prizes, but although there was something un-Chicagoan about it, it appeared to be interesting enough for some sort of consensus to be formed amongst the architectural community, as well as in the practice, that perhaps he was one to be watched. It was pleasing to hear that his name was being favourably mentioned, but not so for the next thing he was asked to do.

It was to work on an extension to a mansion in Oak Brook, DuPage County, a small addition with the essential directive from its new owner being that it should correspond with what was already there. The partners were pleased with this request knowing that its purchaser was a rather prosperous and, according to the Chicago Tribune, a man who was to become even richer. Piero recalled, but only vaguely, an article he had idly read that had described him as 'destined to become one of the most powerful men in Chicago.'

The contents of his lazy read became a little sharper when Samuel, the older partner, had asked him to put his energy into the man's latest acquisition. Piero thought it may have been a piece of in-house satire until told that the practice's relevant employees were otherwise fully engaged and that with his penchant for water colouring he was sure that after visiting the place he could do some impressive sketches for their client.

He was about to respond by telling them that he was the last person to do, or be asked to do, this sort of work when, remembering his quasi-vow to be more tolerant of the things he had to do whilst earning a living and, after all, he had just proved himself on his recent endeavour, agreed to do it.

It had an impressive drive for a place smaller than he was given to believe; with an unprepossessing exterior that, as he drove up to it, could see was an ungainly and inappropriate mixture of pseudo-classic styles. But once the real-estate agent had let him in and he'd squinted against the glare of gilt and mirrors in the entrance corridor, it became a visual assault.

There was hardly any second floor, its space taken up by the twenty-five-foot high vaulted ceiling of a living room decorated with neo-Romantic frescoes below which were reproductions of old masters in baroque frames and an erupting fountain. He went through to the almost two-storey dining room with its carved ivory frieze, onyx columns and the largest mahogany table he'd ever seen. The onyx also extended to the lavatory.

There were tapestries, murals, frescoes, winged statuary, bathtub-sized flower-filled samovars, a Corinthian colonnade, blinding chandeliers and more mirrors. He wondered where its previous owner had sat, perhaps in boxer shorts, to eat his salami or roast beef sandwiches or scratch himself where it itched. If the new owner wanted this opulent style to be repeated in the extension then he had as much taste, or lack of it, as its previous one.

He was just about to communicate his thoughts with the agent who had as yet not said a word, merely following him a few paces behind, when the front door - an ugly Tudorbethan-like object - opened and a tall, broad man stood there in silhouette. He entered. He was a few years older than Piero with a well cut suit, a shirt and tie, and sandy coloured hair that looked a little too pinkish to be a natural hue.

'You're the architect guy, huh?'

The question was posed in a strong New York accent, one that Piero had heard all around him during his time spent in the city.

'I'm David Tern, the owner. What d'yer think of the place?'

Piero hesitated. 'It's, er, certainly opulent.'

'It is, and I want the rest of it, what'll be built out back, to correspond. Can you do that?'

'Yes, it can be done.' He wanted to quickly add, 'But not by me.'

'Good. I need to go, but you can let me see somethin' pretty soon, I'm interested in this project. See yer.'

He turned and went down the front steps to a large chaufferdriven Lincoln and gave a gesture of a wave as the car moved quickly along the drive and into the road.

'There's a guy for yer, eh?' said the agent standing beside him, not bothering to shake hands. Saying 'Shut the door behind you, please.' he went to a car around the side of the house that Piero hadn't noticed.

Sitting on a gold-coloured chaise longue, Piero looked up at the ceiling again, at the paintings and chandeliers, got out his sketch book which he carried with him most of the time now and quickly started sketching rough outlines for he knew only approximate measurements of the extension. He put a few ideas down in terms of shapes and colours then returned to the office to get more information.

Though not caring much about what he was drawing it was nice to be using a pen and brush again and the time moved swiftly by. It wasn't far off dawn when he'd finished a preliminary presentation. It would impress his employers that he hadn't returned home. He would get some sleep in the rest room anyway, then later have some colazione and fette biscottatti in the Italian deli he'd found a block away. He rarely met clients, especially one-to-one, so after a short sleep and before ringing the man's office, he decided to do a little investigating.

In a local library he found that some hundred and eighty yeas ago Tern's main antecedent had established a gun powder mill on the banks of the Redwine River in Missouri which allowed for the manufacture and shipment of sulphur and saltpetre. At one time it was the largest black powder manufacturing firm in the world and the family were amongst the twenty richest in the country, but profligacy, ill health and a non-adherence to the protestant work ethic amongst its younger members meant that when it came to David Tern's inheritance there wasn't a great deal of it left.

But the Tern name still meant something and Piero gathered that by using it copiously and advantageously, the current beneficiary had managed to acquire loans and make property deals in New York before moving west that had gradually built up his income, which, it seemed, was now escalating rather quickly. It also mentioned his East European wife.

In the office next day he had a message to contact Tern as soon as possible. He did. He was asked to meet him with his illustrations at the mansion in an hour. He was there early, Tern arriving not long afterwards in a different suit but with his same business-like movements as he got out of his car, this time having driven it himself.

He nodded at Piero and strode to the offensive door and let them both in. He gestured to the same sofa his companion had sat on two days before, took a seat opposite and asked him to show him what he'd done about the extension.

He looked at the work for a few minutes, not glancing at its creator till he had laid the sheets of cartridge paper on his lap.

'I like these, I like the colours, they're different from, but kinda suit what's already here, and the way you've suggested the mirrors and where the paintings go. But how d'yer know I've got any more?'

'I don't, but I'm sure you have.'

'I have, they're classic ones, the old masters, not that Pickassole stuff. I'll have a look at these again later.'

He stood, looked at Piero silently for a while and said, 'Tomorrow sometime I'm gonna start looking for knick-knacks. They'll be starting on it soon and I like to move in as soon as the contractors have finished, knowing exactly what I have and where it's goin'. If you want, you can come with me, you might have a few ideas. Okay?'

Quickly convincing himself that it would make a change from the office, Piero complied.

As they walked to their vehicles Tern asked, 'Where were you before here?'

'New York.'

'Where'd yer live, Little Italy?'

'No, why should I?'

'I recognise the accent. You're Italian.'

'Your wife's Lithuanian, but she doesn't live in Bridgeport or work in the stockyards.'

He had recently learnt that the city held the largest population of Lithuanians outside Lithuania.

The look he received instantly forced him to realise that whether he wanted this particular job or not, he couldn't afford to offend this rather mean-looking, strong ego'd man. His need to earn a living was of more significance presently than his desire to populate America's third largest conurbation with idealised structures. The look hadn't wavered and it was getting longer. Not knowing what his response should be he just looked back.

'How d'yer know that?' Tern asked.

'Read it somewhere.'

The questioner seemed to grin ruefully and said, 'See yer tomorrow.'

He got into his car and drove away.

Three days later, the in-between filled with some minor alterations and corrections to the 'Snake Building,' Piero was told that Tern wanted to meet him Downtown at three that afternoon.

He was outside Marshall Field's on the dot, both arriving at its columned entrance at the same time, Piero from a subway exit, Tern from a red and white Cadillac.

'Come.' the latter said, gesturing for Piero to follow him into the store. 'I haven't long so there'll be no gazing at the Great Hall or visiting the restaurant.'

The absence of the former was okay by him, its ornateness reminding him too much of quasi-classicism. Instead, they went to a ground floor department where Tern beckoned to a sales assistant then pointed to a pair of ivory door handles. She came over hurriedly.

'Grab those for me.'

She did, adding, 'There's something we think you will be interested in, Mister Tern, just a moment.'

Just as quickly she moved towards a door at the side of a counter and after stepping inside a cubby hole for a short while she came out looking down at something in her hands. She smiled at him.

'We've been waiting for you to come in,' she said, and handed it to him. It was a small autograph book. He looked at the page it was opened at and grinned.

'Yep, that too.' He turned to Piero. 'It's Buddy Holly's, it'll go with my Jimi Hendrix guitar.'

He went towards two large mirrors with gold-leafed frames larger than the area of the glass.

'These as well,' he said, the woman behind him jotting his requests in a notebook.

With both Piero and the woman now following him, Tern went through to the adjoining department and immediately saw a large, glass-topped dining table with gilded lions along each corner. He pointed to it.

'Yes sir,' she said, again writing in her book.

Piero wasn't sure whether to just go along with it, to encourage him in his desires or to modulate them a little with something more tasteful. Once in Tern's eye-line again, he pointed to some Shelley pottery and a pleasant Clarice Cliff vase. They were dismissed with a 'Too boring.'

At the end of a silent trip up an escalator to a bathroom section, Tern grabbed some champagne soap bubbles and gestured to a bath with Dutch metal claws under its curved ends, his wish duly noted by the assistant. They went quickly through two more sections where the New Yorker purchased three large silver vases and dallied over a king-size four-poster bed before looking at his watch.

Saying 'Send 'em to me.' to the diligent employee then telling Piero he would be in touch, he moved quickly into an elevator.

As he watched it descend, Piero wondered how many times a month he did these shopping expeditions, this mishmash of shine, this expensive garnering of glitz.

A week later, time taken up using his energies indifferently on a rehash of a commission the firm had been given a few months previously, Tern rang the office asking for him.

'I've got a project over at Cook I've just started discussing with contractors. I've bought the land. I had a little talk with your bosses before you first came to the house and they mentioned you and your ideas. I don't know much about your views, but you seem kinda different, I usually like that. I'll tell you about...' He hesitated. 'No, I'll send you a letter telling you what I want. Maybe you can come up with something before I discuss it with you then we can see what's what.'

Piero had an odd, pleasing sensation upon hearing the 'we.'

Next day he received the information. It was simply stated: A thirty-two storey office block - apparently tern had had to fight for that height against the local Land Authority's restrictions, Piero imagining him easing the way with dollars - at the edge of Cook County with a specified square footage of office space. Included was a photo of the land it was to be built on. It seemed to be a field with woodland demarcating one of its edges; apparently the enterprise would be a lone tower in a suburb.

This was fine by Piero. He'd had for a while intermittent images of a tall construction curving slightly in from its base and then out again from halfway, and a semi-elliptical jutting platform towards its top to serve as a heliport. The latter would, he knew, look more impressive if the building was over the number of floors specified.

It had been a kind of semi-fantasy at the time; he'd even vaguely predicted its name whilst imagining it, 'The Lip.' He liked that, and maybe it didn't matter what a building was actually called; if people gave a name to it, it meant that it, and the architect, were noticed. He now found himself actually drawing it.

He became engrossed and called in sick, something he'd never done before, and worked long hours at home for three days on his idea knowing he would need specialist help for advice on materials - there would be a hell of a lot of glass - structural steel, thousands of bolts, the stresses, strains, volumes and weights.

Returning to the office, he told the partners what he had been doing during his time off. Their reaction was one of frowning surprise which was interrupted by Tern calling, wanting to speak to him. He was handed the phone. The caller told him to meet him in the evening. They must have heard; Tern was loud.

'You'd better go then,' Samuel said, Piero feeing his eyes on his back as he left their office.

This time he waited over an hour for the man who strolled into the Downtown bar, came across to his table and said, 'Whaddya got for me?'

Piero showed him. Tern looked through the sheets of paper with screwed-up eyes and occasionally nodding in what seemed approval. After he'd perused the last sheet he looked at

Piero, initially without expression then scrutinising, studying him and nodding again. He then grinned.

'I like it, especially the helicopter deck.'

'That's just something I kind of got carried away with I suppose, it doesn't have to be there, it s an addition. It's the concave curve that's - '

'I always wanted one. Keep it.'

He looked at Piero again with that questioning look.

'I didn't tell yer that this is for me, my offices, my headquarters, my building. It's my tower, yet here you are, coming up with a chopper.' He grinned again. 'You got it right.'

'Thanks. I think the partners will like this; maybe they'll let me take it over, some of it anyway. Perhaps - '

'No. I want you to do it. We'll discuss fees, etcetera another time.'

His listener wasn't quite sure what was meant.

'They don't know about this? Not sure I understand, I thought it - '

'You thought wrong.'

'But I haven't the… facilities, the resources to do this on my own'

'I'll help you out with an office, even staff. I know a few architects, civil engineers and so forth, and there's some even younger than you. They can work with you. D'yer want that?'

It was a lot for Piero Ronzi to absorb, but before he could give it a semblance of commercial or rationally emotional thought, he heard himself say yes.

# CHAPTER 7

He had enjoyed his artistic break - a photo of the brick figures he'd completed featuring in the local weekly newspaper, a
copy of which Con had proudly shown to her neighbours back
home - but was also glad to get back, along with Thomasz, to
the nitty gritty of conventional bricklaying on the rest of the
houses, though to give them names like 'Foxgloves' and 'The
Cedars' he felt pretentious.

His wife came down just the once to see him, her brother
staying with her mother. The two days and three nights were
good for both of them. He'd got tickets for 'Cats' and even
'Othello' at the National Theatre, which Con didn't like much
though he did. They walked around the west end and visited
Westminster Cathedral, his wife's Catholic upbringing still
strongly felt, and Madame Tussaud's, a place she'd long wanted to see. When he saw her off at King's Cross Station he cud-
dled her and whispered in her ear, 'I can still do romance, lass,
eh?' They grinned at each other before she stepped onto her
train.

From then, he began after a few weeks to return home for
weekends, occasionally arranging to have a Monday off and
working all day the following Saturday then making it more
regular. It started to become almost the norm for both of them.

The subcontractor's boss was indeed a good 'un as Thomasz
had said; looking after his men, paying them well, accommodating to requests for flexibility in hours worked, and Jim had
no problem joining him on a new site in the city's northern
suburbs.

When he started work there, the first thing he noticed with
dismay was a near-completed building which looked like the
curve of an enormous bird's mouth and almost overhanging
the site he was to work on. It was coloured a deep yellow at the

broad start of it from the first storey to the fourth then turning into a dark grey at its curved down, slender tip. It had a line of small windows running along the middle of it, creating the effect of a closed beak.

He felt it a preposterous design and hardly credible that someone, anyone, would want to work in or look at a building like that. He guessed that the designer and developers would get kudos for its originality. He visibly shook his head - Thomasz just kept staring - put his overalls on and got ready to start a day's work.

Three Mondays afterwards as his bus neared the site, he was thinking of the old Guinness poster of a large bird with its 'Look what toucan do' caption and looking forward to the dinner break when he could open his packed lunch Con had made for him to put it in the fridge at the lodgings with the proviso that he musn't touch it till he was at work. He'd surreptitiously taken a peep and knew there was a stottie loaf with pease pudding lovingly spread inside and a singin' hinnie for pudding. He didn't know the origins of the names, but liked the sound of them almost as much as the food and which she'd made him promise to share with Thomasz.

It was close to lunchtime and he was taking a quick look at his watch - he and Thomasz had just laid their fourth row above the concrete foundation - when he heard Thomasz shout, '*Popatrrz!*' He knew it meant 'Look!'

His peripheral vision registered, twenty metres away, his mate's face in profile angled upward towards 'Toucan Tower' or 'Brainless Bird,' the latter his nomenclature for its designer. The crane on their site - a mixture of flats and three-bedroom homes - was winching up slabs of concrete ready to place on a corner of the third floor of one of the blocks.

As its cargo went higher, the top of the crane seemed to lean a little in one direction, a direction that Jim and probably Thomasz saw was forcing it nearer the tip of the 'beak' on the adjacent construction. He heard the sound of steel hitting pre-cast concrete.

He couldn't understand why two distinct pieces of the building began falling towards and not away from them; certainly not away from Thomasz. The sharply defined shapes loomed larger as they fell. One of then Jim could see smashing through a half-finished roof his fellow brickies had recently worked on, the other thudding just in front of Thomasz, a long piece of alloy ducting striking his hard hat and flinging its wearer instantly to the ground.

Jim hesitated for a second, his mind more concerned with several of their bricks that had been knocked away from the soft mortar underneath them. It was a momentary annoyance, holding in abeyance the shock of seeing Thomasz lying almost star-shaped on the ground.

He went to him. His helmet, still attached to his head, was hanging away from his face which looked as if had suddenly been bleached white, looking more Slavic than he'd ever noticed. He knelt by him; just looked at him.

There was silence then a shout of 'Don't touch him.' and one of the roofers was standing over both of them, a mobile in his hand, bringing it up to his mouth. Jim didn't hear the man's words; he was looking at the top of the crane and the damaged, grotesque tip of the building. The crane was now steady, its load still being raised before its slow turning away towards its intended landing place.

The ambulance came very quickly. Jim had never seen one on a site before; he'd never seen an accident, other than flattening his thumb chopping a brick when first under Thomasz's tutelage. For a moment he felt as if he'd only just began working in construction, hadn't been doing it long enough to experience the relatively commonplace; though this particular happening wasn't.

Two men got out and knelt either side of Thomasz, one with a small machine in his hands, part of which he placed over the casualty's mouth and nose. Another brought a stretcher to them. Jim kept where he was; just looking, knowing he could do nothing to help. They didn't bend over him for long, the three of them laying him carefully on the stretcher, placing a blanket over him then carrying him inside the vehicle. As the doors were closed, with the driver moving towards the cab, Jim took a step towards him.

'Cun I - '

'Sorry mate,' said the driver as he slammed the cab door.

Jim managed to shout, though it seemed to take almost all his strength, 'What hospital you takin' 'im to?'

He just about heard, 'St Georges.' before the ambulance turned around, crossed the site and out, its siren wailing. It was only then that fellow workers gathered around him, some silently, others asking him what had happened.

One of the latter offered to drive him to the hospital. Jim told the others to let the foreman know what was happening and ran behind the man with the car which was parked just inside the edge of the site.

The satnav helped and they couldn't have been far behind the ambulance when they arrived; it was the only vehicle in the parking bay outside the A&E. They went in and asked various people who looked like hospital employees if they knew anything of a patient that had recently been brought in, until a nurse pointed to a door along the wide corridor. They hurried towards it, another nurse asking what they wanted and telling them that they couldn't go in; best they sit on the row of seats behind them.

They sat there, Jim asking his companion if he'd seen what happened. He hadn't, but had heard the reverberating thumps as the large pieces of concrete had landed and seen Thomasz lying on one of the few pieces of grass that were growing on the site. Seeing no point in mentioning the obvious, that they hoped he would be alright, they talked of the building whose highest floor stretched so thinly, the end of which had so easily been toppled.

The wait seemed much longer than it was. After a while they simultaneously stood and walked towards the door again, a large double one that looked as if it was made of rubber then, further on, seeing a bit of green through a widow, walked into and around a quadrangle with shrubs and flower beds then sat on a bench.

There was a tree in a corner. Jim looked at it. That'll live on past me, he thought, perhaps it's already done so with Thomasz. No. Thomasz would be okay, he musn't go, he was a brickie, a master builder in a way; that Ibsen feller - or 'geezer' as Thomasz had started to say since he'd been working in London - wrote a play about it.

'The tree can foockin' go 'cos it don't know it's 'ere,' he thought. And what does it mean to 'know?' He'd heard one of the Irish chippies asking someone that. He wasn't sure, had never thought about it. What he had thought of - only the once - was where 'thought' was in the world. He couldn't answer that one either, nor, he suspected, could the philosopher who'd originally asked the question.

'I hope he's not in too much pain,' his co-worker said.

Jim didn't answer. He was thinking of inanimate objects, of stones, chairs, hacksaws; they didn't feel pain either. He stood and slowly walked around the quadrangle again. What was it that felt the pain anyway? Scientists could go on about nerve ends, the brain and stuff, but what was... The word came to him; consciousness. Was it part of the physical brain; was it some sort of 'mind stuff'? It didn't matter, his mate was injured; he could be dying.

What could he say to Con? She was fond of Thomasz; she'd been so welcoming when he'd first brought him home soon after he had arrived in the land. She'd even taught him some Geordie sayings. He couldn't pronounce them that well but two of his favourites were 'radgie gadgie' and 'canny buy a

Tudor, man,' referring to an old man and a brand of crisps respectively. Thomasz had been back to Poland a couple of times and on the second occasion had invited Jim and Con. They'd politely refused. He wished they hadn't.

He had an image, unbidden and unwanted, of a Catholic funeral in a columned, gold leafed, high-domed church in Krakow with Thomasz's family - his mother, he thought, was still alive - and the coffin carried in sombrely and slowly by funeral parlour employees.

As a bizarre escape he changed them to bricklayers in jeans, with aprons holding trowels and a hammer or two, and bearing the oak coffin with its pattern of inlaid bricks on the sides aloft and balanced securely on raised mortar boards underneath each corner. He let the pictures continue and saw the brickies gently laying down their load and crawling through the narrow entrance of the furnace to examine the brick lining to see if it was of a high enough standard for its new occupant. He stopped himself as he imagined the men utilising their trowels to repoint some of the brickwork.

Then he felt the man who'd come with him to the hospital touch his arm and suggested they go back in and find a cup of tea somewhere. There was little else they could do. They sat at a café near the entrance looking at their untouched cups of tea and saying nothing until Jim said he would go to the room they weren't allowed in and see if there was any news.

They both went. Jim knocked gently on the door. A nurse came out, closed it quickly behind her and asked what he wanted.

'You have a man in there, a Thomasz Nowak. He's been in there for a - '

'I'm sorry, but this room is out of bounds,' she said in an African accent.

She had high cheekbones, a drooping upper lip, slightly protruding teeth and a skin like soft plastic. She was a Somali. As the door closed on him he remembered the time when nurses always seemed to have blue eyes, dark hair and Irish accents. He turned away and went back to the table. He told his companion he may as well go and that he would wait for news, there was no point in both of them staying.

'It's okay lud, I'll be alreet. Thanks for coomin''

His workmate got up and left.

It was the silence, as if it wasn't a bustling, anxious, busy hospital at all. He couldn't see a single nurse, obviously no doctors, and only one patient, walking slowly away from the little café in a dressing gown. The nearest thing to a sense of urgency was two porters pushing an elderly man who hardly looked ill on a wheeled stretcher.

Thomasz would look ill, very ill. That thing had come rushing down on him, smashed onto him. He hadn't seen any blood, hadn't looked, really. He thought of him being no more. Not existing. He disliked the word 'legacy,' but there were houses, offices, a factory, a town hall somewhere, a railway station, and he'd worked on a cathedral in Krakow for three years, parts of all of them built by his friend. He couldn't just stop doing it; there were more bricks to be laid for Chris'sake, thousands of 'em, millions.

He didn't want to think about what he would do, feel, if his friend didn't recover. It was all right for those that believed. Most cultures, especially religious ones, had a strong belief. It gave strength as a consolation for the grieving. He knew that in Nigeria there was a kind of triple heritage of Christianity, Islam and ancestor worship, in the Caribbean Catholicism was mixed with folk beliefs like Voodoo and Curanderism - though not sure what it actually was, he liked the word - and both Christianity and Islam saw death as a transition to a more glorious place and believed in the sovereignty of God or Allah. 'God giveth and God taketh away,' as Con would say. She had her faith. What did *he* have?

You're here for Thomasz Nowak aren't you?'

79

The voice almost startled him. It was a nurse bending slightly over his table.

He almost stammered.'Yes.'

'There's no change. He's - '

'Critical but stable?'

'Yes he is.'

'Sorry, but clichés like thut mean noothin' to me, lass. What actually is it? How is he? Will he live, for Chris'sake?'

'Try to be calm. We can do no more, we'll have to see. It was a bad accident.'

'I know. I saw it. I were there.'

She looked at him sternly, he later realising it reminded him of the old-fashioned Sisters in the local hospital; they could scare the shite out of you.

'He has a head injury as well as shoulder and back damage. He is alive, Mister?'

He told her.

'Mister Salmon, by all means stay here if you wish but I doubt very much if there'll be any significant news for a while. If you can, go home, come back in the morning. If you give me your mobile number we'll be able to contact you.'

After he'd done so, she wheeled away and walked briskly back along the corridor.

He wasn't sure what to do. He didn't want to stay in the hospital but felt an unease; a guilt creeping up on him as if he was betraying his mate by not staying near him though he knew he could do nothing. But to go back to the lodgings and him not be there, wasn't that worse? He decided to return. Thomasz wouldn't be there, but his room and belongings were so he would be kind of near him. He went back and tried to sleep. He couldn't.

He got up, switched the light on, went to the bottom drawer of a dressing table where, if he recalled correctly, he'd put some sheets of A4 when he'd first moved in. He sat on the bed and looked at their white blankness. He wanted to write something, maybe the play he'd never started, maybe it could be about bricklayers, an honourable trade, perhaps about an East European one and another from 'oop north.' He'd make them stereotypes, a confirmation, satisfying an audience's lazy, almost unconscious searching for order, and also to take the piss out of them.

He'd make a parody out of it, a satire. The chief character would go around gripping a trowel and spirit level and saying things like, 'Aa'd better gan canny' and 'If aa had a horse ad wad nev a cairt.' and the Pole, looking bewildered, would keep asking *'Jaki?'* 'What?' He could, for a laugh, set it in a provincial bungalow afloat in a linoleum sea of magnolia woodchip and straw donkeys from Majorca.

He didn't look for a pen; instead he threw the sheets of paper across the room and banged a fist on his knee then stood and thumped both of them on top of the dresser. He smashed them down again, dislodging a cup of cold tea from its saucer and vibrating the table's triple mirrors. He sat again on the edge of the bed and looked at the carpet, feeling tears running down the side of his nose.

# CHAPTER 8

He was passing a girl pasting theatre posters to the font wall of the Princess Theatre in Romford. They were creased, corners peeling. He stopped and went across to her, gently took the cloth from her hands, quietly asking her permission as he did so and explaining while demonstrating that she'd do a better job by beginning in the centre and pressing outwards, and suggesting a firm brush or straight piece of hard plastic acting as a spatula would be better than the rag. She smiled her thanks as he walked away.

Liam wouldn't be seeing Mary for a few days as she had essays to complete and didn't want anything distracting her. 'Even you,' she'd said on the phone. He'd gone to the theatre because he liked the cafe there: the omelettes cooked by Frank the French chef, and there was something about the way he sliced the fresh tomatoes and the taste of the butter on the baguette slices that made him think he should come here more often. As he wasn't far from the station he took a train a little further into Essex and got out at a station he'd never been to before.

He alighted and went into the waiting room under the scrolled metalwork holding the wooden Victorian platform canopies. The fireplace had an ogee arch above the grate, there was an anaglypta dado, a varnished bench and a few Forties railway company posters on the walls. He then remembered seeing a computer-generated image of a new station that was to be built there that looked like a giant, swollen inter-vertebral disc of curved glass hanging over a row of established trees and a main road.

No new lines were to be added and there were, apparently, to be only a few extra trains, yet the old building was being demolished because the authorities, fuelled  by an egocentric burst of adrenalin when seeing the catch-all value judgement of 'progress' and the phrase 'fit for the Twenty First Century' shimmering seductively before them, had deemed it necessary that an arbitrary period of time must be a certain way and everything in it - shapes, buildings, vehicles, cities, attitudes, perhaps even amoeba - should be bought into Evolution's or the Creator's remit; perhaps *had* to be thus.

He crossed the platform and returned to the City. He found a café and sat and looked out at the world as if it was a cinema screen, something that couldn't really intrude, physically harm him. 'Watching the world go by.' That's what he did; look at it, not always feeling part of it.

Outside he saw a woman sitting at a pavement table. There was something decidedly old-fashioned about her, but from a past that was elegant. Her cloche hat framing dyed hair, he could see her as a Russian émigré on Rue St Michel, her gloved hand emerging from blue angora and dabbing a tear from a pencilled eye, wishing her lovers to carry mobiles so she could text how late she would be.

Maybe an art fancier would pass by, a retrospective critic in a fedora waving his walking cane at her, smiling. Moving slowly, she stood almost upright, she was small and thin. She bent to switch on her phone, perhaps, he thought, wishing it was a samovar.

More realistically, there was Mary. For the past few months they had seen each other increasingly, at his place, at hers - a ground floor flat in Stoke Newington where he'd felt a self-regarding, mannered liberalism oozing from the tenants she'd got to know in the flat above - in theatres, restaurants, a bar or two and especially cinemas where, after discussing what they'd just seen, she would quickly move on to other films, remembering scene upon scene and recalling whole chunks of dialogue, particularly from older movies, from the last words of 'Towering Inferno, 'So long Fire Chief. 'So long architect.' to 'Play it Sam. You played it for her; you can play it for me.'

'It's alright,' she'd laughed, 'it's the only way that I'm autistic.'

Finishing his savoury, he recalled some of the definitions of love he'd once read: 'A variety of different feelings, states and attitudes that range from interpersonal affection to pleasure. It can refer to an emotion or a strong attachment, also a virtue representing human kindness, compassion… '

He wasn't sure. And what of 'Falling in love?'' 'Falling' denoting going down, out of control, helplessness maybe. Some of these things he felt for her, not all.

It was also a reification he mused, an abstract concept that felt real and tangible - like duty, loyalty, patriotism, and how many human beings had died for them? The concept couldn't be precisely defined anyway. Maybe he'd speak to Clive about it. His psychoanalyst friend interested him.

Tall, Jewish, grey-haired and some years older than himself, he lived in a large, Thirties pastiche house in an affluent northwest London suburb with a long through-lounge and a white, hand-painted grand piano in the window bay. He was also a lyricist and had written 'Nectar Kiss' and a Eurovision song contest winner 'Ring a Ling' some years before and was still receiving royalty cheques for these and other songs.

When he saw him last he had played some pieces by Gershwin and Porter while Liam was standing by his piano thinking how attractive to women he must be; the patriarchal nose, stern, but sensitive profile, the lilting sounds from under his hands. He'd been brought up in an east London borough adjacent to where Liam had been raised, was divorced and had a daughter who was studying psychoanalysis in Paris under a former student of Lacan.

He saw his clients in a small upstairs room. After some time he'd changed the setting of these sessions to his through-lounge, explaining how difficult some of them found it to adjust to a different environment.

Seeing how serious and absorbed he was becoming in elaborating the idea of how a room and sofa could become not just a home for a patient but a foetal residence for some, Liam asked him what Jewish jokes he knew, liking them because many were created within the Jewish culture, a culture he had, the few times he'd experienced it - at a bar mitzvah, a Ben torah - felt a little envious of the warmth of it, the feeling of belonging.

'Oedipus, schmoedipus, who cares as long as he loves his mother?' Clive asked. 'Okay, why do Jews like watching porn movies backwards? They like the part where the hooker gives the money back.'

Liam liked being with this man and as the Oedipal had been mentioned, he asked him whether it could be true that in prehistory young men who desired their mothers killed their fathers and ate them and, in redemption, forced themselves not to want their mothers, therefore not having to kill their fathers. From this, he'd read, came the idea of marrying out.

'Yes, the first cultural event leading to civilisation, you might say, though you could have added that the sons were also frightened of being killed by each other. There isn't much evidence for early cannibalism though and many have delegated it to mere myth. Who knows? But there's little doubt that parent and sibling unions are virtually universally taboo of course.'

'Virtually?'

He thought of his mother. He had no recollection of desiring her; perhaps it was in the unconscious. As a child he thought he'd noticed her slim legs and how nicely shaped her shoulders were, but those deep-set eyes and long nose made her look... He felt momentarily sickened for thinking it, of being able to formulate the words. It was like someone saying, 'I never fancied mum, she wasn't attractive enough.'

'Yes, even that,' said Clive, 'has probably no absolute taboo. Different cultures have different norms as to which blood relations are permissible sexual partners and which are not. In some instances brother and sister marriages have been permitted, but of course, if you're conditioned in a particular culture then what constitutes an incestuous act is, for the people who've lived it, an absolute.'

He was into his stride and Liam didn't wish to interrupt him, cultural relativism was a familiar and valid concept to him, also. This was a man who he didn't feel a need to argue with, to point out that psychologists adduce mental characteristics of individuals to explain social forms when, it could be argued, these mental characteristics are themselves the result of the very social forms to be explained.

'I had a case quite recently with siblings. It appeared not to affect the woman, though I never met her, but it did the man and he left me in the end when I confronted him with it. I shouldn't have done it quite so abruptly, should have allowed him to get there himself. It was she that had prompted him to come to me, perhaps using him as a proxy to face her own guilt.'

He'd then changed the topic to the increasing use of drugs in his business and had long thought that those used to lessen fear and quieten the internal voice of paranoid conditions were, in essence, counter-productive, a cop-out to helping patients face their devils, to struggle with them and develop a more solid identity.

The subject interested Liam, all of it, as long as there was some depth and not on the level of 'psychobabble' sneering and the latest media-popularized trends.

His friend had, apparently, not long returned from a short holiday in Greece, an area of the Mediterranean he was fond of: Aegean islands silhouetted at dusk, white ferry boats, the light, the landscape and, seeing it through the illustrations in an old Sunday school bible, expecting Jesus to appear any moment on the dirt road in front of him. He'd liked to have gone to Sappho's island of Lesbos, he said, to see its contradictions:

the emerald isle with its eleven million olive trees next to a petrified forest, the *salziknum,* 'daughter-men,' and perhaps he'd get some historical...

'Fuck lesbians,' he'd said, laughing at another contradiction.

Liam ordered a dessert, looked out of the café window again and, seeing the congested traffic, thought vaguely that vehicle congestion perhaps represented us waiting in the birth canal while we wanted to get out, get on, and wondered if his dislike of long, straight, terraced streets represented a bad birth canal experience. He stopped himself.

He then, briefly watching a decorator painting a shop fascia on the opposite side of the street, mused a little on his old friend who had got him back into 'the game' before he'd started where he was working now. It was Chas who had obtained a small subcontracting job in some luxury flats near the Ritz Hotel and who had needed some help.

He had thought it would be good to be with Chas again and have some laughs - he remembered when they were once on a site adolescently rolling putty into small balls and blowing them at each other through lengths of electrical conduit to alleviate the boredom of painting or spraying large areas of wall.

He also recalled Chas saying to him, 'You don't see me much anymore 'cos I can't read.'

His pal was illiterate and thus sharing the things that interested Liam was limited, though they had been close at one time. Working together would, maybe, alleviate his guilt at hardly ever seeing his friend in recent years. It hadn't, but he'd been forgiven.

In the flats the old skills had returned immediately; this was 'west end' work, he was enjoying it, as he was the six-a-side kick-around in Green Park at lunch times with some builders working in the hotel. He wasn't as fast as he used to be - though considering himself just as tricky - but felt re-energised when he got back to the job and they'd top-coated three rooms with time to spare in their self-set targets.

Returning to the flats after the game a few days later he'd noticed, through the grimy window of the area basement, a figure with a woolly hat pulled low over his forehead staring out of a window. There was something rather grim and a little lost about him. He could have been the caretaker. Liam disinterestedly guessed that he wasn't.

That evening he had a call from a man who had taught him at a one-off class as an undergraduate and later had invited him to do his unproductive term at the local poly. He was now, apparently, a director of a large charity which, along with its other work, was currently looking into reasons for homelessness.

After predictable pleasantries, the man said, 'I don't know what you're doing currently, something academic I suspect, but what we were thinking of doing, though we're obviously looking into economic determinants, was a kind of psychosocial study of homeless people, and I thought of you. You were, if I remember, very enthusiastic about your subject. You also did a rather good dissertation they told me on the Underclass theme that was then gaining credence.'

'As I say, I don't know what you're doing these days and you may well not have the time, but if you have we can fund you a little. It's up to you, of course, how you carry it out.'

The request seemed to Liam to concretise his intuition about the man in the basement, it gave him a status: 'Homeless,' though he wasn't sure why he felt he fitted it. It wasn't just his appearance; crumpled jacket, old sweater, and unshaven, Liam, too, had stubble though a little more designed, but just a general impression, and if he was right, here was somebody on his doorstep, so to speak, he could talk to, find out a few things. He told the caller he would consider doing a small pilot study.

'Fine. Thanks. Confirm what you intend to do when you know.'

He felt unsure; the man may live in the block somewhere, he could actually own the apartment they were just finishing, but if he was homeless how best to approach him? As Liam was a decorator working a few floors above him he may as well play that role, get friendly with him; show some sympathy. He had a fancy to see himself as a participant-observer in an ethnographic study pretending to be without a home himself. He quickly deleted the whim.

The question seemed to be answered next day. Liam didn't have his kick-around, he and Chas needing to finish hanging the paper-backed silk in the hall to complete the flat so that they could clear their stuff for the furniture to be moved in. At lunchtime he made a quick trip to peer through the basement window, but there was no one inside, though he could see what looked like a pile of rags and discarded clothes against a wall which could have been used as a bed.

Chas had invited Liam to have a meal with him and his wife at their home in Brentwood so he travelled back with him. At Stratford Station an untidy, unkempt man stepped into the carriage. Liam was surprised but not unduly so that it was, as he internally referred to him, the basement man.

He walked straight to the end of the carriage, turned, and holding out a cupped hand and looking straight into passengers' eyes, began what seemed to be a well- used patter.

'Spare a few pence, guv? Only a few pence. Need a bit to get by. Just a few pence, gotta 'ave a cuppa, an' I.'

He continued from the end to the front of the carriage repeating the same spiel, letting his offered hand stay open for about five seconds in front of each traveller and collecting, Liam reckoned, as well as his own quickly given pound, about two pounds. This could mean, say, fifteen pounds per train for roughly thirty minutes work. It seemed to be a living of sorts, but what interested Liam was where he'd learnt his ritual. The steady gaze and the proffered, almost demanding hand, enacted perhaps daily, must have seemed like a long, bitter stretching of time. He said nothing to Chas.

They began the second flat next day and had finished half the paintwork by the evening. Liam made an excuse tor staying on and, when on his own, went down to the basement door and knocked. He waited a while then went outside and looked down into the window. There was a light on. He pushed some earth with his foot which fell and lightly brushed a pane. The man appeared and looked up. Liam smiled and gestured to him to pull the sash up. He did so, frowning.

'Sorry to bother you, but we're working upstairs' - Liam had kept his paperhanging apron on - 'and I wondered if you had a pair of steps we could borrow. I assume you're the janitor?'

'No. No I'm not and I have no steps, I'm sorry.'

He closed the window abruptly and turned away. Liam hardly recognised the voice; gone were the 'guvs' and 'ladys,' the glottal stoppage, the London 'f.' In their place was an accent of almost lazy elegance allied to a very different personality. For a moment Liam imagined he had acted both personas, as if he were immersing himself in characters he was about to play on a stage.

Next day, after a brief kick-around with the builders, he looked down at the window as he passed. The man was staring at the inside of it from two feet away as if he had an intense interest in the anatomy of the fly in its centre.

When Liam left in the evening - he was to finish the flat himself, Chas beginning another subcontract near his home - he could see basement man walking a few yards in front of him. He decided to follow. It wasn't difficult, it was a sunny evening and there were enough people around to hide behind if necessary.

His quarry got on a Tube train to Stratford, but this time went to an Overground train going westwards and repeated his patter. Liam hid his head in a newspaper. As intrigued as he was, the man was surely an atypical example; the voice he

used when trawling trains mimicking, perhaps, what he perceived as an accent of the destitute.

Liam got off, wearying a little of following someone when
he could have been in a cosy café somewhere. Maybe it would
be easier to talk to the men he'd seen lying around at Charing
Cross Station or the one that seemed to be living at the rear of
the National Theatre.

While working hard and fast the next day, he decided to
stick to basement man as his pre-study. Maybe he was being
lazy, but better the devil you know. He finished what he intended to do and went downstairs and tried the basement door
again.

He knocked twice, waiting a full minute between each one.
As he turned away the door opened. The occupant was dishev-
elled and looked strained and tired. Liam could see beyond
him a rumple of old clothes and sheets of cardboard lying in a
corner.

'Hello, I just wanted to see if you were okay.'

'Why?'

'Because you... didn't seem okay when I last saw you, I
thought maybe I could - '

'Cheer me up? Look, I'm having a rather awful day and - '

'Fancy a drink? I could do with a little company; I'm rather
hungry, too.'

The man looked at him with suspicion.

'Alright. Hard graft is it, painting those apartments?'

He came out and closed the door.

'I'm Russell.'

They shook hands. Liam knew a small café in a side street
opposite. They sat; he told him the meal was on him.

'Do you work in the building? I did think you were a caretaker or service engineer or something.'

'But you don't now?'

'No. It's your business; you can tell me or don't tell me, or
we can talk about football, maybe the weather or something.'

Russell finished his soup, wiping his mouth with a napkin.

'You've guessed then that I don't belong downstairs.' He emphasised the last word. 'You're quite right, of course.' he said, leaning back. 'I'm not your average janitor or your typical tramp, am I.'

They ate their food in silence. Liam watched him eat; it seemed to be the first decent meal he'd had in a while. He asked him how he got by.

'You pick up tips from the others; you wear layers of underwear when you can get it, it's warmer, always wear two pairs of socks, except in the summer, etcetera. You tend to gather where the others do. It's company, you know. I started like that, really'

'Is it competitive, all seeking a finite resource?'

'No,' he looked a little uneasy, 'though I feel guilty using the basement on my own, but I don't think I could stay there if I brought anyone in with me. The places they, we, stay are pretty institutionalised, been there a while; you can find evidence; little nick-knacks, syringes, dog ends, tins of tobacco, all sorts. Could do a sort of contemporary, urban archaeological study, I suppose.'

He looked at Liam steadily for a while.

'Going to ask me why?'

'Yes. Or is it too painful? And how long?'

'Too long. You wouldn't know what it's like would you, to wake up so cold it's... the wind, it's so bitter.' He halted. 'You have to give so many damn details to get a job; your life story, NI number, your last job.'

'What was that, then?'

He looked aggressively at his questioner as if he'd never been asked the question before.

'I was stage manager at the Coliseum. As you've guessed, I'm not now.' His fists clenched. 'Do you know, some people don't believe anyone's homeless unless they see them lying in a gutter, you can tell it in their eyes.' He was getting angrier. 'What do they expect me to do then?'

He bent forward and rested the side of his face on the table. He looked up pitifully.

'Please think of the homeless. I've nothing, nobody. I need food.' He rolled his eyes imploringly. 'Please.' He sat up. 'I can't do that.'

Liam quietly asked him where he got his money from to live on.

'Well, it's certainly not from shares in Coca-Cola.'

He drank his coffee, used the napkin again.

'I get it from trains. I sometimes ask people on trains. D'you know; I though about volunteering for the Samaritans at one time.'

Liam casually enquired if he chose any particular line and what criteria he used, feeling embarrassingly coy as he did so.

'I sometimes toss a coin. Mostly over ground, but the Tube in the late evenings when there's less people, but never in the early morning; nobody wants to give you anything then. You pick up things from the old hands as if it's a trade and you learn the tricks.' He bent his head down briefly. 'It's hard.'

They left and walked back to the flats. Russell thanked him and asked him to have a drink; he'd saved a little wine from somewhere. Liam accepted. In a larger room than the one where Russell slept, the apartment block's boiler filling a third of it, there was a table with an opened bottle of wine in the centre, two doilies, a wilting vase of flowers and three chairs. Russell took a quick look around him.

'The caretaker's quite a nice guy. I look at the boiler from time to time, though I don't really know what I'm looking at, just keep things tidy, put rubbish in the bins, you know.'

As Russell drank, Liam asked about his childhood. Staring into mid-distance, he answered.

'I took it all for granted, of course. The money - dad earned most of it - the talented mum; privilege, I suppose you'd call it.' He was quiet, then, 'I got a third class Physics degree, it should have been a First or a Fail; either would have suited. I was too bright for them. Most of the lecturers didn't understand me; what I was arguing... their syllogisms with undistributed middles, they'd never heard of Kuhn's paradigm shift, couldn't see that science is a self-contained conceptual system, a belief system that cannot of itself, be wrong, is no different to magic or religion.'

'Why did you do it?'

'Because my father fuckin' did. He and his team won an award from the Royal Society for working on, whatever it was, DNA stuff. He just went along with the research, there was money flung at it. He was conventional, predictable, no shattering insights from him, no breakthroughs, no... You can imagine how we got on, can't you.'

He'd been looking around him while speaking. Now he looked at Liam.

'Once, when I was a boy, seeing our cleaner out - I liked her, there was something warm about her - and he probably thought I'd left the house, I heard him shout at my mother, 'Damn, bloody child!' and then a crash. I'd never heard him swear, or shout before. I was so scared. He'd smashed a teapot.'

He fell silent for a while.

'I found some old coins the other day, they're mnemonics aren't they. It was their clinks, their whisky malts, the cigars, tips for the tradesmen. He tried to be a well- met fellow, the firm handshake, fake laugh; a kind of honorary member of an imaginary club. I was in bed when he shouted; I was curled up, foetal. I ran out across the Heath, flung myself into the grass trying to push through the earth.'

There were no tears, but Liam guessed he was crying internally.

'You're a good listener,' he smiled, and took a deep breath.

'I used to paint, draw, I wanted to act, I don't know; but not a scientist. Rigidity, classification, that's what they do; quantify the qualitative to create an illusion of control, and it's engendered an academic and cultural ethos in which creative, intuitive intellectualism is penalised.'

He stood and went into the small kitchen and made coffee. Liam watched him; hurried, efficient, agile. He brought their coffee to the table, took a gulp; placed the cup back on a doily. He turned to Liam.

'I've got a conviction, I've done time. It was a child. You may have heard the theories: neuroscience says that where the wiring in the brain is that creates feelings of protection and caring when looking at a child, for people like me there's desire. This wiring analogy's such baloney. But it means, of course that it's not my fault, doesn't it, it absolves me. But, it *was* my fault.'

He was suddenly restless, put his hands to the sides of his head then on top of his knees, then to his head again. Liam thought he would cry.

'The word 'paedophile' comes from the Greek, meaning friendly love for or friendship with a child. I loved my brother's girl, my niece. I stroked her hair, it wasn't really sexual, it was... I kissed her gently, always gently. I touched her a little bit, she was... I loved her.'

His voice was rising. He looked around him almost wildly, then calmed.

'You're shocked. Yes?'

'You must have seen a therapist or somebody, surely.'

'No. My family didn't want me to see one. They didn't want to think, 'Oh, poor Russell, it must be some sort of abnormal condition, it wasn't his fault.' They wanted me put away, they wanted to blame me. Somehow they made sure I wasn't diagnosed, treated; I don't know how. I think if anybody attempted to help me, they'd stop them somehow. My father's cruel. They're nasty people.'

'Is there nobody in your family who's willing to help you?'

'What do you think, after what I did?' It was the rhetoric of anger.

'I have nothing. I haven't a home; I don't even know whether my parents know that I'm out. You'd think they would, wouldn't you. They don't want to see me, they have no son. I have no - '

He put his head in his hands again. He was crying. Even then Liam couldn't help but take a second's absence from what he felt to wonder if this gesture of anguish was the only symbolic absolute, the universal symbol of pity.

He reached across the table and squeezed the man's arm. Russell nodded silently then suddenly stood.

'I think you should leave me alone now. I'm sorry. Thanks for listening, though I'm not sure why I told you.'

Liam left him. He'd finished the flat two days later and hadn't seen him again.

He sat and thought about Russell's relationship with his father, it seemed something of a classic: the pressure to pursue the career he himself had chosen, to be like him, but he'd said little of his 'talented' mother, she was in the background. He'd probably got his artistic characteristics from her, though it was, perhaps, an ideologically fractious household with a science-art split and...

Liam couldn't help him; he wondered who could, or if he would accept help. He could put him onto Clive who dealt in cases like this, in destructive, familial horror. He could write down his friend's number and slip it through Russell's letter-box saying he was sorry that they wouldn't be seeing each other again. He would, of course, warn Clive of the man's potentially hostile family; though without money available for any fee, it was hypothetical.

And he wasn't sure whether he really wanted to rummage around in the psychosocial reasons for the non-scheduled status passage of homelessness. He felt he could give himself neither to the academic part nor to trying, somehow, to marginally ease the situation of the people he may meet.

He'd been attempting, he supposed, a thoughtful and even empathetic understanding of them. He had talked with one of them to find out about a too-common social situation he'd been asked to investigate. He had heard one man's story. He couldn't generalise out from it; that would be vulgarized inductive thinking. Using his craftsmanship, his hand knowledge, had been a welcome change from academia, but it was familiar, easy, there was nothing really… worthwhile.

He'd decided to return the fee for his little study for which he hadn't written a word.

Liam looked around to order a coffee. There was a girl looking impatiently at him and he realised that there were chairs stacked on the tables behind and that she was waiting to do his.

As he went out into the growing dusk, a man with a woolly hat, his back leaning against a shop window, legs stretched on the pavement and a label saying simply 'homeless' hung around his neck, looked up at him. But he'd spotted, further eastwards, a building going up, another trophy tower engendered by the populist cry of 'affordable homes,' a slogan utilised by developers to increase their annual profits. But this was office territory; it would be another money market edifice.

Using a mental map he worked out roughly where it was; this was a different market, Linden Market, a covered market of early Victorian shops which still had a furrier, cheesemonger and poultry dealer. He tried to recall the gist of the objections that had been made to the skyscraper that was planned to abut it. It was its 'obvious inappropriateness' and the 'detrimental impact' it would have that were the valid comments.

He'd seen an impression of the proposed construction, an ungainly thing that seemed to be held together by crisscrossing stainless steel struts, something that would, perhaps, seem okay for Houston, Texas, but not here in this city. It would obviously compromise its setting; such a huge break in the local skyline would make the market look like a lost relic.

He remembered the blurb from its developer saying it would 'engage with the historic market and enhance its viability and setting as a heritage asset… '

How stupidly anthropomorphic, he thought. How can a building 'celebrate?'

To break his annoyance he thought of Russell once more. He recognised that unthinkingly, automatically, he had assumed, as perhaps others did, that to be homeless was the individual's own fault, even a choice.

He retraced his steps, returned to the man still staring expressionlessly down at the pavement, placed some coins in the upturned cap between his thighs, went down the escalators at the station and returned home.

# CHAPTER 9

The office Tern found for Piero was a loft on West Adams Street in West Loop, some six miles from where he'd been working. Piero moved into the narrow, high, church-like space with desks, assorted chairs, stacks of A4 sheets of paper and four computers already installed three weeks after the deal had been proposed and a week after he'd left his employers.

He could afford the week off - allowed him by his client-benefactor whose new-found architect had told him that a few days away would refresh him, answered by Tern's, 'Okay, but you better come back all guns firin'' - and wanted to explore more of Chicago and the State it was in.

He started off with the three-thousand-feet long Navy Pier and its fifty acres of parks, entertainments, gardens, shops and restaurants. He'd visited the Victorian pier at Southend-on-Sea when in England which, compared to this one, seemed, although longer, almost cute and innocent. This one was noisy, highly populated and almost towered over by the downtown skyscrapers. He fancied visiting Aurora, Joliet and maybe Cicero, partly because he liked their names.

He caught a tram to Union station. He'd seen a few photos, but wished to see the building its architect, Daniel Birnham, had alluded to when he said, 'Make no small plans: they have no magic to stir men's blood.' He entered through a Canal Street entrance and into the Great Hall with its barrel-vaulted skylight a hundred and twenty feet above him.

Two large figural statues on its east wall, one representing 'Day,' holding a rooster, the other, 'Night,' holding an owl in recognition of twenty-four hour railroading were also imposing. He appreciated that the statues required intricate craftsmanship, but so did embroidery; he cared for neither a great deal. He went out under its limestone, columned façade. It was grand but, again, another large and famous building with, anti-climactically, Romanesque capitals and fluted columns. He couldn't seem to escape his childhood city; it was as if it was following him.

The next day it was an Amtrak to Aurora where he saw a few Frank Lloyd Wright residences and some bits of Mies van der Rohe which had a marginal interest, the early Deco of the Paramount Theater having hardly any, though he enjoyed a walk along the bank of a tributary of the Fox River.

The following day it was Cicero and a neo-Gothic church, the old Hawthorn Works with its Disneyesque, Rumpelstiltskin castellated tower and the neo-classical Beaux Arts Morton High School, but little new. No high sheets of glass, no low, flat ellipses of steel, buildings that looked as if they were, or could be floating, no … Piero Ronzi.

He cut his holiday short and hurried back to his new office. The - his - new staff weren't expected to arrive for a few days so he made himself finish the blueprints for the mansion's extension before continuing with Tern's new building. He was losing himself in doing this when two of his new team arrived.

They introduced themselves and asked where he was up to in his work. While they were looking at some graphics on his computer he fished out some drawings from his desk drawers, including originals, grabbed a few scattered on a desk and gave them to the newcomers. They immediately grinned with pleasure, one of them telling him he'd sketched something a little like it a few weeks back but without the vertical curve, the height and, of course, the helicopter pad.

'I bet Tern liked this, huh?'

'Yes, that's why we're going ahead with it' - he noticed the 'we' was from him this time - 'it's the prime reason you're here.'

He asked them if they were both designers. The one who had first spoken to him, Tommy, was, the other, Lance, was a civil engineer. Piero was pleased, they were all needed, especially the engineer. Henry, tall dark and skinny from New York's Bronx and a graphic designer then came in. They all seemed to know each other. They were to work three days a week there - the rest of the time plying their trades freelance - with most of their salaries from Tern, the rest from himself, though Tern hadn't finalised his fee yet.

The civil engineer, like the other two, was younger than him, but from a family of engineers; perhaps Tern was a good judge of expertise and of people connected with it. Piero guessed he would have to be to occupy his financial position - that and, he assumed, a penchant for ruthless business. Lance hadn't long returned from working in Los Angeles, where, he'd said, 'the sunset sky turns shades of red and orange that you'd expect to see only in the painted backdrop of a movie set, with cloud formations rippling pink like just-scooped strawberry ice cream.' It was of course, pollution. 'The world's briefly more beautiful,' he'd added, 'but only because we're screwing it up.'

There were, apparently, tsunami warnings at Venice Beach, stores that sold ready-packed earthquake survival kits, and annual sprinkler bans in a drought-prone city that probably ought to be a desert. Any desire that Piero had to visit California was extinguished.

He liked Lance, and could see within a couple of weeks that the three of them worked well together. The engineer was unthinkingly privileged: privately educated then on to Columbia University, while Henry was more competent with the sophisticated graphics Piero realised he needed for this particular construction.

Tommy, his fellow architect, was solid in both temperament and ability, occasionally and sometimes fortuitously questioning Piero's ideas on his taken-for-granted details of certain fittings, thickness of glass, air vent sizes, even, at times, floor thicknesses.

The land had been cleared, exact measurements, acreage, soil samples and other information had been sent to the small band of architects - Tern pushing through a leasing deal with the owner of adjoining land for access to the site who, the rumours went, was holding on to it to increase its purchase price for a permanent road to be built on it from North Cumberland Avenue half a mile away.

Piero had had only two telephone calls from Tern as the plans for the building were finalising. The first was to ask if everybody had joined up and were 'working like hell', the second to tell his protégé that the extension to the mansion was well on its way and that he would like the latest drawings of his skyscraper sent to him.

He was specially interested in illustrations of the foyer which Piero, along with Henry, had just begun work on and knowing Tern liked impressive first impressions had visualized Creole and Fauske marble floor and walls, large paintings or prints of recognisable old masters, chaise longues and, hanging from a high, vaulted ceiling, the crystal chandeliers Tern seemed to like so much.

A week afterwards, Tern came into the office, had a quick glance around, nodded to Piero's three aides then went across to his recently appointed designer and congratulated him on the entrance hall.

'Guess you're workin' out my style now, huh? Well, you're gettin' there.'

He turned to leave.

'Carry on with the work,' he said over his shoulder and gave his flippant wave.

As they watched him through the door pane entering the creaking lift and descending, Piero again noticed that he was wearing a tailored blue suit, white shirt and red tie, this time striped with pink, the pointed end of which hung two inches under his belt like an affectation.

'You can see the American flag, apple pies and eagles coming out of his ass,' said Lance.

They laughed and carried on with their work. Piero didn't laugh, he supposed he rarely did, the work was the thing. It was all, or had become that way, and the man he was working for was powerful, he wanted to stay with him.

Although knowing little of the man's ambitions, his deals, his financial interests, he guessed that he wanted to build more than his personal monument - he'd heard from somewhere that he was angling to buy a large construction firm. He knew it was a time of laissez-faire capitalism, of Reaganomics, more economic expansion, more jobs, and that manufacturing multinationals were relocating to countries like Thailand, Taiwan, Mexico and even China.

He felt Tern was a kind of multinational himself; if a large conglomerate could look like a man it would look like him: Hard, straight line of a mouth, a slight, almost-pout when he disapproved of something, the narrow grey-blue eyes that seemed at times almost hidden in a half-frown as if suspicious that whoever he was talking to was out to better him, perhaps to cheat him.

Piero had picked this up from only a little acquaintance with him; a few minutes in his mansion, a few just now in the office. Maybe there was a lighter side, there had to be.

He was aware that his own lighter side had never really developed, certainly not with his family and only a little as an undergrad; to create something was more important. Even the few times he'd been intoxicated in the students bar in Rome, he remembered labouring other students with diatribes against the columns, capitals and podiums of ancient Rome, and what was all the fuss about the Renaissance anyway?

The few girlfriends he'd had didn't seem to keep with him for long, there were no common interests they could share, except with one or two of them in art, maybe in film, but not literature, contemporary or otherwise. He didn't read much outside of his degree subjects, and there were few women doing his subject at his places of learning in either his home country or England. A student friend had once asked him if his short-lived relationships bothered him. They didn't.

Tern phoned him soon after he'd left the office and told him to meet him at his mansion the next afternoon. Piero wasn't keen to leave what he was doing - yet another think about whether the helipad should have curved edges, which, according to Lance, was rather difficult to build - but he was there on time.

Again, the red, white and blue sartorial motif; the wearer seemed pleased to see him.

'Seems like you're all gettin' on okay, I hardly know the others, they were recommended. They start pile-driving soon, once that's done we're go. Gotta contractor lined up, your stuff'll be finished and it'll rise.'

He began to put an arm around Piero's shoulder then the phone rang. He seemed to have had it changed to his own number already. He strode over to it, picked it up and listened for a few seconds.

'No, that's just EPS, it's a penny stock, not worth it, a kinda analysis paralysis, and those lots are too small; it's the market value I'm... Yeh, the investment commandments, some are okay: 'Thou shall set clear goals, Thou shall question authori-ty, Thou shall not follow sheep,' sure, but 'Thou shall be hum-ble, be patient,' and the 'Thou shall not ogle thy investment.' To hell. It's what I fuckin' do; ogle it.' He laughed. 'Okay, bid 'em down, way down.'

He replaced the phone. 'Come and see outside.'

Before following him, Piero noticed the American football helmets on a mantle shelf and magazine covers including some old 'Playboys' on a desk, as if it was a first year college stu-dent's room, but bigger.

The exterior rendering of the addition to the back of the house was almost finished, a roof in place, windows installed and a doorway ready for its doors. It had been done quickly and well, the process feeling part of the owner's business style.

'Come on then,' said Tern, 'let's go.' and walked around the extension into another different car, a red and dark blue Chevrolet this time.

'Get in,' he said, holding the passenger door open.

Piero couldn't drive, had never really thought about it; rarely had the need to do so, until lately when buses, trains and the occasional taxi seemed to be interrupting his flow, both physically and creatively. He asked where they were going.'

'Just wanna show you the land it's goin' on. You can see the whole site then.'

They'd gone a mile or so when Tern asked him what he thought of politicians.

'I haven't thought much about them, I suppose. I admire them though.'

The driver turned his head to him and frowned.

'Their coordination, really; I mean, they can be verbose, inarticulate, corrupt and naive all at the same time. Well, Italian ones can.'

Tern looked at him again.

'I like it. You're right. Politicians are like diapers, they should be changed regularly and for the same reason. You know what democracy is? Three wolves and a sheep voting on what to have for supper. I don't approve of political jokes really; I've seen too many of 'em get elected.' He smiled. 'Guess I'll stop now, I'll think of some more for later.'

For the first time Piero felt himself warming a little to him.

They didn't talk much for a while then Tern said, 'It's up here a way.'

A little after that, Piero could hear the intermittent thuds of a pile driver.

'It s a diesel drive for the piles, they're goin' deep. Hell, if anyone knows that, it's you, you got it all worked out, well, you and your computer guy. Hope they go deep enough man, it's a big building.'

They came off the main road, turned into one with a slight incline then onto a roughly laid gravel drive that was still being worked on and onto the neatly hedged field Piero recognised from the photos Tern had shown him. There, a gang of workers were doing things around a pile driver, its explosive thumping seeming a little at odds to the out-of-town setting.

Tern got out the car and leaned against it, watching the men working while Piero joined him. They looked at the site: the trees, grass; the elevated road they'd just come off and the buildings going up on its far side.

'There's gonna be quite a large development there,' he said, nodding towards the road. 'There's some residential, but it's mostly commercial. But this one,' he pointed towards his site, 'is gonna make it for the whole area.' He glanced at his companion. 'It wasn't easy to get planning permission for this.' He looked away again.

'You know how it is, 'No new building to be higher than the highest building in the curtilage boundary.' It's only applicable 'cos there's some residential stuff over there, as mentioned. 'No new building to exceed gross floor space of...' etcetera, etcetera, and there's the zoning ordinances. I did a deal with the developers on the other side of the road as well as with the municipal people.'

He was silent for a few minutes then said casually, 'Oh, I forgot to mention, you've got thirty six storeys. I left it till now to tell you 'cos I knew it wouldn't take any real design changes to add another four floors. They haven't started actually piling just yet so you got time to tell 'em to go deeper.' He laughed and looked at Piero again.

'You pleased?'

He was. 'Thanks for telling me.'

'Had to dig a bit deep, and I don't mean pilin', but I did it.'

He paused again and looked across at the workers.

'Aintcha feeling good that these guys are workin', or will be along with lots of others, from your drawings, from your ideas?'

'Yes I am. And thanks.'

He couldn't tell him how pleased he really was. He thought, deep down, that it might happen one day, but not as early, not so randomly, serendipitously, almost. He wanted to get back, tell the others about the four extra floors, get to work, add to the graphic images and, mainly for his own satisfaction, begin a final watercolour sketch of the building. He'd put a few more trees around its base, he'd make it look as if it was rising from them, as if growing from a forest. No, that was too fanciful. He'd stick to just the building. His creation.

They looked across at the site once more. Tern looked up at the sky, blue with criss-crossing contrails.

'God Bless America, huh? You know, I like Jesus, but he loves me, so it's awkward.'

He laughed, patted Piero on the back and they got into the Chevy and drove away.

Tern had the look of being quietly pleased with himself on the journey back though they didn't travel far before he stopped outside Cumberland Station.

'I'll drop you off here 'cos I'm getting my jet at O'Hare and flyin' to La Guardia. I've some business in Queens. Not that I need to tell you any of this. Carry on with the work.'

He nodded to his driving companion who got out and turned to raise his hand as Tern was fast disappearing.

There was only the architect in the office when he returned, the others doing their freelancing work, and though pleased about the extra storeys, wasn't as satisfied as Piero was. Henry would be glad; he could do some more graphic stuff.

He left Tommy to lock up while he went on his own to the bar on the corner of the block and had what was a rather rare intake of alcohol. It was a glass of champagne. He'd seen the

site, could envision his building clearer now: its mass, the
curving, its height.

# CHAPTER 10

Not wanting to wait in a queue of people being offered 'To use ring-back press 5,' knowing he wouldn't be rung back, and a recorded American voice informing him that he was 'number fordeen in the coal queue,' Jim Salmon went to the hospital early the next morning. He went straight to the rubber doors and rapped his knuckles on them a few times till a passing porter asked him what he wanted.

'I want to know how soombody's gettin' on. He was admitted yesterday, he was on a life-support thing I think.'

The porter parked his empty trolley against a wall, told him to wait a moment and went through the doors. Jim began walking up and down along the corridor for what seemed a long time until a nurse asked him who he wished to see. He told her.

'He's still in ITU, there's no change I'm afraid. You can stay here or we can ring you, it's up to you.'

He decided the latter would be better, gave his number again and left. At least, he thought, she didn't tell him to pray. If she had, he'd have felt like telling her that God was either a well-intentioned deity who was obviously not omnipotent, or was all- powerful and therefore a bastard or, a third alternative, was both weak and a bastard, and anyway, he didn't create us, we created him.

He should have gone back to the site right way, the others would want to know how his mate was, but he didn't want to sit on a bus, wanted to be on his own, to walk. After a few minutes he glanced at a passing Amazon delivery van and thought of the giant organisations that ran the world, and of people no longer being citizens of countries, of nations, but consumers living in International Market States, and imagined Britain one day being officially known as Amazon IMS 32 or some such number.

He wondered what Marx would have thought of it all. There was a small park on the other side of the road and he pictured him strolling along a path with a jumble of books and papers under his arm, looking around and upwards and bumping into a bench. He'd sit, beard resting on his belly and staring at a tree. He'd found himself in Starbucks an hour before looking across the street to a golden M, with oddly dressed people offering strange currency to bargirls and shouting at things held to their ears, and he would hear the familiar accents of *bitte, wievel kostet, prosze.*

Disorientated as he was, he'd look for escape in a magazine he'd brought with him. He'd frown, shake his head. No, he didn't say that, perhaps it was the translation. He'd look in disbelief at page three of a newspaper, on the next page a picture of the American president on his first visit to Asia and somewhere before 'Gazza 'Aza Dazzler' two lines that say India gets a McDonald's - did he not say that the State is but a committee for managing the affairs of the bourgeoisie?

He'd think back to his coffee and gazing out the window seeing vehicles flashing past posters saying 'my ipod,' 'my music,' 'my life.' Smiling, his lips would shape the words 'technological determinism' then he'd look up to see pink-clad young people with aggressive, blind eyes and tight pony tails all around him, pointing at him. 'Loser,' they'd chant. 'Loser, foockin' loser.'

Back on site, he made for the foreman's cabin to tell him there was no news. He saw him before reaching it.

'Tell the others then,' he was told, 'and you may as well lay a few if you're up to it; keep your mind busy anyway.'

He went back to his bricks, on his own this time.

'I'm 'ere doin' me job,' he said quietly to an image of Thomasz in his head. 'It's startin' to rain, getting' chilly, it'll get muddy again and you're in thut clean, warm place bein' looked after by bonny lasses with African arses and...'

He took a deep breath, knocked up some more cement, spread a large wad of it on his board and, scooping up trowels full, evened them onto the last course and began laying them, faster, as if to make up the time lost by his old 'marra' not being there.

'I'd like to know who the idiot was who designed that buildin', what a prat.'

'What was that, Jim? Talkin' to yerself are yer? 'ow's yer mate, seen 'im?'

It was one of the first-fixing joiners. He shook his head and worked faster.

Just before lunch his mobile rang. It was the hospital telling him that Thomasz was no longer in intensive care and that he could see him for short while.

One of the labourers drove him there where he immediately looked for a nurse, a porter or a Sister, though not sure whether they still had them, to tell him where his mate was. He went to a kiosk selling chocolate, doughnuts and newspapers and asked the woman if she knew where he could find a nurse. She told him to go to the Outpatients across the hall.

At the Reception desk he hurriedly explained why he was there. One of the women working there told him to wait while she finished seeing to someone he'd jumped in front of. He moved away from the counter, looked around and saw about a hundred people sitting on long rows of chairs, occasionally one of them disappearing into a room as a number was called. He guessed they were having blood tests. Thomasz hadn't bled much; or rather he hadn't seen any.

He paced about in front of the desk, looking through some windows behind more waiting patients and seeing a side wall in the usual Flemish bond.

'Foock bricks,' he said to himself, turned and went to the desk again.

The woman began speaking into her phone as he approached her. She nodded a couple of times and put the instrument down. He wondered why people nodded, shook their heads or gesticulated when on the phone, there was no point. She told him it was Ward G. He moved quickly away.

'Don't you want to know where it is?' she called after him.

He went to the kiosk lady again and asked her. Following her directions, he hurried along the corridor, ran up six flights of stairs and went to the door of the ward, pushing it open. A male nurse immediately came across to him asking who he wanted to see. When told he pointed to the end of the ward,

'It's the end bed on the right. There may be a nurse with him, if not she will be shortly.'

He went towards the end wall, his steps slowing as he saw the curtain around the bed. He didn't want to open it; he wanted to wait till Thomas was better, walking; cheerful. He almost turned away till he realised how childlike this would be.

It was the nurse inside the little, medicated, sanitised white cave that opened it for him. It was the Somali, seated by the side of the bed, looking at him crossly.

She then gently said, 'You should not really be here, and you must go soon. He is conscious and he has spoken a little but I don't understand what he is saying.'

She looked back at her patient. Jim could see him lying there with dials and counters around him, a tube in his mouth, another taped to his forearm. Bizarrely, he wanted to take a quick glance under the bed to see if there was a chamber pot there.

'Not long,' she warned, wagging a finger at him.

He sat on the vacated chair and stared at his friend. He was pale and his face thinner, though looking better than when he'd last seen him lying struck and spreadeagled. He leaned forward and carefully touched his forehead. Perhaps he should kiss it, maybe Poles did that sort of thing, but he didn't. He looked at the tubes and technology again and back to Thomasz.

He thought of the times they'd shared, though nothing exceptional: the laughs, the pubs, some of the lads they'd known on various jobs - Thomasz probably calling them 'oppos' now since being in Cockney land - and the crap greasy spoons they'd used, his pal insisting in recent times that they find Polish ones.

He recalled, soon after he'd started working with him, when Thomasz was a foreman and had forgotten to book in some Saturday overtime for a brickie who was an ex con and proud to admit it. When he'd received his wages he challenged Thomasz, asking loudly why he was short. He was a Glaswegian - the only time Jim had visited that city he'd stepped out the station into the cliché of a broken bottle and spatters of blood in the gutter and someone saying loudly, 'Wha' yer fockin' doin', Jemmie?'

Thomasz had told the brickie that he, also, was short because he hadn't booked himself for those hours either.

'If I don't get it I'm gonna kill yer,' Jim had heard him say. He could imagine him doing so. His intended victim had calmly emphasised in clearly enunciated English that the mistake would be rectified. He had handled it well. When the man received his money next day he left to work on another site.

He remembered also when a young, macho brickie had come on site and soon began letting the whole gang know just how strong and tough he was. He picked on Thomasz, asking him if he could accomplish certain feats of strength, Jim forgetting now what they were.

Thomasz had pointed to a wheelbarrow, saying slowly, 'I bet you a week's wages that I can take something over to the other site and you won't be able to wheel it back.' The young one had said, 'You're on, old man.' Thomasz had grabbed the barrow and said, 'Get in.'

It wasn't just the jobs they'd done together that he remembered most - there was one where it was so cold the cement froze solid and the bricks were like rectangles of ice; and they weren't getting paid if not laying bricks - but when Thomasz came for the occasional meal at his place and he made Con laugh, invariably explaining some Polish phrases  to her, especially the saucy ones.

He used to tell Jim of differences between Polish and English culture.

'An English person calls you a friend after knowing you for a week and getting a beer. A Polish one will only call you a friend after knowing you for years and when you've helped him move out of his apartment and attended his grandmother's funeral.'

They weren't hilarious, but very Thomasz.

One of his eyes had opened. It seemed a little misty, unfocused.

Jim heard a whispered, *'Wiem, ty Przyjaciel.'*

He understood; 'I know, you friend.' He could feel relief, a joy.

The eye closed then opened again. *'Gdzie modje zajecie?'* He understood this too, 'Where my job?' as well as *'Wtoz ylem cegta.'* 'I put brick.'

As Jim was about to answer in the little Polish he knew, a hoarse gushing of his native language came from the speaker, his listener recognising nothing.

Then, attempting to move his head forward a little, he shouted, *'Achtung* Spitfire, Messerschmitt, Junkers, *esturaium'*

Thomasz had once told him that his father had been a Battle of Britain pilot over here when he was twenty; he seemed to be harking back to his parent's experience. He was silent for a while then said softly, both eyes opening and looking down at the end of the bed, *'Nie moge uszyc noga.'* and kept repeating it while tears slid down his cheeks. Jim had never seen his friend cry before.

The curtain swished back.

'You must go now.' It was the nurse.

'He turned to her.

'I cun understand soom of what he's sayin', but... he's distressed, isn't there soomone here who cun speak Polish?'

She frowned again.

'I will see. Don't make him tired.'

Again the admonishing finger as she went.

Thomasz was still repeating the phrase, but hardly audible now. Maybe he was merely mumbling past imperatives, random ones that were no longer there.

The curtain was drawn back again. A casually dressed man said, 'Is he still speaking?'

He glanced at the figure on the bed.

'He seems quiet now. Does he speak English? Someone said he wasn't English.'

'He speaks it very well. He's Polish.'

'I'm half Polish, I speak the language. What was he saying that caused you concern?'

Jim mimicked the repetition as well as he could.

'His leg; he was saying that he can't feel it. It could be damage to the brain.'

He looked at Jim, shrugging his shoulders.

'It's not good. I will tell his doctor. I've just come in, I'll get changed. He did say something about him recovering quicker than he thought he would. Unfortunately, he seems to be wrong.'

He went away, closing the curtain again.

Thomasz was quiet, unmoving. Feeling more apprehensive, Jim placed an open palm on his chest. It moved slightly but regularly. He leaned back in the chair. He would like to speak to the crane driver. He pictured again how quickly the end part, the tip of the 'beak' had broken away. It shouldn't have done. Maybe the design was at fault; the part that had broken away was too narrow and weak. Perhaps the contractors had taken short cuts with fixings, materials, maybe all of these things, or their permutations.

He didn't know the name of the building - they all seemed to have nicknames now, he had given it his own - but it had probably been called a 'statement in architecture.' He'd seen the phrase before. But what was it a statement of? Stupidity? Nonsense? Had its creator seen, as a child, some sort of flying creature in his dreams and wanted to turn its shape into a building, a 'Look what I did mummy!' statement?

Jim could see a piece in some building magazine saying something like, 'Taking his inspiration from the natural world, he has created from an airborne creature a dormant structure that... '

'What a load o' shite,' he said aloud, thumping his fist on his knee.

'Why are you swearing? It is wrong, you must not swear.' It was the nurse again. 'You should go now. The doctor will be here.'

'I wanna speak to 'im.'

'Sit outside the ward and wait. I will tell him. Go now.'

He left the bed and the ward, sat on a bench outside the doors and wondered why Africans seemed so authoritative. Perhaps because they had a colonised tradition of being told what to do and when in a situation where they did have some authority they used it, especially with their children. It was merely a disinterested generalisation, it didn't matter.

He stood up and started restlessly pacing. He would sooner be back on site than just sitting, waiting, feeling trapped.

A man in a white coat with a stethoscope swinging from around his neck came quickly into the corridor and entered the ward. Jim mused on whether medical men really needed a white coat and whether the stethoscope really needed to swing. Couldn't it be fastened somehow? And why wear white footwear whilst operating, was it to show blood? Did they want to look like butchers? He wanted to see Thomasz again.

After more walking back and forth, Ms Somali, as he'd named her, leaned her head outside the door and beckoned him in with her versatile digit. He walked behind her back to the end of the room with the doctor standing outside the closed curtain writing notes on a clipboard. He was young, with designer stubble.

'Hello,' he said, looking up briefly. 'He's not delirious now but, I'm sorry to say, it could be that he does have some brain damage. One potential clue is that he's speaking in his native language, he's been speaking it again, he may have forgotten his second language, I may be wrong of course, though I doubt it, the scans did show what could be damage there. I'm sorry but it's better to be realistic. We'll do more tests and do all we can. Goodbye.'

He hurried away. The nurse looked out of the unclosed curtain.

'I will be with him for a while now. You should go.'

He got a taxi when he left the hospital. Not many bricklayers, he knew, got taxis to their job, but he wanted to do something with his hands, his body.

He stood in front of what he'd been working on. The cement on his board was hardening. If he could work twice as hard then he would, in effect, be doing Thomasz's work for him. That's what he'd do. Until he came back to him.

# CHAPTER 11

Liam was walking through a local conservation area on his way to a hospital where he'd been referred for an x-ray on his lumbar spine which had been giving him intermittent pain. He felt no real need to go, but thought he would anyway. He wasn't crazy about bungalows but some were large chalet types with long gardens and built on gridded Thirties streets.

He'd never seen such an estate so near central London. He hadn't walked through it for a while and it had changed somewhat. There were increasing number of run-ins enabling occupants to gaze out at cars' arses instead of an evergreen bush or a few flowers, PVC windows where the area of the plastic was greater than the glass panes, and large roof tiles causing the bungalow underneath to look squat. But there were some good things, such as wooden window shutters with small heart shapes cut out of them and a smattering of original Deco front doors.

Turning a corner he saw a bungalow with yellow ochre and black bricks forming crescent front walls with gold-tipped railings and double gates the height of the building. He had a brief, cautionary dialogue with himself questioning whether there was any racial prejudice present, knowing there wasn't and knowing equally that it was the Asian aesthetic and its sheer incongruence that bothered him.

He thought the owner of this residence was, perhaps, proclaiming his wealth, his status and his right to do what he wished. Conservation: to conserve. Was he to do battle with the council again and this time point out what the concept meant?

He wondered why congruency was important to him. Perhaps it represented a visual calm, something uniform, regulated; order, maybe. These inappropriate colours, shapes, proportions disturbed - as did eight-hundred-foot buildings scattered around the city - a metropolitan order, *his* order. Maybe developers should employ thousands of therapists to attempt to convince people, especially atheists, that visual and physical order didn't matter; that they could turn their search for it to a belief in a supra-human deity to give it them.

He'd been in the waiting area of the Outpatients Dept. for a while and, feeling no pain anywhere on his body other than the sound of the dying of RP and its manifestations in the receptionist's 'You might 'ave to wait firty minutes 'cos the uvver patients ain't gone frew yet,' was thinking about leaving.

'Ooh, 'e do like 'is football, 'e used to play it all the time when 'e was little; knew all the names, the stars, oh, 'e did like it.'

It was a patient wearing a dress that looked like the result of an exchange of bodily fluids between a polar bear and a leopard, who hadn't an idea in her head and hadn't stopped talking about herself or her family since he'd been there, making herself heard even above the sound of a mindless TV show that had its captive and equally vacuous audience seemingly mesmerised. A man joined in and after six 'know what I means' in as many sentences, Liam got up and left.

He walked to his local station and took a train to one near the Lea Navigation, where he'd once walked its length from Limehouse Cut to Ware, sat on the towpath and gazed at moored and slowly passing canal boats with their painted scrolls and names: Emma Darwin, Water Floater, Passing Wind, Granny Spice. He strolled along the towpath until the day became misty and left it for a parallel lane.

After a while, a Victorian tower rose from the mist and he looked upward at its balconies, quoins, its barely discernible Palladian roof then stopped and gazed at its arching curves, its symmetrical, dusk-like loveliness. For a second he yearned to embrace it, glass starting to sparkle as the sun twitched on glazing bars and rested briefly on soft bricks and high wisteria.

Gazing upward, he wanted to pull it all inside of him, not knowing why.

Mary had recently asked him why he enjoyed walking in the city, why certain buildings and streets meant so much. He'd explained to her that there was a spirituality in that most basic form of travel. And it wasn't always the feel of a whole building or a line of them. It was, maybe, a tree at the side of a Georgian window or looking up at the finely crafted details of a capital with ovolo and dart, an Edwardian window or an unexpected row of dentils and feeling their past, their history - even if imagined and knowing little of it, nor all the classical orders or their concomitant ideologies.

Maybe the images and what he'd got from them had come from films seen as a child, but It was the feel of them: a house, street, a crescent, mews, a mansion, riverside houses, the sense of... magic maybe, of a kind of peace, like the Georgian street they'd turned into and were walking along while he was answering her question. He'd pointed out a cannon head chimney, some eaves, the shine on an old front door that had coat upon coat of paint; there was something about the depth of its shine.

She'd been silently listening and had said nothing after he'd finished then said, 'You've made me interested in buildings now.' She'd given him a fond smile. 'You draw me into your world.'

He went to a cafe back at the station before heading home. It was Turkish, outside were expatriate patriarchs with gold-slivered grins drinking coffee in awning shade, fingers playfully prodding each other, their open gestures brushing a potted fig tree. One leaned his head against a St. George flag painted on the side of an adjacent pub; Liam could hear the beer-belly laughs and glottal roars. They lit cigarettes, maybe tasting like the Abdullahs they smoked at twelve, and letting the English think they'd haggled bargains in the bazaar.

He got out at the station before his stop just to walk through a park. It was a reasonably pleasant diagonal from entrance to exit then a few hundred yards along a main road. He walked on the grass by the path. On it, across from him, was a woman, walking easily, her jilbab swirling in the breeze, her gaze straight ahead on the back of a husband.

An Islamic possession, she must, he thought, quietly know that her cover-up was as useless as its irony as her eyes briefly caught his and he imagined dark nipples and smooth legs as she moved along, female and hidden in her oppressive black, and Nike trainers.

He wondered what Mary thought about Islam and Allah, he'd never thought, or knew, much about it, though she probably had as she was quite religious - one of the few areas of belief they had rarely talked of - even inviting him to some sort of course on Christianity. It was this evening and he'd agreed reluctantly that he would meet her at the church.

It was in Aldgate, a Fifties redbrick with a large concrete cross above the entrance and Mary was waiting just inside its doors. The course was being held in a large ground floor room in which there were a dozen people inside, comprising three or four different ethnicities, mostly women.

'Before we begin, let us pray,' said a large, bearded man with a Dutch accent named Aalderk who sat at the head of the table and who, Liam assumed, was a pastor. They did, then were asked to introduce themselves. Liam told them nothing except that he was interested to see what went on. The pastor pulled in his chair, rubbed his hands and said, 'God is good.'

Liam couldn't resist.

'God is not necessarily good. Your statement's either a tautology or it implies that goodness is independent of God's credence.'

Mary looked at him with a frown while the pastor smiled indulgently then looked around at the others who began asking questions directed at their leader and each other about specific parts of the bible. The bible was, as Liam expected, their bible.

There was a white Zimbabwean woman there, Bethaan, who talked of The Garden, apples and snakes, of original sin, while her eyes shone preternaturally, her skin holding a slight yellowness, both, perhaps, a testament to pathology. Her belief in borrowed myth was manifest in her eager mouth. The others, looking towards her, nodded emphatically. There were several 'Amens' - evolution for them, thought Liam, was probably something to do with the Bolsheviks.

He exaggeratedly shook his head disbelievingly while they matronised him with subtle smirks. He told them that they could only infer God's existence. A teenager who'd been quiet till then cut in, neatly turning around Liam's positivism with a mature 'Believing is seeing.'

Ignoring Liam, they talked amongst themselves about their 'evidence' for God; personal incidents, biblical happenings. He was about to give them both barrels of his secular shotgun when the pastor announced that as this was only an initial meeting, they would finish. He invited them to pray again.

Liam lowered his head, trying not to listen, looking across at Mary smiling at him, and feeling as uncomfortable with prayer as he had as a child. He wanted, rather sulkily, to be disliked by them, wished them to react to his iconoclasm with suspicion and anger, even perhaps ostracising him, but during and after soup, tea and buns, they were open and friendly, even interested, asking him where he'd found out about the course, what he did, where he lived. He mumbled a few answers and moved away.

Mary went to him briefly and whispered, 'We need people like you.'

Attack Christians, he thought, and they become more Christian; turning the metaphorical cheek, courteous, smiling warmly as they gently surrounded him. He felt himself reluctantly responding, relaxing; making mildly amusing pleasantries; Bethaan, tall and earnest, was talking to the pastor.

She wore high heels; her legs were long and shapely and she was, he told himself, unwell. A few people asked if he was coming again and maybe finish the ten-week term. He wondered if he'd had any effect at all, if they had even considered anything he'd said; his entrenched views versus theirs. The pastor was still talking to Bethaan as he and Mary left and walked to the station.

'Should I ask you what you thought of it?' she asked.

'They seem nice people, Christians, although delusional, but....' He put his arm around her. 'Maybe it gave them food for thought, but I doubt it.'

'I won't ask if it gave you any.'

'I'll come back with you and look at your latest essay, proof it at least.'

He did, and after they spent the night together she was up early and off to her place of learning.

Initially, he had no intention of going to the church room again, Mary was still working hard, he was bored with his rather repetitive work and though he saw a friend for a drink and went to two badly chosen films on his own, feeling a need for a little proselytizing and intellectual stimulus, he went.

Once they'd begun, Mary absent but glad he was going, he went through most of the basic arguments against there being a god - some of the people around him seemingly not having heard them before - attempted to offer proof that there can be no proof then, after a silence, bore the brunt of a fervent battering by their beliefs, dogma, and the occasional use of biblical quotes like back-up sniper fire. The pastor, who'd been quiet for a while, then joined in, enthusiastically explaining chunks of the good book to his delighted flock.

Liam watched Bethaan again; she wasn't saying much, she hadn't the week before. He knew little about her. She was younger than him, but could have been married, had children, he didn't know what she did for a living or where she lived.

After the soup he walked out of the room to the staircase and looked through a window at Commercial Road.

'You're frightened to feel God, aren't you. Release it, let it go.'

He turned. It was Bethaan. He felt almost startled, this didn't seem like doorstep preaching, it felt as if it had been said specifically for him.

'What drives your intellectualised disbelief in faith then?'

'look… there's a need to create a god, we search for an ordered world, comfort, a deity gives us that. If God *did* exist we'd still have to invent him.'

'There you go again.'

He asked where she lived.

'Here. I live here.'

'What d'you mean?'

'There are rooms here,' she said, as if explaining to a child. 'I've lived here for two years, since I came. The pastor knew my parents, the rent's cheap.'

'And you're nearer to God?'

'I'm tired now. Come next time; try to shake us up again.'

She grinned for a moment. He walked with her to the lift.

She turned to look at him.

'Do you want to do some good?'

Before he could answer she told him that she was helping out at a south London Christian Centre assisting people coming off drugs. In his naïve, secular way he asked if she was supporting the medical staff in some capacity.

She frowned and said, 'We pray. They're helped through prayer.'

She was going the next day. He wasn't working, he'd be on the phone at home for a while assisting a surveyor with some cost estimates. He said he'd go if he could. She gave him the address.

They went back in. The meeting finished soon after and as he and Mary left the building he told her what he said he would do the next day, unless she had some free time herself.

'No, it's good of you. I'm a little surprised, but yes, go.'

It was a small, nondescript public building, and another warm welcome, this time by two Jamaican women who appeared to know who he was. There was a young African pastor he was introduced to in a room just inside the entrance. Bethaan hadn't arrived yet. He went into the hall.

Long tables were laid with food, mostly cold. There were piles of sandwiches provided by a large chain of coffee shops with 'Donated to the Homeless' promotion wrappers. Following instructions, he moved some chairs around, blew up a few balloons, pinned them to a wall then went to the kitchen and washed and dried with some of the other helpers.

He went out to the hall again where Afro-Caribbean, East European and other nationalities took their places at the tables and a young, possibly born-again Christian told him how he had been cured of his drug addiction through prayer.

The pastor said some blessings. When he'd finished and people began to sing hymns, with the Polish group smoothly word-perfect but in a hurry to finish and start eating, he came over to Liam and told him that Bethaan wouldn't be coming, she didn't feel well enough.

He talked to him about her; she'd been coming there three or four times a week for a year. Liam told him that she'd asked him to come. Unasked, he was given her phone number. He left; the yellow street lights against the black sky seemed rather cold and hard.

At work next day he intermittently thought of her; the pallor, the quiet mystique, spirituality, the belief and faith she carried with her. He felt jealous, envious of the constant drip-feed of assurance, of… certainty. He wanted that belief in him - realising it was his baby again, wishing mummy to be interested in nothing but him. He rang her from home.

'Oh, hello, you've surprised me; did you go? What did you think of it?' Did you help out?'

He told her he'd blown up a few balloons. He was going to ask how many of the needy had been religious before they'd arrived at the Centre or if it had been a sudden conversion when they saw the free food, but felt it wasn't fair to unload more cynicism onto her. He asked how she was feeling.

'Thanks for going,' she said.

'I'd have done more if you'd been there.'

'Such as?'

'Whatever you'd wanted me to.'

She laughed. 'Are you always this compliant with women?'

'Are you going to have a coffee with me?'

There was a silence. She quietly said yes. There was a period of exams and appraisals for Mary beginning and he wouldn't see her much. They arranged a time and place.

He met her outside Aldgate Station where she suggested a nearby cafe. As they walked he watched her. She was casually dressed: flat shoes, jeans, small earrings, and the spirituality again, which had a depth, a core.

He was aware that he had a proneness to be attracted a little too easily by the physicality of a woman, especially if she was tall and slim - his mother was, thus that physique was the norm, short was unthinkingly inferior.

It was a fixed-chairs-broken-yolk kind of place, but it didn't matter; she was there. They sat. She asked him what he thought of the church meeting.

'Well...'

'They seemed to like you.'

'Why?'

'Because they're Christian,' she grinned.

'Precisely. I should save this up for next time, I know, but the only way we can know anything is through sense data, and God isn't amenable to that.'

'Oh dear; cynical again.'

'Like God, everything's some sort of construct, really. Language is a kind of ultimate one. We can't get outside of it and-'

'You know that I'm not well, don't you.'

Maybe this was a way of shutting him up, to make him feel guilty, knock him off another hobby horse which, with its bit between its teeth, he was about to let ride on. He told her that he knew. She looked down then smiled again.

'But you're getting better. Yes?'

She gave an awkward grin.

'Hope so. Look I've got to get home, welcome a new boarder, I think he's from Canada; I should have done my homework. But you'll come next time?'

He asked her what she was doing the weekend, knowing he was seeing Mary.

'More church work I'm afraid.'

She got up to go. He offered to accompany her on the short walk back. He asked whether they could have a chat if he came early next time.

'Okay, I'll see you half an hour earlier. There'll be a service afterwards of course.'

She looked tired, worn out.

The morning before he saw her, a friend who had moved back to the north east after living in London rang to say he would be around locally and would like to have a drink with him. When Liam saw him he realised he'd missed his bright, jocular, crassness and enjoyed the short time they spent together. He then drove back to his local station to get the Tube to the church meeting.

It was attended by less people than last time and there were fewer comments from Liam. After Aalderk had pleasantly wished him and Bethaan a blessed evening they sat there on their own with tea cups and remnants of bread and scones on the tablecloth.

'Do you get fed up with me keeping on about God?' she asked.

'Perhaps it should be you asking me that.'

'Sometimes I wonder why you say anything at these get-togethers if it's all so pointless. In fact, should you even be listening?'

'I'd like to see your room.'

'Why?'

'Because… you're in it, you live there. Here.'

She looked at him dubiously.

'Come on then,' she said, like a young Girl Guide leader.

They went up the stairs to the top floor, along a corridor and into a room at the end. There was a sofa bed, table, chairs, religious books and the inevitable collection of halo'd Jesus's on the walls. There were also some photos of red earth, large trees and a house with a veranda which he guessed was the parental home. It was, she said, near Harare, which her parents had insisted on calling Salisbury, still referring to themselves as Rhodesians. They were dead, she had no siblings. She'd begun training as a lawyer, and then … God.

She made him tea. He asked her if she wanted to tell him what was wrong with her.

'It's malaria,' she said it as if the subject bored her. 'It develops within three months of leaving a malaria region, ironically there's little in my country. It affects the red blood corpuscles and my type is plasmodium falciparum.'

She said it almost by rote as if she'd heard it a hundred times, the reciting of it objectifying, detaching it from her for a few seconds.

'There won't be much discussion this evening, Aalderk will want us to eat and then go to the service in the main hall. I'd better help get the food ready. Do you want to come?'

He found himself washing up and laying plates again. This was the prosaic, pragmatic side of belief; no searing orange light, no illuminating epiphany, just mundanity, getting things ready, preparing; cleaning. He spoke a little to a few of the others, they were friendly as always. He felt dispirited, wondered how long she'd had the disease, what its prognosis was.

They went into the service. There were a lot of people; he was separated from her. After a loud, booming Nigerian pastor had finished his spiel, a small band with a young soprano played gospel music. People began singing and dancing. Bethaan stepped into an aisle and he watched her throwing her arms heavenwards. He, too, began moving with the rhythm.

As he looked at her again she turned her body towards the people behind her. Then she crumpled and fell on her side. He hesitated, went to go over to her, but others in the congregation already had. A couple of people on the course lifted her, another shouted into a mobile.

The music stopped, the singing petered out, the drummer continued for a few seconds, then quiet. Aalderk was there and went out behind two people half-carrying her to, Liam suspected, her room. The teenager came across to him and told him that it had happened before, but was now occurring more frequently.

He went to the back of the hall and sat on a pew. He heard the siren of an ambulance getting louder then stopping. The congregation looked rather lost; some left, others sat, including the singer.

He should have gone to the ambulance, but felt he had no right to, felt cut off from her; didn't share her conceptual system, these people, this place, this faith. And what *did* drive this intellectualised disbelief? 'Let it go,' she'd said. But he knew he wouldn't, couldn't.

He went home, half-heatedly willing his intellect to crumble, to make himself believe something. She was ill. He wanted to want to pray, but knew who his God was: God the father. Not a bearded man in the sky, benevolent, wise and seemingly righteous, but his late, indifferent, rigid, unaware, weak parent. He rang the church. A caretaker answered. He knew nothing. He went online. The malaria variant she had was mostly fatal. Before he deleted he saw 'Coma.' 'Major organ failure.'

'Dad, fuck you.' he heard himself say, but there was little feeling, it wasn't even a genuine attempt, just a gesture.

He realised he knew so little about her, wondered why he hadn't asked her more, discovered more. Was there a little bit of him that was wary of getting close to her, to feel something for her because of Mary, or because he knew she was ill? Perhaps he wanted her as some sort of proxy God; an intermediary between that great illusion in the sky and himself.

He didn't ring again, was scared to; didn't want to know that she was getting worse, didn't want to emotionally face the concept of death. He was frightened. He knew he wouldn't go to the church again. He would tell Mary tomorrow, though she would probably have heard what had happened in the church to her fellow believer and that he had been present. He would console her, pushing away want of consolation himself.

Trying to sleep that night, he thought of when he'd first spoken to Bethaan while he was looking out of a staircase window in the church and glimpsing again the new building being constructed at Linden Market, a little higher now.

He mused on narcissism, architects and buildings; a solid, deterministic link. 'The pursuit of gratification from vanity or egoistic admiration for one's own attributes.' He knew it originated from Greek mythology where the young Narcissus fell in love with his own image reflected in a pool.

He imagined a contemporary building's creator not seeing him or herself when they looked at a reflective surface, but their work, and not seeing its often ugly, visually painful results.

Maybe designers of buildings saw their profession as a religion: 'a cultural system of behaviours and practices, symbols, societal organisation' - architect, archbishop, archdeacon, - with them as high priests, their juniors being vicars or pastors, and those that designed the toilets or photocopied their betters' 'brilliant, radiant work', merely novices or janitors. Any criticism would, for them, feel like a religious persecution, an attack by philistines on their belief system.

When he did intermittently sleep he was plagued by an image of Bethaan, ill, bowed, carrying on her back a huge mound of a building full of pre-cast concrete caves, then suddenly standing tall and well, holding aloft, all at once, the stepped towers of Central Park, their shimmering glass and marble foyers, things created by other designers, those with a sense of majesty, with space inside them that allowed influences from a visionary past, from the Egyptian, from... He then slept.

# CHAPTER 12

It was a year and one month to the day after he'd sent the final design details to Tern when, at the topping-out ceremony, Piero, who was one of forty or so people present - city dignitaries, representatives of the contractors, Tern's wife and his friends and business associates - applauded the man as he waved to a crane driver based forty floors up to raise the last beam. It was a steel one painted white and signed by most of the workers involved. On his orders The Stars And Stripes would be tied to it.

These months, for Piero, had been a succession of trips from the office to the building, to the contractors' office, though they had often come to him, to interior fitters and a specialist engineering company in Schaumburg for the heliport - a few girders for its base protruding from the main structure were visible - and to Tern's mansion after he'd moved in six months previously. Here, he would answer any questions about the project and listen to the owner's occasional jokes.

They were all gazing up now. Milda, Tern's wife, looking particularly appealing, her mouth half open - 'gape' he thought too ugly a word for her - and her eyes under the perfect brows holding a quiet pride in her husband's achievement. She sensed Piero was looking at her and gave him a hint of a smile. She had expressed little emotion the few times he'd seen her but this small manifestation was friendly enough. Term gave him a quick look and a brief thumbs-up before looking skywards again.

Piero's co-workers were there, standing together behind him looking pleased, but having left his office to pursue their freelance work, Tommy now directly employed by a firm, they would leave pretty soon. He could, however, always call upon them when necessary, though having only one small commission since finalising the main work on the tower - a minor developer's rather cheap and pragmatic block of apartments which he hadn't really wanted to do - he presently didn't need them. There was a minor slow-down in the Chicago economy currently but Tern was certain that as it picked up so would the number of suitors for his work.

He could now see the crane's load disappear from view as workers waited to unhook it and place it on top of the building. Its owner hadn't wanted a mast of any sort, which Piero thought was rather out of character considering the ostentatious ten-foot silver block lettering of 'TERN' he intended to have attached near the top or, if taking Piero's advice, placed directly under the heliport apron.

When the 'yeahs' and 'whoos' had finished, and a small brass band had played The Star Spangled Banner, people in the ensuing 'what to do now' hiatus began looking at Tern for guidance. Nothing had been collectively arranged after the topping-out, but Piero knew he would be with the building's owner, his wife and friends at a long-standing restaurant in the south suburban area, 'Gibson's Gardens,' owned by a friend of Tern's and a descendant of the namesake.

After Milda had briefly straightened her husband's too long tie, another variant of red, white and blue, he began walking to his car, this time a Buick, interrupted by several people coming up to him wanting to shake his hand, he obliging them. Piero followed Tern's friends into the first of the two vehicles behind, sharing the front seats with its chauffeur.

It should have been a pleasant journey, it was sunny, there was lots of greenery, they passed a golf course or two, Piero still thinking the game was merely the interruption of a pleasant walk. But the three men who sat behind him were talking loudly about business deals in a restricted code of 'capital asset pricing,' 'leveraged buyouts,' and even more obscure financial abbreviations. They didn't talk to him, not even when the chauffeur mentioned the building they'd come from and Piero told him of his role in its construction.

The driver's look was rather disbelieving at first then he nodded and said, 'You're pretty young. I suppose I have an idea of architects as older.'

He didn't say any more until they were outside their destination, wishing him good day in his polite Chicagoan way.

They climbed out the car and went into a rather nondescript, but comfortable place with black-and-white photos on the walls of the restaurant in its heyday. The owner was vigorously shaking Tern's hand and patting his shoulder then turned and smoothly gestured for them all to follow him. They went through to a spacious back room with a long table and waited until Milda had seated herself before they did the same.

Piero, not sure of the appropriate seating hierarchy, assuming there was one, sat towards the end, briefly looking at her and that now familiar, not-quite smile again. Although quiet and appearing almost to lack confidence, she had a presence; he wondered whether it was because of whose wife she was or it was her own personality, he wasn't sure.

He thought of when he'd been first introduced to her as he was approaching the mansion and she leaving it, briefly waving behind her to its owner. Tern had shouted, 'Hey, this is my wife, Milda. Milda, this is Piero Ronzi, I was tellin' yer about him.'

The architect felt hurt for a second that Tern had used his surname. She'd paused and slowly held out her hand. If she'd offered it more enthusiastically, Piero felt, it would have been too forthright, too aggressive for her. He gently touched it. He'd wanted to again.

He'd thought of her intermittently during the next two days, then more continuously. He was aware he had a proneness to seductive images that were, often, meaningless pictures; filmic, theatrical, transient, but this time he kept seeing her face in the car as she'd been driven away: the still profile, unblinking, slightly elongated eyes, mildly prominent cheek bones, the not-quite blonde hair.

Her mouth reminded him of Chiara's. No. He musn't go there. It was a long time ago. *Non e' successo.*

As other people sat he could hear the restaurateur telling an obvious tourist about the early days of the place when it was a speakeasy and a popular hangout for cops and politicians. Those were the days when diners would drive out to the country to enjoy a decent steak and freshly butchered chicken or their famous hash browns. For entertainment there would be a bear-boxing ring out back.

Tern, at the table's head, looked expansively around telling people to order what they wanted. Most had Greek gyros or Chicago hot dog, an all-beef sausage with green sweet pickle relish and peppers, and they all had, at the owner's insistence hash browns. Piero chose an Italian beef sandwich, the nearest the place had to the offerings of his native country.

He pretended to listen to the talk, literally business as usual, their host dominating most of the wheeling, dealing topics, his cohorts chiming in sporadically and largely in agreement with familiar, quasi-tough talking clichés. He tried, albeit half-heartedly, to join in and began asking a few basic questions about their symbolic world of market capitalizations, stop-limit orders and Keynesian economics, the last quickly responded to by one of the diners, cheeks bulging, almost spluttering, with 'Hey, forget that interventionist crap, no swearin' at the table.' eliciting a few chuckles and a brief nonplussed look from Tern.

It went on; 'margins,' 'Dow Jones,' interrupted only by the ordering of desserts, most going for trifle or marina cake. It was a pity for Piero that Tommy and the others couldn't be here, though he would sooner have been with them on the work they were doing, or alone back in the office.

He could see that most had finished their drinks; root beer and whiskey were popular, Tern ordering some Swedish liquor, obviously having had it here before. He hadn't finished swilling it when he stood and tapped a knife a few times against his glass. Piero had thought this was a particularly English thing to do to get attention, he'd seen it only in the rather posh restaurants in London the few times he could afford to be in them. The others looked up at Tern as if choreographed.

He went straight into his spiel.

'We're all aware of the local economic dip at the moment but I was surprised yesterday when I had a cheque bounce from my bank marked 'Insufficient funds.' I rang to ask if it meant me or them.'

There were a few appreciative and knowing chuckles.

Somebody said, 'Yeh, a recession is when a neighbour loses his job, a depression is when you lose yours. Let's hope Reagan don't let it go that far.'

'More significantly,' Tern continued, 'I was in trouble with the cops for alleged assault recently, but I pleaded self-defence. I was in Walmart when a man in overalls asked if I wanted deckin'.' More chuckles. He paused.

'Forget that. Recent news: George did okay with the Cicero deal, though it may have been a bit lucky, Chuck gave his all for the, let's say difficult, transaction on Michigan, and Bill had to work hard on the Rush Street operation but made it in the end.'

'What about you with that deal on Roosevelt? You were goin' at it hammer and tongs when I left.' one of them said.

'I sent you away, Al, if you remember, thought my shouting might frighten you.' Again there was knowing laughter. 'But I got what I wanted; got the price.'

'You bethca,' said the man who'd asked the question.

This banter was confirming to Piero that Tern's interest in a deal was more one where he could be seen as a winner, rather than in the content of it.

'Enough of this,' he was saying. 'A marketing manager, married to a woman  previously married three times but still a virgin, told him that her first husband was a sales rep who'd told her throughout the marriage, 'It's gonna be great.' The second was a psychiatrist who just wanted to talk about it, the third was in technical support and kept saying, Don't worry, it'll be up any minute now.' Expectantly, she looked at her new man who said, 'I know I have the product, I'm just not sure how to position it.''

The laughter was louder and, Piero thought, more syco-phantic.

Tern looked around the table, paused and said, 'I've told no one this yet, even Milda.' He looked down at her and squeezed her shoulder, smiling; she was expressionless.

'I'm having another tower.' He almost smirked. 'This one, though, I've gotta get the okay on.'

Amongst meaningful looks from the others, he glanced at the man sitting next to Piero and winked.

'But it's gonna be higher than the one we're celebrating.'

There was a hiatus of almost head-shaking admiration then clapping. Piero felt suddenly lost, hollow. Who was going to design it for him? Did he already have a visualisation? Why hadn't he told him? He heard a mini-chorus of 'Well done, Tern,' 'You're the man.' and 'Great, congratulations.'

'And if the deal comes off, and I see no reason why it shouldn't, who knows, the one after, or the one after that, could be in my home town, New York.'

Piero felt left out, alienated.

'Why is Christmas Day,' Tern asked, 'like a day on a con-struction site? You end up doing all the work and some fat guy wearing a suit takes all the credit.'

There were a few smiles.

'But the guy I'm talking about ain't fat and he's not wearin' a suit. He's my architect. And he should take the credit.'

He looked at Piero and grinned. There was another silence. The others seemed unsure what to do. They didn't know him, who he was; none of them had really spoken to him, but as Tern started to clap they followed suit.

Piero felt relief, the room didn't seem so large, he filled a little more of it. He bowed his head slightly toward the big man who responded with, 'No helipad this time, I've got one. I want something different, stately, maybe. What d'yer think of that word guys? 'Regal's okay so is 'majestic,' but, no, 'stately' sounds about right.'

Piero was wondering if, as it appeared, nothing had been finalised, perhaps even begun, then maybe he would be asked to submit something. He could draw something for him he'd had in mind for a while. He imagined going to Tern's mansion, handing him an illustration of his creation with a proud look on his face and Tern, frowning, asking him what it was.

'A building,' he would say.

'I can see that. What's it for?'

Tern would, perhaps, hear a timid 'You.' and then say, 'What am I supposed to fuckin' do with it; give it to the Graham Foundation?'

A waiter came across to the table and told Tern there was a call for him. He got up, excused himself and followed the man out of the room.

'Didn't know you did his building,' the person next to Piero said, turning to him. 'Guess we're kinda more interested in the figures, the margins and so forth, than what a thing looks like. I suppose it blinds us to the looks a bit.'

'Aesthetics.'

'Yeah, that's it. But it is a fine-looking thing. Wonder what people'll call it, huh? Guess the big man would like it to be known as *his* building, guess it will.'

'Maybe it'll be called 'The Lip.''

'Meaning that it'll be noted for the design and not the owner?'

'Maybe.'

'That'll be a win for you, huh?'

Piero smiled.

'So, what are you working on now?'

'Not much.'

'What's your next thing? You gonna do Tern's one?'

'We'll see.'

'Well, let's hope you do, huh, who knows?'

'Yeh.'

'Don't see that many Italians in this city. Mostly in New York I guess.'

'I lived there.'

'Little Italy?'

'Gotta go boys.' Tern had returned. 'See a guy about how high we can go with the next one.' He grinned. 'Think it'll be higher than he wanted.'

As Milda stood, he said to them, 'You do what you will. Enjoy yourselves.'

He held his wife's hand, gave his little wave and they left.

The people around the table continued talking more business amongst themselves. Piero rose.

'Perhaps I'll see you again,' he said, glancing quickly around him.

'Ciao,' replied the man who had spoken to him.

He took a train back still feeling a little empty, went into his house, idly thinking that though it wasn't trendy to live where he did, he liked his habitat and he wasn't going to leave it while he had work to do. He went straight to his study, rummaged through the drawers in his desk, hastily throwing papers on the floor till he found what he wanted.

It was a rather creased, swiftly-executed watercolour of a structure like a vertical cluster of various sized metal rods, the taller at the centre. He'd been unsure of the floor plan but thought a Y shaped one with curved lobes buttressing a hexagonal central core would be an interesting idea.

There were a lot of external walls and windows with the first twelve floors or so fairly bulky, making a wide stance on the ground, but then there was a spiralling sequence of set-backs - he was no lover of these, preferring a smooth, increasingly-narrowing shape, but various authoritative bodies involved with Chicago buildings would see their appropriateness.

About a third of the way to the top the building gently metamorphosed into a slender tower and narrowed until only a central section remained. He was uncertain of the appropriate engineering possibilities and problems, but Lance would know.

Pushing away the idea of his sometime co-worker's input being, at this moment, pointless, he looked again at his sketch and decided to do it again; more detail, a bit more exterior emphasis of the lower floors, a little more bulge maybe.

He made himself coffee and, still wondering if Tern had yet asked anyone to design his next project, began. Again, he worked into the small hours.

# CHAPTER 13

Dusk was rolling over the site and he was still using his trowel. Everyone had gone except a security guard who came over to him and asked when he was going to finish.

'Can't lay bricks in the dark can yer?'

Realising it was well past home time, he'd dropped his trowel into a bucket, shooed his wad of muck off its board and said, 'Actually, I cun. I'm goin' now anyway.'

He looked at his watch. There was a bus due that would take him to the hospital. He still felt that he shouldn't leave his mate on his own. He removed his overalls, pushed them into a workbag which he dropped inside a corner of the wall he was building and went to the bus stop across from the site's entrance. He paced restlessly around till the bus came. It seemed to take a long time to get there. He hurried in, went through the ward door and looked towards the end of the bed-filled space. This time there was no curtain. Maybe Thomasz was better.

He took a few strides then saw that the figure on the bed wasn't Thomasz, it was a young girl. This time a different nurse asked him who he was. He told her. A flicker of interest had come when he saw that she looked like his remembered archetypal Irish one.

'Oh, I'm sorry Mister Salmon, but Mister Nowak passed away a little while ago. I believe someone was going to contact you.'

He immediately heard his mother, wearing the perpetual headscarf that hid her curlers, saying, 'tis the grim reaper la.' For an instance he saw the robed skeleton with a scythe robbing Thomasz of his life, cutting, slicing him in half at the waist as he lay on his bed.

'Oh Christ, it canna be.' But it was. It had happened.

'But where is 'e? I wanna look at'im, joost - '

'We had to move him. We're congested at the moment. I'm sorry; we need beds, all we can get.'

He thought of Con, she was coming down tomorrow.

'Aah, me God,' she'd said when, after leaving it a couple of days to see how bad it all was, he'd told her what had occurred.

'I think you'll be better outside,' the nurse said quietly, lightly squeezing his arm.

He sat on the now familiar bench outside the ward. What did she mean when she'd said Thomasz was dead? That he wouldn't be working with him anymore? Be loyal to him? Have a pint of Broon with him? Death. What was it? He recalled a definition he'd read: 'The cessation of all biological functions that sustain an organism. Phenomena which commonly bring about death include biological ageing, malnutrition… and accidents or trauma resulting in injury.'

But it was more than that, the causes irrelevant. It was 'Nothing.' And what the hell was that? A speculative image of the universe came to him and the primary question of how something could be made from nothing. And when people said, 'He's better off out of it.' the sentence may as well have been translated to 'blah blah blah' for all the sense it made.

Before he could face the notion that the questions were useless, facile escapes, a voice asked him if he was Mister Salmon. Another new doctor.

Jim looked up at a bearded Asian and heard himself say aloud, 'How can I tell Con?'

The man turned away. 'Come with me. Take your time.'

They walked to the end of the passage where lift doors were opening. He wasn't sure whether he should speak to him in the lift or when they'd got out, knowing it didn't matter a shite.

As they walked along a basement corridor the man told him that, officially, he shouldn't be doing this and that where they were going he could be left on his own for only a few minutes.

'When you've finished, the ward nurse will answer any questions. I'm sorry.'

Asking Jim to follow him, he opened a door.

'I'm bending the rules a little. As said; just a few minutes, Mister Salmon.'

A young, competent looking man sitting at a table attending a laptop looked up and nodded towards them and as the doctor closed the door behind him, got up and went across to a cold-chamber at the end of a line of them backing onto a wall. He opened its door.

Jim nervously asked him how long the corpses were here for. He said the word intentionally, to detach from it all, to attempt to be curious, interested in the processes of a mortuary.

'Up to several weeks.'

'Do these things prevent decomposure?'

'Well, it continues to decompose but at a slower rate than room temperature'

'All wine is served at room temperature,' said Jim drily, staring at the open door.

The technician looked puzzled then slowly slid out a flat metal slab. It seemed to take an inordinately long time before Thomasz appeared; on his back, head first.

'You may look.'

Jim walked hesitantly towards the covered form. 'In the beginning was the body' came to mind. Maybe it was biblical, Con would know. Would she wish to see him one more time, like this? He had a mother in Krakow, well, he thought it was there. How would he find her? How - '

'I'll be just around here, don't touch him,' the man said, pointing to the hidden space at the other end of the row of chambers.

Jim stood over the figure whose face was now almost colourless; he had never seen a face so pale. His fair, greying hair was fine; Jim had often taken the mick out of its owner's habit of flicking it away from his eyes. For a rather crazy second he wanted to get back to the job and say to his mate, 'There's a bloke who looks just like you in that mortuary place at the hospital.'

This was merely skin and flesh, bones and animal-like organs and dark red blood and nails and... This was it, the nothingness of not existing. He bent and kissed the forehead. He didn't know what to feel.

The technician moved around him, his movements implying that he wished to push the slab back, to seal in the aftermath of death.

'I think that will have to do now, the autopsy will be quite soon.'

Jim mumbled a 'Thanks' and, feeling disoriented, looked for the door he had entered by. The technician was there before him and opened it.

Feeling just as lost, he returned to the lift which now had an 'out of order' sign stuck to its door. He slowly climbed the stairs back to the ward. The same nurse was there. He asked her what would happen now.

'We need to inform his next of kin, of course. Do you know who it is?'

He didn't, had never thought about it. Perhaps it was on a piece of paper somewhere, in England or Poland, he had no idea.

'Has he a wife, children; a parent perhaps?'

He told her he thought he may have had a mother in Poland

'Thank you, we'll try to find out. Sorry, again. Try to rest.'

He took a last glance at the bed Thomasz had occupied, thanked the nurse and left the building.

He stood at the bus stop thinking of euphemisms for death, thinking, perhaps, it would stop him from screaming. 'Bite the dust,' 'go west,' a 'sticky end,' and the cockney 'brown bread.' Thomasz had 'popped his clogs' in action, he'd 'died with his boots on.' Con would have said that he'd 'gone the way of all flesh' and was now at peace in 'Abraham's bosom' after having taken the 'last train to glory.'

She still may say these things when he told her. He would do so tomorrow after meeting her off the train. Thomasz would have said, if he could, *Kopnac kalendarz*. He'd explained to him once what it meant: 'kick the calendar.'

Back in the house he made himself go straight upstairs to Thomasz's room. The landlady was away somewhere; they'd had the place to themselves for a week or so. He stood outside the door wanting to go down to his own room, lie on his bed and pull the duvet over him, all of him, be in the dark, remain there. He pushed the door.

It was a tidy room, Thomasz was tidy, too. It was hard to accept the past tense. He glanced around. There were photos on the wall above a couch, one of him kicking a ball inside the Bochnia Salt Mine, another of the Tyne Bridge, and in pride of place the Corpus Christi Basilica in Krakow, the 'City of churches' he'd called it. The spiritual sharing of their religion was a prime reason for him and Con getting on so well.

There were no photos on his dresser, and he drew another deep breath before opening the top drawer, thinking irrelevantly that professional burglars started with the bottom drawer so that they didn't have to close it before pulling out the next, thus saving valuable seconds.

There was an old silver lace brooch which, he supposed, could have been his mother's, and a framed photo of a dark-haired girl with grey eyes which may have been an old girl friend, though he kept that part of his life to himself, at least he didn't share it with Jim; Thomasz had sometimes gone out for an evening on his own but had never mentioned a woman. He was still thinking in the present tense, he should stop it.

In the next drawer, underneath neatly folded Y-fronts, vests and T-shirts, were black and white photos of a slim child with square shoulders and long hair hanging over an eyebrow, it was obviously him. One of them showed a fair-haired woman smiling into the lens, the likeness suggesting his mother.

There were also some postcards and a few letters. The former had pictures of the Mazurski Lake District, the Old Town Hall in Warsaw and another which had been sent to him some time ago by Jakub of bison in the Bialowieza Forest.

He turned the letters over, one, sent to his old Newcastle home, had a name, 'Agnieszka,' and an address in Krakow handwritten on the back. It could, possibly, be his mother. He opened it knowing he probably wouldn't understand a word, thus not feeling guilty in looking at it. It wasn't dated, so he could have received it just after he'd moved here.

She could no longer be in the world; Thmasz never talked about her. Thinking of this, it appeared that there were large chunks of his friend's emotional life he knew little of and thus couldn't retrospectively empathize with.

He had a quick look in the wardrobe. 'Tidy Thomasz' he'd heard Jakub call him. There were two suits he had never seen him wear, shoes looking rather bespoke, and quite a few expensive-looking shirts, some having Polish labels.

He looked around him again. Curtains tidily open, bed neatly made; he had a sudden urge to lift the valance to see if Thomasz was hiding under the bed, ashamed that he'd given his mate such a scare. He sat on the edge of the mattress and banged his fists against the side of his head.

'Why d'yer die, Thomasz? Why are you fuckin' dede?'

He began to cry. He wailed for a few seconds, got up and, still sobbing, punched the wall, shut the door behind  him and went down to his room.

There was no sleep. Several times he reached across to pick up his mobile to ring Con, but knew he had to be with her when he told her. But where? In the middle of a crowded platform? In a café? On a bus? He wanted to wait till she was with him here.

Walking to the station early, he gained a short-lived comfort from the great brick-built double-arched entrance. Almost sub-liminally he internally rattled off a few things he knew about the place: that it was designed by Lewis Cubitt over a hundred and thirty years ago, was, at the time, the largest station in England, and that the thirty-four metre clock tower once held large tenor and bass bells. There were other things about the place he had probably bored Thomasz to inertia with.

Not wanting to wait for her inside the building he walked around a little and, finding an old, tucked-away café, he felt a muted, perverse joy in its atmosphere of speckled lino, fly-spattered blinds, sunlight filtering through smeared windows hitting a cloud of steam, and the eternal smell of ketchup and frying oil. It was almost like a day-care centre for window cleaners, artists and escapees from rehabilitation centres. It was also just right for him and his situation, his breakfast-less mood and sudden desire for a fry-up.

He sat for a while after finishing his meal then made himself face the walk back to the station. He usually liked trains; especially when, watching them as a child, the steam from the engines hissing sideways across platforms and blowing out the chimneys with long puffs which got shorter and shorter as the trains began moving.

In the main station in Newcastle he would draw things: engines, brown and cream carriages, a tea urn in a waiting room, a lady in a fur coat. Sometimes he'd sit on a bench and write phrases in his notepad like 'pulsating pistons' or 'a steam hiss of motion,' though not sure what he meant by the latter. He remembered drawing a porter pushing luggage, bent over like a scarecrow wearing a cap. He recalled sketching a signal box and some bushes. But this was now, and he felt apprehensive.

Her train was a little early, he began walking down the plat-form. She hadn't rung him while on it or even told him if she'd caught it, she wasn't one for using phones. She stepped out of a rear carriage and saw him immediately. He went towards her.

'How is he?' she asked hurriedly before he could cuddle her.

After he'd done so - a long hug in which he was partly comforting himself - she asked again. He'd forgotten what he'd rehearsed.

'It's er, not good, luv. Let's get back. I'll tell yer about it at the house.'

'Why canna yer tell me now? Tell me. Is it very bad?'

'Come.' He held her hand tightly, almost pulling her.

'He hasn't died, has he? Not that.'

He stopped and pulled her to him, holding her again.

'He's dead, Con. Yesterday. He's bloody gone, lass.'

'Oh Christ.'

She pushed her face into his neck. He could feel the wetness of her tears. Easing her from him he put an arm around her shoulders and told her they'd get a taxi.

He held her in the vehicle then the walk across the pavement from it and into the house. He sat her down in his room.

'You better see if you can contact his mother,' she whispered, wiping her face. 'Do it now.'

Ringing the international directory, he found there was neither an address nor telephone number listed. He knew it was pointless to attempt to trace Jakub. She asked him when he'd last seen Thomasz. He told her about the morgue. She was quiet, it becoming a long, silent hiatus till she stood and said, 'Best to arrange a funeral soon as we cun, it won' take 'em long to let him go, will it?'

He rang the hospital. They gave him clearance for a funeral; it was brain trauma, and pneumonia had also set in as a direct result of his Injuries. Nothing had been discovered about their ex-patient's mother.

Con had decided there shouldn't be a procession from the undertakers to the crematorium - a cross-bearer at the front followed by a priest and clergy - she thought that would be too

much and Jim knew Thomasz had been a rather sporadic at-
tendee at the local church.

They sat in the car behind the one with the coffin, followed
by others carrying workmates and other workers on the site
Jim had rounded up. There were nearly thirty of them. They'd
lost pay but Jim heard that there would be a whip-round for
them from those who remained working on the site.

As a boy, Jim hadn't liked churches, he would sooner have
been over the park and its see-saw and sand pit escapes from
their God-fearing Gothic that he'd had to endure most Sundays. He sat on a front pew with Con and looked around at the
gold and glitz - a double standard, he'd always thought, considering that most Catholics inhabited the world's poorest
countries. But even the brightness of the place couldn't push
away the memory of dad's sharp elbows accompanied by his
'Stop bleedin' fidgetin.' in a cold Victorian church.

He had, in recent years, when needing some quiet, some
calm, occasionally looked around graveyards; He would look
at the winged angel monuments, a testimony to Victorian pi-
ousness and order, at the leaning, mossy headstones and cher-
ubs, the long grass, the wilting flowers.

A sense of peace was to be found in spreading, unkempt
cemeteries with their large trees and wild bushes hanging over
blackened, eroded tombs and headstones, and long grass growing over inscribed slabs of granite.

He had once walked briefly around this one, which was built
in the Thirties: low, cream-painted buildings, Palladian style
roofs with a tall chimney, the neat symmetry of rose bushes
measured along red-brick walls, sculpted hedges bordering
curved paths and small numbered plaques telling whose ashes
were uniformly spaced in the earth with its cropped, tended
grass and plastic-wrapped flowers. Its peace was, contradicto-
rily, marred by its ordinariness.

The coffin, borne by bearers from the undertakers, was put
down in front of an altar and candles placed around it which

were lit and burned throughout the cycle of prayers. There had been no vigil the previous day, Con wanting to keep it simple and relatively short. The priest then conducted the liturgy: the Mass and Rites of Burial plus readings from the Bible, the singing of hymns and Holy Communion.

The Catholics in the congregation knelt and spoke the prayers and sang the hymns aloud - certainly most of the Irish workers present did - the majority of the people, which included two neighbours and a local newsagent, stood. He recognised the Liturgy of the Hours, bits of some prayers but hardy any pieces from the Bible.

The service concluded with the Rite of Commendation for Thomasz and the coffin sprinkled with holy water and incense placed upon it. As the cask slid into the furnace opening, Jim held his wife's hand tightly, noting with utter irrelevance, that the oven curtains were embroidered with gold thread. There was a small and father tatty columbarium in the crematorium's grounds where Jim and Con would place a funerary urn containing his friend's ashes in a day or so.

For the wake, he had hired the hall of a working men's club a few hundred yards from the crematorium, the lads from the site walking there. Inside - the buffet organised by Con - he listened to the workers talking of Thomasz, of his jokes, the speed of his brick laying, genial disposition, how they'd miss him, some indulging either in a rather fake jocularity and often superficial memories; ''e liked a good laugh, did Thomasz.' 'Yeah, 'e once said that if 'e couldn't take it wiv 'im, 'e wouldn't go,' or an earnest sadness.

He did like a laugh. Jim recalled putting on a posh accent to recite the old joke about two upper-class types that hadn't seen each other for a while. ''I say,' says one, 'are you still in the club? I'm a town member now.' 'Really. I'm a country member.' 'Yes, I remember.'' Thomasz hadn't got it.

He asked himself whether any of it hid the reality of their pain; how many there actually felt it. But he knew the animated conversations at such gatherings weren't only because people hadn't, perhaps, seen someone for a long while, but a kind of relief that they were talking about somebody who wasn't any more whilst they were; a kind of confirmation of their own existence. Funerals were rituals reminding people that society continues, *they* continue.

Guests began leaving. 'Nice spread, mate, thank the missus.' 'Reckon 'e 'ad a good innings.'

He'd have liked another one, thought Jim. He and Con, he felt, had become Thomasz's ersatz family, perceived now almost as a de facto one.

In the cab taking them back to the lodgings Con was silent, holding herself rigidly upright. Her husband, looking out of a side window, glimpsed a familiar shape in a gap between buildings. He hadn't realised it could be seen from here. It was the 'Toucan' building. He wondered if there would be some sort of official enquiry into the accident, whose shoulders the responsibility, the blame for the accident would fall on.

He began feeling angry again. They could say what they liked about faulty materials, corner cutting; the carelessness of the crane driver, perhaps blame the local council or the Mayor of London, or whoever gave permission for its construction, even declare it a series of random events, an act of God. He didn't care. This was Brainless Bird's fault. And he could do nowt about it.

# CHAPTER 14

Clive was telling Liam of a case he'd handled a few years ago he called the 'Movie Man' one, which was sparked by his listener mentioning Mary's ability to remember the names of so many actors, lines and scenes in movies, and her almost childlike delight when doing so.

They were sitting in a restaurant - its interior a reasonable attempt at art nouveau, with Mucha prints on the walls and William Morris cushions - in Highgate Village, with its artisan bread, craft beer from the small brewery next to it and surrounded by Georgian, Victorian, Edwardian and Thirties houses, Fifties Blocks of flats, five churches, six pubs and effortless, understated affluence.

Liam and Mary had seen one of their favourite films the evening before, a rare respite for her from working on degree assignments, after which she'd repeated yards of script, described, sometimes in minute detail, the contents of shots and, as always, insisted on staying for the end credits to hear the theme music.

The man Clive had begun talking of seemed to have had little joy in his filmic recalls.

'When he first came to me - a middle-aged man, maybe older - the first thing he said was that he'd just bought a poster of 'Gilda' with a shot of Hayworth that, he said, was a reversal. Not sure why I remember the words, they were innocent enough. 'Her cigarette,' he said, 'was in her right hand and the smoke, drifting slowly upwards like a kind of helix, is really a symbol of Noir, like contra jour shots as in 'Build My Gallows High' with Mitchum in Acapulco heat, slatted light across his jacket and Greer walking in against the sun.'

He mentioned Dietrich's films, 'Strolling a highway, headlights stroking her back before she becomes the night, the palms, fedoras, wise guys, bars...' It was a sort of visual composite of those sorts of movies I suppose.'

He had asked him why films were so important to him.

'They're an escape,' his client had said, 'just as they are for everybody.'

Clive had felt that the second part of his sentence was a deflection from his awareness that his 'escape' was, perhaps, unhealthy and wanted to present his intense interest as a mildly eccentric foible. He'd wondered if the man was also aware, as Clive was; that they were part of a larger running away, a much bigger avoidance.

''I rarely get carried along completely with a film,' he'd said, 'there's always a part of me, I think it's located above my right ear,' he'd smiled, 'that's continually aware of the camera angles, the framing, the script, the... it's always there, but sometimes when I do things I become characters in the films I've seen, like when I once kissed a girl when I was younger, I was really the boy kissing the girl in the porch in the background of a foreground Danny Green in 'The Lady Killers.'

'It was interesting that when he talked of a soft-focused Bergman lah-lah-lahing it next to Sam's piano in 'Casablanca,' I felt we were experiencing the same nostalgic frisson, the same, if you like, pre-pubescent meaning. I knew, of course, that I should stop this implicit sharing; an interactive process like this wouldn't do the man any good. He was a client. He wasn't a friend.'

Clive then saw him in a local cinema. He was sitting at the back when his client came in after him and went straight to the middle of the front row; it was a matinee, few people were there.

'I looked occasionally at the back of his head, it didn't move. I wondered whether he always, when able, sat front-centre whatever the cinema or film, and if so, why. It could be merely for room to stretch his long legs, he was pretty tall, but the nearer he was to the screen the bigger it was and there was less peripheral non-film area to distract him.

I imagined his expression: still, intense, eyes wandering, occasionally widening, trying to let the film occupy his head, not so much identifying with this or that character, but empathising, almost becoming them.'

When Clive had left he was still sitting there, just as motionless, perhaps wanting to see who the Second Assistant Director was before the shock of an empty black screen and someone in casual uniform picking up an empty drinks bottle from under the next seat; and reluctantly having to accept the need to leave this warm, dark space and face the harsh light and the traffic outside.

'Next day, he came exactly on time, almost having to stoop to miss the top of the door frame as I let him in. He sat and tried a smile.

'Yes, I have seen some good films lately. Well, not really. I saw a recently-made silent film, but wasn't impressed. But those pencil moustaches did bring back a magical world, magical I suppose because it was so unlike *my* world, my rather grimy life.'

'I asked him where this world, this life was. He waved a loose hand as if flicking a fly away. 'Doesn't matter,' he said. Then off he went, describing, at times vividly, scene upon scene from film after film.

'I can see the back of the head of an actor who I haven't seen for years and recognise him instantly, as I do sometimes from the first syllable uttered by a minor off-screen character I haven't heard for ages.'

I asked him if it was his 'bit above the right ear.'

He shouted, 'Yes. Yes it *is*.'

I had to quieten him. When I asked him if he was obsessed with film, he laughed, swinging one leg over the other restlessly.

'No-o. Some people drink, others take drugs, this is *my* addiction.' He'd laughed again, took a deep breath and carried on with his 'addiction.''

Clive had gone through the motions of listening to his client while wondering whether the speaker was imagining himself as an observer on the film sets or actually dwelling in the scripted fantasies. He stopped him when he realised he'd run fifteen minutes over time.

During the days before the man's next appointment, Liam's friend had wondered, in between seeing other patients, how real the world was to him. He'd never said, in quiet desperation, that it wasn't, but Clive felt that underneath the relentlessly detailed memories of movies the world outside of them wasn't quite real. How unreal he didn't know, nor how long it had been so.

When he next saw him he'd enquired about his relationships with women.

'What did, do, you feel? Love?' A nebulous word I know, but... what?' He told me he'd left his wife for a woman who looked like Faye Dunaway.

'Remember her?' he asked me. 'I know it seems superficial, but there it is.''

He'd then started yelling. 'I act, all the *time. All* the time.' He kept punching the arm of the sofa. 'Everything's an act; I'm acting with you now. I don't *want* to anymore.''

The silence after that was, as Clive said, 'like something hard and heavy hitting the room.'

His client had stood, gone towards the window and looked out.

'He was completely still for a while then raised his shoulders, turned quickly, took some money from his jacket pocket and pushed it into my hand. He'd then left; slamming the door.'

After he'd gone, Clive had sat in his study thinking about him.

'I don't like using the phrase 'classic case' for it depends on what period of psychoanalytic history a quintessential example of a condition comes from, but it was tempting. Peter - I shan't tell you his full name of course - when dealing with people generally or in significant relationships, would have used characters he'd seen, mostly in movies, and squashed into an amalgam of different pieces of a constructed personality. This would have been a fluid, shifting plasma of protection.

'I was pretty sure that this was the first time he'd hinted to anyone that his behaviour had been, was, influenced by filmic images, how much of his actions had been internalized from the picture palaces of his childhood onwards; fused into multi-layered bits of behaviour in which he could artificially respond to social situations, not just everyday ones, but intimate ones.

I was suddenly convinced that his real self wasn't bearable, had become fragmented, impoverished, unreal. He had created a false self.'

Liam interrupted him. 'I'm no analyst, but did you examine other possibilities? Forget I said that, you obviously did.'

'I did. I examined my diagnosis, contradicted it and attempted to put other conclusions in its place. I'd seen the man only three times and had been told very little until his last emotional speech. But, assuming I was right, I tried to think of what this experience would have meant to him.

'I dredged up my knowledge of the patients I'd treated over the years, trying to find symptoms, characteristics, actions that I could validly relate to this man. I didn't look at past notes, the experiences were virtually all in my head; but a correct analysis depended on whether I was right about the man's lack of reality.

'There had been, I guessed, a perceived destruction of himself, an annihilation of self as baby, at birth perhaps or, a contentious view, in the womb. Whatever the source, he had pushed it away from him all of his life. Every perceived incident of neglect, however trivial, every raised voice as a child, would have left him unutterably estranged and lonely, carrying a pain unbearably harsh.

'He would have filled his emptiness not only with the technicolored and monochromic conjuring of childlike emotions, but with an intellectualisation of the world; perhaps constantly, relentlessly looking at his every thought, every action, wondering why and where they came from and analysing them in discrete, staccato bits of introspection; a prohibition on *feeling* a self.

'I tried to imagine what it would have been like for him in a relationship with a woman. If she told him she loved him, he'd have forgotten it the next day as if it had never been said, there would have been no emotional memory of it. I imagined him, hours afterwards, writing down the exact words she'd used in a notebook he'd secreted in a bedside chest of drawers to look at repeatedly to convince himself that they had been said.

'The pain of the bad things that had been magnified throughout his life would have been remembered, but rarely the few good things. But, he wouldn't have loved; he couldn't, except for the fantasising of it, the fantasised emotions.'

Clive stopped and looked away from Liam for a while. He then asked his friend if he wanted another coffee. Liam signalled to the waitress and ordered two, thanking her with the one word he knew in Lithuanian. Clive continued:

'I decided that when I saw him next I would probe deeper, shake him a little, interrupt his flow of excited, beguiled escapism, and to elaborate on those revealing last sentences.'

He was silent again till he'd taken a few gulps of his coffee.

'You know, Liam, over the years I've had some upsetting phone calls from patients, some calling to see if I'd give them free time to listen to their talk of small, often mundane things, yet crying inside for help, others literally crying for some sort of salvation, from God, from anything, but none so alarming and confusing as this man's call on the day he was due to see me.

'He rang at exactly the time he should have been lifting the knocker on my front door. I didn't recognise his voice at first.

'Hello. Mister Jelien? I won't be coming today unfortunately, because...'

'I heard a momentary squeaking sound, slightly muffled, like someone trying not to laugh in case it tipped into hysteria. Then I heard: 'I've killed someone.'

'I think my mind went into inertia for a few seconds. The voice asked if I was still listening. I asked him to explain what he meant, to tell me exactly what had happened and if he wanted to come to me. I heard: 'No. No. I hit him. I hit him.' Then the line went dead.

'I rang back. There was no answer. I was tempted to drive to his address, but this was a mobile number, he could have been anywhere. I did nothing for an hour except, mostly trying not to believe what I'd just heard.'

Clive looked at his listener and said ruefully, 'This indecision was a weakness that I knew would tell me things about myself I wouldn't like. But then I'm not a god, I'm fallible. Some people when they come to me; seem to think they're going to meet some detached, forgiving, merciful, angel-like figure metaphorically floating serenely above their fragmented, dystopian world with a magic wand.

'Anyway, then the phone rang again. It was the police. My patient had seen one of their cars slowing down at traffic lights, had knocked on its window and told the driver what he'd told me and then asked them to ring me. Apparently, he hadn't told them who or where the victim was. They asked me to hold for a minute. It became ten. Then a different voice was saying that they'd found something and they would contact me.'

Liam could imagine the fretful night he'd had after that. At their request he'd gone to see them. He waited for an hour in a small room till two plainclothes policemen came in and spoke to him. They told him briefly what had happened. It was related, he said, in a matter-of-fact, almost casual manner, ritually not wanting to show what they felt, or perhaps partly inured to the aftermath of violence.'

Clive resumed. 'They contacted me. My patient had smashed a hole above a man's right ear. It seemed, from an early pathologist's report, that it was the result of repeated blows from a house brick. I wasn't told who the victim was or the context. They then had to leave, telling me that they may need me and, if so, would let me know 'in due course.' One of them shook my hand.

'As soon as I heard where the wound was a thought had flashed: Had this man, in an ultimate act of projection, been attempting to smash his *own* intellect; that detached, obsessive game which prevented the films and maybe plays he saw from completely taking over both his undeveloped and fake self, prevented him from giving himself up to complete, bewitching, comforting fantasy, or was it merely a meaningless coincidence?

'I wasn't sure, and I realised that I hadn't been fully aware of the man's anger. Depression is often anger frustrated, perceived as having nowhere to go. This time, for him, it had found somewhere.'

He was silent for a while, looking wistful and troubled.

'I do think of him from time to time. I, also, wasn't real to him I suspect.'

He took a breath and squared his shoulders.

'Quite unlike your cineaste girl friend, eh? Her sort of, well, let's very loosely call it a branch of autism however arbitrarily defined, is quite healthy. It seems, from the little you've said, that she enjoys it, you do too; it's part of your relationship with her.

But it is disheartening, you know; when the knowledge that you can't really help someone makes itself clear. Though, I did manage to make a breakthrough once when a patient who hadn't spoken a word to me after sixteen years of monthly visits, suddenly did so.'

Liam asked him what he'd said.

''Dad.' He then began to cry. But that was reward enough.' He smiled. 'Well, that's some of the vicissitudes in what *I* do. And here are you, a skilled artisan working with your hands and with your mind free to think.'

'That's the problem, it's too free, there's no goal, I guess '

'But there seems to be a direction though, doesn't there? at least from what you've said to me previously.'

'Such as?'

'Perhaps a kind of crusade against the architectural world? Your interests, passions, if you like, do seem to be coagulating, perhaps the jigsaw analogy is more apt, pieces locking together. Maybe you could burn down the RIBA Head Office, but don't let it spread 'cos the nearby BBC Deco Headquarters hasn't long been refurbished and that *would* upset you. Shall we walk? We can have a dessert up the hill a little, there's a place that does a great almond and pear tart.'

They left and talked of inconsequential things, both glad to be away from thoughts of the events that had just been described. Liam didn't wish to talk, or think, about death. He thought briefly of Mary, still vaguely puzzled at why she had only recently told him she was Italian.

She had briefly mentioned Rome and nothing more. She must, he'd suggested, have lived here quite a while as there were such small traces of an accent. 'Yes,' she'd said and hadn't referred to the subject again.

As they approached the top of the rise, they could see between trees the Heath and, beyond, some of the City. They stopped and began pointing out some of the buildings, Liam recognising a few more than his friend.

There was one that neither recognised.

'It probably needed little engineering and less imagination,' Liam said. 'A group of Nineteenth Century buildings in keeping with the city's spirit was probably mercilessly razed to make way for it. That and others have become an infectious obsession on the body of English architecture. Furuncle, pustule; architectural aberrations.'

'You're waxing lyrical now, Liam.'

'That's the way I feel about what's happening to this city. Look, there are reasons for restraint over exhibitionism and understatement over extravagance, also privacy over revelation, it's part of the civil; why doesn't it seem to apply to architecture?'

They were at the almond tart place now and entered. The delicacy was as good as Liam expected it to be.

'If you're saying that we have a culture of endless self-exposure and self-revelation, I think you're right,' said Clive. 'If so, it's being driven by the mass and maelstrom of modern communications, and architects don't seem to have escaped it, so we get trophy buildings, narcissistic creations and vanity projects indulging in showy engineering tricks.'

'Like a building getting wider as it rises or leans to one side, or appears to be made of coconut shells. I'm not against all contemporary design. I mean, there's something appealing about a building that relies on the most advanced engineering but doesn't flaunt it.'

'Isn't there a Plaza somewhere, voted the ugliest building in England?'

'I've seen it, all adhesive balconies and frenzied facades.'

'Though, perhaps the citizens of Barcelona thought something similar when Gaudi's Casa Mila and Casa Battlo or even his House Museum was built.'

Clive looked sideways at his friend. 'And don't look so disbelieving, Liam, it could have been so. Bet you'd like to meet one of these narcissists one day, eh? Tell him what you think?'

Liam nodded emphatically.

'Perhaps they've had arrested ego development.'

'On that subject, here's my theory. The more self there is, and I don't mean selfish or what's called ego but just being a... person, the more of that there is, the more feeling, then the less intellect, less awareness, perception; a pure intellect, if you like, with no emotions to cloud it.'

'You're positing a limited psychic space then?'

'I am.'

And so they went on, with Lam looking out of the café window seeing the sun hitting the green pantiles of the Deco house opposite, reflecting from a polished door knocker on the Regency house alongside and glinting off the water lying over a blocked drain at the kerbside.

Clive had a client to see in the evening, while Liam was visiting Mary, and other than the steroidal thrusts of oppressive structures, his world was, he felt reasonably okay.

CHAPTER 15

After a tense, frustrating week waiting for the call from Tern, it came; a casual, almost deadpan invite to the mansion. Over a drink sitting at the counter in the ornament-laden kitchen, its owner casually asked him if he had any more ideas for a construction he might be interested in. Piero had certainly wanted the question but would have preferred it to be a formal request and certainly asked with more enthusiasm.

He had the detailed watercolour sketch with him. Pulling it out of a brief case he presented it. Tern took his time then nodded his head in a kind of hesitant acceptance.

'Not sure how many floors you got here, but... '

'It doesn't really matter; it narrows towards the top a little as you can see, so there's adjustment for more storeys.'

'Yeh, guess there is. Excuse me, must go to the john.'

He seemed to be in there a long time. Piero was restless and becoming a little disappointed with the reaction so far. Tern came back, slowly picked up the drawing again and looked at it without expression.

'Yeh, it catches a lot of light, there's a lot of glass.'

'That's the idea. There's over forty thousand square feet of office space, there could be something like three hundred apartments, a restaurant, plenty of shops too. It would be easy to put in a viewing gallery. There could also, of course, be a combination of these and other uses.'

He remembered a particular discussion with Lance.

'You know,' he'd said, 'one advantage of this configuration is that because the building's shape varies slightly at each level, wind can't create an organised cortex around it, and stress on the structure is reduced. The set-backs, though you have them sloping slightly, kind of confuse the wind.'

He was about to mention this when Tern, who had looked across at him then down at the illustration again, said, 'Got any more or is this the only one you've come up with? I had one sent to me the other day that was very slim and tall with a kinda pole or steeple on each corner at the top a lot higher than the building, I liked it.'

'Er, the only one I do have is an outline for a rather different shape, not as tall, more curved, following perhaps unusual planes but, as I recall, you wanted... 'Stately,' was it?'

Tern smiled. 'Okay, you got it, not just the word, the building too. It's fine. Well done.'

He stood up and shook Piero's hand firmly.

'I'd like you to stay for another drink, but needs must. Gotta see Milda.'

He made for the door and, before telling him that he'd be in contact soon, asked if he could keep the sketch.

'What do you think?' grinned Piero.

As Tern was giving his customary backwards wave, he halted and turned.

'Hey, at the moment there's no rush, the site ain't finalised yet, but I'll get it. Why don'tcha take some downtime? Ever been to Seattle? Got a pal there, runs a place overlooking a marina on Bainbridge Island. You're rich enough now to buy yourself a good time but he'll put you up gratis. Ring my secretary, gotta new one now, she'll give you the details, then let me know when you wanna go. And as you seem rooted to the spot; when you do leave, close the door behind yer.'

He went out, climbed into his car, this one large and in metallic silver, and was driven away.

Using one of Tern's gold-plated phones he rang Lance and asked him to work for him permanently, hoping optimistically that there would be more edifices on the way.

He went out for a drink that evening - on his own because Lance couldn't make it - where he got himself really hooched up, as Chicagoans would say.

Spending much of the flight seeing in the clouds fluffy dogs, countless chicks and an elephant stamping on a mouse, he arrived at Seattle Airport.

After an overnight stay at a bland, beige airport hotel, he got the light rail to Downtown Seattle, wandered around Central Market and through the small square under the rooftop cantina with its samba band and hip-swaying Mexican Seattleites.

The ferry trip to Bainbridge Island across Elliott Bay was like a mini-cruise, with the distant Olympic Mountains ahead of them and the city dwindling away at the stern.

Tern's associate owned a large house with plastic clapboard cladding and rocking chairs on the wraparound porch and overlooking a cluster of yachts. Piero had to smile, it was so American: the automatically sprinkled, front lawns, two cadillacs, smaller than Tern's, in front of double garages with pine trees and elms behind them.

The owner, a large pasty-faced man who had a drink in his hand which Piero guessed he carried around perpetually, led him to his guest room past an office with an over-styled mahogany desk and a card leaning back on it saying 'CEO.' Downstairs was a large carpeted area with kitchen bar and more beige ceilings and walls.

Next morning, not sure quite where to go, Piero jumped on a bus marked 'Perben.' It didn't matter where he was, he hadn't been here before and, as he was refraining from working on his design and filling in more of its details, had energy to spare for walking. He would, anyway, hear when he got back to the city that Tern had got his site; he had little doubt of that.

The town's Nordic origins could be seen in the flags and shop names; the deeply cut fjord-like bays surrounding the town would have held a comforting familiarity for its early immigrants. He ate in the Mexican 'Casa Luna' overlooking a bay with the waiters' constant, 'D'yer wan' it boxed? as they scraped the remains of meals into polystyrene boxes, and then wandered into the Perben Marine Science Center. He had little interest in things piscatorial, but a fluffy, sponge-like creature in a large glass tank caught his eye.

'We call it Ginger, it's an octopus. It's kinda small and pink, but there yer go.'

She was tall, slim, with dark frizzy hair, deep set brown eyes, olive skin, and perhaps in her late Twenties. He asked her if she knew a lot about fish.

'A little. I'm part-time, I help out back with the kids some-times, it's mostly voluntary.' She bent down. 'Lenny, go back in the room with Debbie. Good boy.' He did.

'You're not working your way through college, then?'

'Well, yeh, but not here. I'm majoring in Developmental Psychology and I have a job.'

He asked her what it was.

'I'm a lumberjack.'

She laughed; the white teeth, one slightly crooked, the flesh puffed a little under her eyes.

He enquired how she became a lumberjack.

'My father was one.'

'The son he never had?'

'Maybe.'

He asked her where she worked. It was near the rain forest north of the State.

'It's full of virgin lumber.'

'You've just commoditised nature.'

'Maybe we're all commodities.'

He asked her if she was reading Freud, the only psychologist he knew anything of.

'Yup. And would you accept that a child with a good birth experience will tend to draw circles rather than angular shapes?'

He suggested that it could be a compensation for a bad one.

'Interesting. And what do *you* do?'

He told her.

'Have you had any stuff built? Would I know it?'

'I doubt it unless you're interested in the subject, maybe not even then.'

'I prefer nature to men's constructs, but... '

'What about buildings that copy nature or are influenced by it?'

'You mean shaped like a tree or an amoeba or something?'

'Could be. But curving, flowing, undulating forms and... Think I'll stop there.'

He'd felt suddenly stimulated; that feeling when he'd prose-lytized at his colleges and occasionally with Lance and the others. He hadn't done it with Tern, he'd just wanted to know what something would look like and what he could make from it in dollars and, especially with the upcoming one, more pres-tige.

'Guess I'm more interested in the nature-nurture debate, though I guess it's been closed down in favour of science.'

'I think you've got to ask who benefits from the power ac-corded to science to 'settle' this debate, and the answer, other than the vested interests of science, are those making money out of it, the drug companies, for example.'

'Are you always this cynical?

Piero didn't answer.

She narrowed her eyes a little. There was a smile in them.

'What are you running away from?'

He'd been asked neither of these questions before. He felt, for a second, a confusion; a kind of emotional interruption.

'Look, I've gotta get something out the car. Be back. Inci-dentally, I'm half Jewish.'

'And I'm fully Italian.'

'Thought I recognised the accent.'

She walked towards the entrance and into the small car park. He watched her through a window go to a red, Fifties Eldorado convertible with a bonnet as long as the rest of the car and a MIZZROZE license plate. She returned with a piece of paper.

'It's a logging itinerary; I want to keep it on me. Sorry about the number plate, my dad bought me the car and the plate came with it.'

'I assume your name's Rose.'

'Yep, and I'm at a private university and feel very privileged.'

'I could count on the fingers of one hand the Jewish female undergraduate lumberjacks I've met this week.'

'And I never expected to meet an Italian architect in an aquarium in Washington State. I need to go.' He didn't want her to.

'I lunch with the guys sometimes at the Junction Diner down the 101 a ways if you're ever there.' She gave a take-it-or-leave-it shrug. 'See yer.'

And out she went again, all flower-patterned blouse, black tights and hair. He went back to the window of the arts and crafts room and saw Lenny quietly running around in circles watched by Debbie.

He left the aquarium to get some groceries - feeling he had to contribute something to his host's generosity - then walked around a little, past a dirt road behind 'Silver City Tattoos' which would have had a view over hill-ringed Freedom Bay had it not been for the chalet-like condominiums obscuring it.

He then saw a poster nailed to a telegraph pole informing its readers that there would be a bus trip to Crescent Lake beginning from the bus stop opposite. It had the day and time. He read it and looked across to the stop. The bus was there. He had an image of blue tranquillity. He wanted it.

As he boarded, it drove off, its occupants all elderly women except for a baseball-capped male. A few miles along the highway, with its occasional yellow smudges where paint trucks had veered off the lines, they passed the steeple-less First Church of Christ The Scientist and then more dark green hills as they neared the peninsula.

They were held in a queue while trucks with long trailers full of logs passed them. He thought of Rose. On the lake jetty listening to Larry telling him he owned twenty acres and a cow, he thought of her again

As they tracked casually through the forest surrounding the lake Larry told him what he knew about logging and about the resinous cedar wood he built his stock fences with, while Piero stopped under the biggest tree he'd ever seen. He looked up and imagined her at the top balancing in a harness, seeing just her boots and hair through the branches. The sun came through. He saw it light up the skin on her arm. He couldn't see what she was doing. He felt protective towards her, ridiculously proprietary then excited; her thighs, knees, boots, pressing against the trunk, her upper body swinging out. He caught up with his companion and went across the log bridge to the falls.

It had been a pleasant few hours and after saying goodbye to Larry back at the bus stop, he returned to where he was staying. After living on his own for so long he couldn't get used to sharing a house, despite the plea from its owner's wife, Pam, delivered from the fake leather sofa she seemed to constantly lie in, to 'Treat the place as yours, our home's your home.'

The following day, feeling restless, he wandered into the local, windowless Wal-Mart. As he left he asked the check-out girl why she'd wished him a great day and told her if she knew him she'd probably wish him a bad one. She frowned, put her grin back and said' 'Have a...' and turned to the next customer.

He wasn't quite sure why he was in this mood; perhaps it was because he was hungry. He went to the Junction Café a mile away at the side of the highway: melamine walls, gingham tablecloths, ketchup or gravy on every square inch of steak, omelettes and biscuits applied by large men sitting on high-backed bar stools. One of them, looking out at a lumber truck in the parking lot next to a 'Honey Bucket' mobile toilet, was wearing an 'old guys rule' t-shirt. There were a few pony tails and backwoodsmen beards, but no Rose.

He still wasn't certain why he kept thinking of her. Amongst the women he'd known, he could think of no-one he'd met just once who had caused him to think about them till the next time, the next class they'd attended, the next date. In his few relationships with women, each had gone back to something, or someone.

He went back to the Island and walked along the jetty where high-bridged boats with names like 'Geisha Gal,' 'Vegas Virgin' and 'Same Old Story' were moored. Wanting something more restful than conspicuous nautical consumption he went around the back of a nearby Unitarian church, part of which was a pre-school with a cosy allotment of sweet peas and rhubarb with the Stars & Stripes planted firmly in a corner.

Out of curiosity he thought he'd have a quick look inside the building. He went in. Someone was awkwardly spinning a ball off a bat over a table tennis table. It was Rose. He went towards her,

'Hey, what are you doing here?' she asked, glancing up.

'Wandering. I'm not stalking you, honestly,' he said lightly,

'I do voluntary work here too, out of semester. Coincidence, uh? The kids have gone now. D'you play?'

He remembered when he'd first learnt the game at thirteen in his school in Rome, using partly open books triangling across a desk for the net.

'I'll beat you,' he said. 'You serve.'

He hadn't held a bat since playing for a youth team. She was good; a little gauche, but effective. He childishly felt he had to beat her, to impress, he couldn't let her win.

It all came back: smashes, devious serves, defensive chops, backhands. When she served he watched her enthusiastically hitting the ball, breasts moving beneath a white T-shirt. He won two games, the next he didn't, possibly because he was watching her, intrigued by the way she smashed down, the irregular tooth showing as she grimaced, her crouch as she chopped back, the firm slap of her flip-flops.

'Wh-hey, I beatcha. There's coffee through here.'

She put her bat down and went into a small room with a coffee machine and a table. He followed and sat down.

'How are you going to psychologise that then?'

She thought a while. 'I could say that, like all games, it's rule-bound behaviour, thus its competitive nature affirming the capitalist ethos. But I won't.'

'Tell me about logging.'

'Well, there's forty three saw mills in Washington State, though some are stopping production 'cos of the recession, and some are exporting to China and India and - '

'You're telling it by rote, why?'

'Well, I don't really relate to that side of it, I just like getting out there, working.'

He asked her to tell him about the different kinds of trees she worked on.

'Western red cedar, Alaskan yellow, and don't forget it's not tie hacks and axes any more, it's chain saws. Douglas firs - '

'What about the sequoias that are so big the trunks are carved out and cars drive through?'

'That's for tourists, and I know that word's got all the vowels in, and I don't want to talk about this stuff anymore.'

He felt a little hurt. He asked her if she was finished here and perhaps wanted to eat.

'I need to be going, but we could go to Alessia's on Thursday, if you want. About eight?'

'That's another two days.'

'It's in Perben.'

He'd seen the place. He said goodbye to her as she hurried out. A few seconds later he saw the red car drive away up Madison past a Fifties blue and silver diner he'd had a coffee in earlier.

He walked along a beach next morning then to a small cinema which was, surprisingly, showing a film from his teenage years, *'Divorzio, all'italiana,'* then more ambling around the Island till he caught a bus into town. The aquarium was shut.

He got to Alessia's early. It was an old schoolhouse converted into an Italian restaurant with a spacious bar at the back and favouring Dean Martin and Sinatra numbers. He sat there thinking, as he intermittently did, of the differences, the little ones, between here and his home country: the light switches going down for off, the high water in toilet bowls submerging the testicles of the unsuspecting, the lack of people walking.

She came in with her usual black tights and no make-up, but with a red band around her hair. While waiting for the waitress he started telling her how filmic he found parts of America, how, for instance, some of the inhabitants of Perben had made him silently ask 'Weren't you in…?' and 'Surely, you played the sheriff with…' and the courthouse clock he'd glimpsed a couple of times seeming stuck forever at four, with 'Jimmy Gill's Gun Store.' on a nearby corner and its wares on trestle tables on the sidewalk, so alien to his Italian eye.

They ordered Alessia's 'secret recipe lasagne' and talked about films. He liked sharing them: those he'd loved as a young man, American as well as Italian. He began talking about a few, but she didn't react because she hadn't seen them. He assumed she had and, he realised, adolescently wanted her to have the same interest as him in movies, in buildings, similar enthusiasms about… everything. He felt disappointed.

'What sort of music d'you like?' they asked it in unison. The music he mentioned she either hadn't heard of or wasn't interested in. Again, his disappointed child. He told her he didn't analyse music, he liked it or he didn't.

'It's like John Doe asking about a piece of art - and 'art' is that which is an art gallery of course - and saying 'I don't know much about art, but I know what I like.' which is just as valid as the art critic of the Chicago Tribune calling it 'A turbulent arabesque of significant complexity.''

He knew this was a populist thing to say to her, to help her see him as unpretentious, 'trendy' even. She didn't answer. He subtly suggested she change her mind and tell him more about her work.

The meal came. It was good. They hardly spoke except to comment on the food. They were both hungry.

When they'd finished she said, 'Okay, there's a European tradition that we're sworn enemies of werewolves, vampires and Mormons and also immortal. We're still sometimes called professional assassins by the way, and I didn't get into it because of my father. There was a high school competition for axing and sawing logs. I won it. I got my proficiency certificate in one year instead of two and I've been doing the job for four years.'

He asked her what happened at the tops of trees, partly because he'd pictured her there.

'We tie lines sometimes to help the direction of the fall, but not often. There's not many camps now either, though there may be one where we're going, it's pretty wild, we usually use a motel if its too far to get home.'

Feeling a kind of pre-jealousy in anticipating her reply he said, 'Do you have trouble with - '

'No. I put 'em down, they don't make passes any more.'

She said it with a quick flint of hardness in her eyes. He felt a ridiculously childlike relief.

'So, what about you?'

Before he could begin, she asked if he lived on his own. There was a slight mocking in her eyes.

'D'you want to talk?' she asked matter-of-factly.

He had his hand flat on the table and suddenly felt the slightest touch. She'd put the top of her middle finger on his. He'd been looking down. He looked up at her. She seemed very still.

'Tell me about things. I dunno, your parents maybe, we've still got a child in us.'

He thought of his parents, something he hadn't done for a long time. His mother's deep Catholicism, his father's oppressive conservatism, their prejudice against incoming migrants, the tenseness between himself and his father and the oppressive meal time rituals, feeling unable to move, bound to his chair. He wasn't sure how to answer, whether to feel sorrow or pity for them, to feel love, a loss.

Then it seemed to flood over him, into him. He could feel the tears shivering across his face, down the side of his nostrils, into the corner of his mouth. He raised an arm a little, like a wounded animal.

He didn't know what to do. He had no behavioural guidelines for this. It was an internal anomie. He felt she'd cut through some sort of emotional impoverishment, ripped it till it was hanging open like bloodied entrails, felt he had to grab it, pull it inside him again; bind it tight with his drawings, blueprints, his creations, his...

He looked up. She was watching his eyes, her head slightly to one side; her whole hand now on top of his. He tried to pull it back.

She pressed down, gave him a slow, serious smile, and said gently, 'If you don't talk to your pain, it will talk to *you,* shout and scream at you.' Then, just as gently, she suggested they sit at the bar. 'There's no one there.'

They did. He forced himself to point out that the large baroque mirror at the back was for cowboys to shoot at while the barman ducked behind the counter just in time.

'You really have seen too many films, haven't you.'

And then her cell phone rang. She said several 'okays,' nodding in between them. She put it back in her jacket pocket and looked at him earnestly.

'Look, I know it's not right, but I have to be going, more big man sawing tomorrow. I'm sorry. That was Rick, he's got my stuff and he'll pick me up on the highway. We'll share the bill.'

He told her he'd pay. She thanked him.

'You don't want to listen to more Perry Como then?'

'Never heard of him,' she said, smiling. He went to get up.

'No, it's okay.'

He asked her when she'd be hack, if he'd see her again. She moved around the table. He felt her near him. She bent over and quickly kissed his forehead. He felt her hair brush an eyebrow. She walked away quickly.

He stood. 'How did you know...?'

His voice sounded weak, inarticulate. She always seemed to be leaving. She half turned her head, lightly touched her puckered lips and bent her hand away, then just before she pushed through the exit door she became a silhouette; exaggeratedly upright, in profile; the high frizzy hair, straight shoulders, aquiline nose.

He stared at the door then sat again. He heard her car pull away. He didn't want to leave, wanted to keep where he was, where she'd been. He wiped his face. He tried to rationalise what had happened. Was it just his parents or something else? Maybe he should attempt to forgive them, his father especially; they were victims too, of the time, circumstances; their class.

And then Chiara came crashing through, like a subterranean drill grinding up through a thick lead floor he had fastened down over turmoil: what they had done, what *he* had done. Was all that coming through once more? He wasn't going to answer his question, wasn't going to think about it again.

The waitress came over, asked if he wanted a refill. He absently shook his head.

'Hey, I noticed before, you got an accent.'

'You haven't,' he murmured sarcastically.

'No, I'm an American.'

He gave her a tip and left.

He went back to the house, its beigeness drooping over him like a spiritual blanket. He felt tired; tired of people walking beaches with dogs that howled most of the night in gardens, of having to ask for 'war-der' in cafes to save minutes of baffled frowns and complex negotiation, of obese women living in solipsistic bubbles loading dipped fries into their mouths and licking their fingers surrounded by chrome boxes of napkins, the dead racoons he'd seen on sidewalks and, what he saw as another example of America's technological obsession with the unnecessary, a crank-operated 'for emergencies' TV set in a shop window.

Laying on his bed he tried to let the good things sift though: the courtesy of drivers unnecessarily reversing to let people cross a road, the politeness, the occasional 'sir,' the friendliness of the local bus drivers and the non-stop joking of the two female ones both seemingly named Daphne. He thought of the nearby hills, the green-blue, clear water lakes, the seventy foot cliffs leading down to them, the mountains that looked from a distance like pink-grey cloud banks.

After walking around Bainbridge the next day, passing a man on a freeway bridge waving a twelve-foot American flag and by the side of him cars honking; he went to the aquarium again. She wasn't, of course, there. Nor was she on the Seattle Ferry the day after.

Not wishing to go anywhere new he visited the market and cantina again. He was about to leave a café when he heard a man seated on a stool and holding an evening paper say to another, 'There's a little piece here about an accident; logs and cables and a ravine and stuff - what's 'high-lining?' - down in North Oregon, some sort of tornado.'

Piero went out. He didn't want to know about trees and forests.

Returning to the house for his last evening there, he picked up a newspaper. Idly going through it, he saw the article. There had been an accident, one fatality and others injured. The former was a 'Miss R. Gold.'

He couldn't quite equate 'accident' with 'Miss R. Gold'. Then he did. He didn't know her surname, but knew it was her. He felt paralyzed, not knowing what to feel. Larry had told him about high-lining: slinging a cable across a ravine to carry a cab with logs from the side with no roads to the one that had them. He wondered if she had ever done it before.

He slept badly. After thanking his hosts for their hospitality he returned to the city on the ferry, looking over the rail listening to bits of meaningless conversation: 'Two hundred Starbucks have opened in China, two in Vietnam.' 'Yeh, he's the seventh best hand surgeon in Seattle.' He missed her.

It was soon after the aircraft took off that he felt the longing. He saw the grin, the red hair band, then a still, white face partly covered in leaves. He pushed the images away. He was going back to help create the building he'd designed, his tallest so far. He would become known, recognised, he deserved it.

And it was as if he hadn't done anything else for the last week than go to an aquarium, play table tennis and have a meal with Rose, as if he hadn't seen deep, cloudless skies, nor sat on a beach looking at the silhouettes of Seattle's towers through the swaying, tick-tocking yacht masts, nor watched a deer in the garden of the house and, almost, as if he hadn't spent precious time with an attractive young woman.

He attempted to think of tiny, unimportant things as, in the house on the Island, trying not to wait for the sigh of the lid closing on the kitchen's automatic bin and Pam's fat, white, squiggling feet in all that sofa; and try as he may, he couldn't see any fanciful shapes this trip, just the merging lines of grey land, sea and sky.

As he fastened his seat belt for the descent into O'Hare, he thought he knew how Rose had died; falling silently, just the shattered air screaming through the leaf-stripped branches above her.

Someone at his London university had once lent him Galsworthy's 'The Forsyte Saga.' A line from it came back to him: 'Beauty is a rose that a fair wind blows...'

# CHAPTER 16

Having just been treated by an implant surgeon in Harley Street, Liam was now at home. It wasn't really his scene; he could barely afford it, but having a high gag-reflex and unable to tolerate dentures, he'd opted for an implanted ten-unit upper bridge. After several root fillings and apexectomies his teeth had given up. He sat in one of the outlets of a retail coffee chain in Oxford Street thinking about it.

In the waiting room there'd been a life-size bronze female nude, exotic plants, a painting of an Arabian teenager with very large hands, a wall entirely devoted to the certificates the surgeon had gained, ranging from a college in Lucerne to the Royal London Hospital, and a smooth-skinned woman who looked like, and probably was, the trophy wife of a Russian oligarch, There was also a statue of Buddha he'd glimpsed in the garden before lying down on the dentist's chair. It was the largest surgery he'd been in, complete with a healthy palm tree and prints of lotus flowers and golden fish.

After the obligatory naming of remaining teeth and their condition - upper-left canine, eye tooth, occlusal, palatal excursion, etcetera - he'd glanced around, seeming to be surrounded by plaster casts, chrome plates and porcelain and acrylic molars. The Romanian nurse occasionally winced whilst putting various pieces of metal in his mouth during the process and before he left she'd commented on how brave he'd been. He'd refused sedation. Perhaps he shouldn't have.

Stirring tea, a sliver of blood whirled like chocolate on a hot cappuccino as he thought of the ratchet torque wrench which had crunched implants into his jaw and of Mary that morning, lying still, her legs loosely closed, telling him how contented she was.

He was pleased that Mary had said what she had. Also relieved. Other than guilt, jealousy is the most corrosive of emotions and he had recently experienced its pain. He'd once looked up the word: 'Present in animals that reproduce through internal fertilization and is founded on the instinct of keeping genes in the gene pool and... ' He wondered why he'd bothered to do so. Tautological definitions couldn't capture the reality of what was felt.

It had begun, innocently enough, when Mary had finished a complex piece of coursework and had wanted a break, to relax, enjoy something a little different. He'd taken her to see a comedian he'd heard good things about from an acquaintance whose own amateur stage name seemed to be Jimmy London, with his 'I go to a draper's warehouse; get my best material there' puns for beginners.

The comic they'd come to see was Bill Bunden, the venue The Crooked Billet pub in east London on a Thursday comedy night. They were standing at the end of the bar; the room was full, dark and the six-inch high 'stage' barely illuminated.

During the five-minute spots the hyper-active MC hovering nearby would, after a designated four minutes, put one foot on the side of the stage, stand on it thirty seconds later, and then threaten to kick the arse and grab the mike off a performer if he ran over time.

Bunden came on with rouge on his cheeks, his eyebrows accentuated and an almost clown-like persona.

'Have you noticed,' he asked, all skinny jeans and stubble, 'that the parents who complain loudest about paedophiles are those who have kids no one would *want* to shag? I lie. *I'd* shag anything.' His next was, 'Did you hear about the woman who thought that Muffin the Mule was a sexual offence?'

His metier was obviously sex-based and sick humour, and in this context it was a competent beginning, earning satisfyingly outraged and knowing laughter - Mary's slight shaking of her head in disapproval being belied by her amused eyes.

Liam had seen and heard lots of comedy and was generally more interested in subtlety and the calmly surreal, though moments of shrill hyperbole, building from everyday comments a whole pyramid of ludicrous narratives and bizarre incidents, could also be genuinely funny.

He wondered what characteristics this comic had. He tried not to bundle them into a genre, humour wasn't as neatly contained as that, though something must be called something.

He'd heard that Bunden was a successful comic and well known at venues in both east and north London and had done a gig or two at the Edinburgh Fringe.

'This one's more up your street.' Jimmy had said.

Bill Bunden continued in the same vein as he'd begun; blasting the sensibilities of the few older people in the audience while seeming to make the rest love him.

After lots of clapping and whooping, he vacated the mini-stage, stood at the back for a little while and left. Liam felt rather surprised that the man would play a venue like this - there was little talent on show, mostly first-timers and others a little more experienced trying to hone their spiel.

He forgot about him for a while then quite accidentally he discovered that in a few days Bunden was appearing on a Friday evening at a small theatre in suburban north west London. They went.

The place was small, most of the seats taken. Not wanting to watch the second-half acts - retro music hall jugglers, ventriloquists, a couple of impressionists - they went in just before his last-on slot.

He was barely recognisable: well groomed, hair shorter, smart jacket, open-necked shirt and shiny shoes He stood motionless, saying nothing, eyes slowly scanning the audience, who, after a long hiatus, began to get restless.

'*All* wine is served at room temperature,' he began, deadpan and slow.

It took a while then a few people began chuckling.

'I took the dog for a walk round the block. It fell off.' Again an expressionless delivery.

'My friend's a radio DJ. When we walk under a bridge I can't understand a word he says.' More chuckles.

'I divorced my wife. We split the house fifty-fifty. She got the inside.'

The audience began a spell of almost continuous, modulated, appreciative laughter, his act becoming increasingly surreal.

'When I woke this morning all the furniture in my apartment had been stolen and replaced with exact replicas. I asked my secretary out but she said if I had sex with her and she found out, I'd be in trouble.'

The slight frowns, the relaxed sharpness were all of a piece, a whole. Liam gazed briefly at Mary. Her eyes were shining.

This was a different crowd than at the pub: a rather older, well-heeled demography, one that appreciated his crafted, urbane performance. Again he left the building soon after vacating the stage. Liam and Mary left, too, and watched him walk to a soft-top Audi, his posture different from the first time they'd seen him; more erect, casual, in control. He opened the door and sat behind the wheel almost elegantly; not the loose-limbed, often crouching prankster of the other evening. He was beginning to intrigue Liam.

Unlike last time, it was intentionally that he found out where and when Bunden was next appearing. It was a club in Dalston. This time Mary had work to do and couldn't be with him.

It was a small venue; dim lighting, a pale spot on the stage-less space at the back and a mike. He started off similarly to his pub act; crude, almost gross, lots of emphasis, but not as funny. Then he stopped, looked around him for a while, again the slight crowd restlessness then, slowly, deadpan.

'My friend has sideburns *behind* his ears and wears braces on his false teeth. I do *very* abstract paintings, no paint, brushes or canvas, but I did buy some second hand paint,' he paused, 'in the shape of a house.'

People didn't really respond, they looked a little confused. They'd been given a genre, offered a mindset they'd taken willingly. Now, here was another, a very different one. Only towards the end did they, rather warily, respond. The clapping was muted. He went out of the room quickly, carelessly, annoyed.

As Liam was leaving the building he walked through the foyer. It had obviously been a Thirties cinema and although its original function had, presumably, long gone there was enough of it left - the lamps, curved handrail, chevrons engraved on a broken mirror - to prompt a flash of teenage excitement, anticipation. He went to the car park at the back and saw Bunden's Audi move away.

He thought of his disparate acts: the zany, exaggerated crudeness, occasional wild-eyed look, the stooping, pacing restlessness, and the calm, unhurried, perfectly-pitched delivery of the other. Were these projections of some sort of classic schizophrenia - roses are red, violets are blue, I'm a schizophrenic and so am I - or was he trying to find the comedic presentation that most suited him, worked the best? Perhaps they were both rather desperate efforts to find himself. He wondered what Clive would say from the depths of his years of psychoanalytic experience.

A fortnight afterwards, Mary had mentioned that a local drama group were rehearsing a play the next evening to be put on in a few weeks time. As a child, her mother had taken her to a local Theatrecoach for a short while and which she'd also attended in her teens. She'd enjoyed the experiences and wanted to see this rehearsal and, as her term was coming to an end, thought perhaps she could do a bit of acting again and Liam, maybe, 'join in' with her.

The latter had an aversion to being one of a crowd, especially starting cold, knowing no-one, but said yes. It would, he rationalised, hold some interest for him: seeing how a show was built, a script changed and tightened, actors growing into their roles.

The rehearsals had begun three weeks previously at the studio, once a school hall that now had black walls and ceilings with matching curtains and floors. They stood quietly inside the entrance door. They were obviously late. Twenty or so people were standing in a half-circle facing them while a man in the centre paced repeatedly towards and away from them, mostly away.

'Think of a number from one to ten; trace it with your fingers on each others backs, those with the same number stand together.'

He seemed immediately familiar. They separated into small groups, scrawling, being scrawled upon.

'Look at someone's eyes, same colour; same group.'

Some women had two or three men looking closely into their faces.

'No, you're dark brown; she's hazel, different groups. Walk about, just walk, don't act. You're walking anti-clockwise like all the groups do, walk straight. You're trying not to act, it shows. Relax till I give you a quality. Right; anger... excitement... vengeance.'

They seemed to be warming-up exercises. The light was dim, they could see only his back now; the others, if they'd seen them, took no notice.

'Okay, so you're traffic wardens, and you love it, the uniform, the peak cap, all of it, you're full of hubris, move like it, look in a wing mirror to comb your hair before you book 'em. Now I'm holding a beach ball, see it? I'm going to throw it to someone, then they throw it to someone else, let's have five balls and shout out the name of the person you're throwing it to. Stop. How many have we got now? Where's the missing one? You've got dirt phobias, clean something; get manic, more manic.'

They started throwing invisible balls to each other, most of them scrubbing floors in ever-widening circles, using imaginary brushes while some polished tables or scratched away tiny bits of non-existent dirt from invisible furniture, others vigorously dry-washing their hands.

The back of the Director's head seemed increasingly familiar to Liam, as was his energy and enthusiasm and that quick crouching when he wished to emphasise, and of course the voice, though occasionally sounding rather posh, drawling, luvvy. A second before glimpsing his profile, he embarrassingly knew who it was.

The unexpected had blunted recognition, though a part of him had known from the beginning. He didn't really want it to be him, though unsure why. Mary, with her large, sensitive eyes, was almost quivering with excitement in anticipation of being part of it. She looked up at Liam, grinning. Perhaps she'd recognised him.

Bunden carried on with his quick-fire instructions:

'Speed-dating. Anyone done that? There's more men than women, put the chairs in facing pairs, women sit opposite the blokes, the ones left can stand at a bar, put some chairs there. When I blow the whistle all the boys choose another partner and so on, then we'll have the girls doing the same. Go on then.'

They quickly moved the chairs.

'Can we be ourselves?' someone asked.

'Up to you.'

Off they went.

'You nervous?'

'Yeh.'

'First time?'

'No, I've been nervous before.'

'Hi, you don't know me, but I'm Mister Right.'

'Yeh, my wife's so fat that wherever I sit she's always next to me.'

'Your legs'll start aching tomorrer, they'll be runnin' through my dreams all night.'

Mary's fascination was palpable.

They continued, not always sure whether the people they were facing were being themselves or acting created personalities. He watched a diffident teenager walk across to a young Eurasian girl.

'Do you, er, live round here often?' he asked.

Liam wasn't sure whether it was intentional or not.

They waited till the coffee break before going over to Bunden, Mary leading. He greeted her warmly, Liam perfunctorily as he mumbled his name; then left the room.

Mary went across to a small group and talked to them while Liam slowly sipped coffee. After a few minutes Bunden returned and gave sheets of paper to everyone, including Mary who he talked to for a while, pointing at what Liam assumed was the script and then wheeled away to stand towards the end of the hall. They began again, more or less still roughly in a half circle, while Liam leaned against a wall and watched.

A large skinhead with a cockney accent; adopted or otherwise, began with, 'Don't forget, some day you're the pigeon, uvvers the statue.'

One by one the others' joined in, Mary too, speaking with a surprisingly realistic east London accent.

The setting of the play was obviously local; the physical and cultural characteristics were all there, summed up by one of the cast's, 'The posh bits, the dirty bits, the swanky and the wanky bits, big houses with dog shit on the pavement, wisteria up the walls, piss in the gutter.'

The fatalism was contained in Len and Hazel getting ready to win the night's bingo overlaid with a sound track of Roy Orbison singing 'All I Have To Do is Dream. The humour: 'I started out wiv nuffink, I got most of it left.' 'Whatever look you're tryin' for you've missed.' 'I told him I wanted to practice safe sex, he said he'd put more paddin' on the 'eadboard.'

and an Asian rhetorically asking, as if he was a comic stand-up, 'What's the favourite name for Asian lesbians? Minjeeta.'

There was a whole potpourri of tenuously connected scenes: a character, Girly, with a blow-up male doll, Orbison singing 'Only The Lonely' in the background, 'Thug', with fantasies of using his controlled savagery to destroy the figure that was always looking at him from across a road, a park, a room, and which turns out to be himself,

This was interesting Liam now, and it was obvious who'd written the show. The author was quite still, not looking at the script in his hands, just silently mouthing the lines, occasionally nodding or suggesting someone read something in a different way, to make it quicker, slower, lesser or more emphatic.

There was an old view that saw actors as, deep down, shy people hiding behind their roles, escaping from themselves, but Bunden appeared to be neither running away from nor coming to terms with any ontological lesions, perhaps he just wanted to express his creativity in the field he'd chosen or had, perhaps, chosen him.

The reading went on for an hour or so then, as a caretaker came in pointedly swinging his keys, Bunden called a halt and they all, gradually, left, but not before he asked Liam whether he wanted a part in his play. Liam thanked him but refused, saying he was merely an interested spectator. Bunden just nodded and then, with a smile that made Liam aware that, when dwelling in this apparently more relaxed persona, he was, with his thick, dark hair, wide smile and patrician nose, a handsome man. He could see that Mary agreed.

He decided not to go to the next rehearsal after Mary told him that she wouldn't be going. This was a little surprising after her obvious enjoyment at, as she put it, 'treading the boards again.'

A few days later, she rang to tell him that she hadn't gone back to the group again because 'the Director' had invited her to have a drink with him and she'd accepted. This seemed to be a contradiction - unless she didn't want to mix pleasure with business.

'I'll see you soon.' she'd said.

She hadn't done anything like this before, not that he was aware, and he intuitively knew that it hadn't, or soon wouldn't be, just a drink. He felt suddenly shaken, as if a more or less taken-for-granted relationship, a complacency which had cloaked him for a long while had been torn away. He became aware that she meant more to him than the interests they shared and the affection they'd built for each other. Now, he emotionally recognised just how attractive he found her, how much time he spent thinking of her, how much she was inside him.

He remembered her recently saying to him that she wasn't sure where she ended and he began. He wanted to remind her of this and ask her why she had accepted Bunden's invitation. But then it would imply that he didn't trust her, she would see the immaturity.

Mary was, he realised, loudly repeating his name, almost shouting it. He put the phone down, detached, in slow motion. He then picked it up and rang her back. He asked if the college had found a work placement for her yet. They hadn't. After talking of mundane things they arranged to see each other the following day.

He didn't know if she had gone for a drink with him or if 'anything had happened' as people say, she had said no more about it. Perhaps she never would. That would suffice, though it didn't stop him from briefly imagining a near-future in which he would be in a waiting room somewhere, maybe the implant man's place, idly looking through a celebrity magazine with a shot of Bunden stepping out of his car with a laughing, groomed Mary, her hand touching her designer windswept hair, alongside an article about Bunden's new TV show.

Hell, he had better things to do than this. One of them would be in a few evening's time when he'd attend a meeting at the local Town Hall to give, along, he hoped, with many others, his adverse opinions on a local tower that had been planned.

He had helped someone living in his street to send out and encourage people to sign an email petition against it. From what he could glean from an artist's impression, he would, unfortunately, be able to see this ill-favoured, misshapen thing from his back garden.

# CHAPTER 17

Piero Ronzi was sitting comfortably with a cappuccino in a deli on Franklin Street, off Broadway. He was gazing at the ice-packed fruit under its counter top and the Mexican staff, most sporting neatly trimmed moustaches and in beige uniforms and caps, ringing tills, clearing away cups and plates, cleaning table tops, tidying stools and chairs and occasionally chatting and shrugging shoulders with customers.

He caught a glimpse of himself in a mirror then held his gaze a moment. He obviously looked older than when he first came to this city almost twenty years ago and his nose seemed a little longer, not surprising, as it was, he knew, the only human organ that continued to grow throughout a person's life. He'd also put on weight, though still looked pretty good, he thought.

It seemed both strange and familiar to be back in New York. Almost the first thing he'd heard when arriving at La Guardia two years previously - the pilot actually crooning 'Those little town blues are melting away' on the intercom as he came in to land - was a yellow cab driver saying in a Bronx accent to an offloaded passenger, 'It's forty-nine-fifty, you wan' I give back the fifty cents?'

On the way to viewing the ground floor apartment of a brownstone in Chrystie Street, where he now lived, he'd passed 'Joe's Bar' on Canal street with its wall murals of football stadia and screens showing baseball, silhouetting its clients, and then dropped off at Sam's Delicatessen for brunch followed by a coffee at Remo's where, again, he was now sitting.

Chicago had been good for him and, as far as he was concerned, he had been good for Chicago. He was thinking about the buildings he'd designed for Tern and which the latter had built with the construction company he'd taken over in that city.

Piero had kept the same office in the loft, tripling the space by leasing the floor below, and employed Lance full-time, his engineer now heading the engineering staff and living only a mile from his employer, while freelances Tommy and Henry had worked for him most of their working time. He had also added some draughtsmen and some admin and general office staff, but as Tern had increasingly become the pathway for the fruition of some of his ideas, there was little incentive, or time, to tout for other work or to submit designs to any other developers. There'd been no need to.

It had taken twenty months from planning approval to completion for the 'Stately' tower. The topping-out ceremony for this one had been a colourful extravaganza featuring, as well as the usual city stalwarts and business people, Chicago's mayor, his attendance pulled off by one of Tern's 'Gifts to the community' entailing, Piero guessed, some not easy-to-trace cash.

The after-event meal was again in a homely, traditional venue, 'The Berghoff,' where natty waiters had handled corned beef sandwiches, *wienerschnitzel* and house-made root beer with pride and aplomb for nearly a century. Mira, at her husband's side looking every inch the prize wife, smiled quietly throughout the proceedings, including a short speech by her husband vowing he would change Chicago's skyline, adding with a smirk and a quick glance at the mayor, 'If allowed to, of course.'

This time, Piero, though mentioned first, was just one amongst a handful thanked for their efforts in the development. Tern's PR people, seemingly quieting down his potential hyperbole, had spread the idea that 'At the heart of the design strategy is the aim to unlock and realise the extraordinary potential to meet staff and residents needs. The crafted forms, proportions and architectural expression will ensure that this new addition to the skyline defines this unique part of Chicago.'

There was no mention of the 'TERN' lettering, this time in chrome and a little larger than the first time he'd used it. The 'unique part' was near Fulton River Park, the site previously occupied by a large Gothic building that had been demolished, much to Piero's gratification, very speedily.

Though rarely reading architectural journals and their opinions, Piero had happened to see a comment that the design was '... boring, a glass tower that apologises for its existence by becoming more transparent as it rises higher.'

If these people wished to wrap the security blanket of the past around them, he had little desire for changing their minds.

Tern's next project was one of the few times whilst in Chicago he'd accepted a commission from a developer other than Tern. The latter had told him of it and, as Piero suspected, the company was a relatively small one and not in direct competition with him. It was in an area where the height had been restricted, though there was quite a wide yardage that could be built upon.

As it was fairly near a fairground in Park Brook with its well-known helter-skelter ride, Piero used its curves to ease the eye into his design that, as someone told him he'd read, 'looked like a plump, tail-less aircraft that had made a belly flop landing, its wings slightly narrowing as they curved obtusely to the ground.'

To heighten the 'aeroplane' effect he had made circular windows on the main body.

The one after this, ten floors of part workshops and part residences and situated merely a mile away, was loosely based on a Fifties radio design plus some Mies Van der Rohe moderne. It was a minor challenge for both he and Lance, the latter enjoying it more than the former, as Piero had created it knowing Tern had a soft spot for the moderne. He was right. The man was pleased.

There were two or three months of relative  inactivity after this, filled, other than with some insignificant, rather boring but well-paid jobs for two of Tern's business associates, by travelling to various places in Chicago State, almost exclusively by train and bus - his reluctance to drive making him, according to Lance, perceived by some as a European eccentric.

He went to Auburn in Sangamon County, again simply because he liked the names, but other than its university and football team there was little there, except a High Street that could almost have served as a movie-set background for the Earp brothers.

Next was Springfield, Illinois'largest city; the State capitol being another classical municipal building he tried to avert his gaze from. He hadn't known that the place was home to Lincoln at one time, and couldn't be bothered to look at his museum nor his monument or tomb.

Then came a steady stream of jobs from Tern. Another was in Chicago, this time on the edge of the South Loop where he'd used a simple idea he had first played around with during his degree in Rome. It was a series of circular floors like hard-edged inter-vertebrate discs or thick peppermint sweets. There were few windows at first, he wanting it to look distinctively solid and, for a change, using less glass, Tern wanting more light both within the construction and reflecting from it. They compromised, and had more glass and light.

The next was a bit of a coup for Tern. Oak Park, in the Metropolitan Area of the City, had a history of preservation for what was initially a village, especially as Frank Lloyd Wright's old home and studio were there.

A new bus station and depot was said, by the Council Committee, to be needed by its inhabitants. After a demographic downturn but the population now rising, it was thought a good idea. Again, Tern, this time in complete accordance with Piero, pushed for light and glass.

It wasn't just the design that was so new in the town, but that Tern's ever-present hunger for optimizing square-footage and maximising income led to the incorporation of apartments, offices, shops, restaurants and bars in the same construction above the station.

Later in the design stage, a performance space was mooted by Tern who, it appeared, financially backed an advertising campaign persuading, educating and swaying the populace in an affirmative direction despite the popularity of their old thea-tre which a development company - Piero suspecting it was a Tern subsidiary - wanted to get rid of to build apartments. If it was Tern's, he hadn't told Piero.

It took over a year before the station - dwarfed in the end by Piero's idea - was given building permission, a time mostly filled by the architect, with the help of Henry's expertise, per-fecting its lines and details. It had a huge glass galleria topped by three towers like a curved 'W,' each of twenty eight stories above the space occupied by the city's original transport need.

As well as the apartments, offices, shops, restaurants, bars and a small hotel, was a performance space named, 'Tern's Theater.'

This was followed by a municipal library near the down-town square in Bloomington, Illinois. Though being some two hundred and fifty miles from the nearest water at Lake Michi-gan and having little nautical history, Piero created slightly convex squares of stainless steel with stretched corners like sails, some covered in ceramic tiles and forming mosaics of locally significant places.

'For the public good' was a concept that didn't lend itself easily to Tern's persona, thus Piero was a little surprised that he was involved with it - it contained only a few offices - but was probably politic for him to be so in the context of a move away from his increasingly pushing, deal-making image. Piero wasn't surprised, however, when Tern told him he was writing a book to be called, 'How To Make The Deal.' His listener would have put money on his conviction that it was being ghost-written.

On three occasions he'd travelled to sites in Tern's hired helicopter while Tern, assiduously reading a stack of papers, studied whatever financial business he was currently involved in, rarely speaking to his travelling companion, or when accompanied by his accountant, loudly helping him push the boundaries of fiscal creativity. Piero, meanwhile, again resisted the temptation to tell him that his necktie was supposed to end above a belt, not hang down to the knees between his testicles.

Before the building was finished, Tern had asked him to work on an office and apartments-sharing project near Rockford Regional Airport, the height for obvious reasons being limited. This was the first time Tern had asked him aboard his private jet.

He met its owner at the airport and as they went up the steps into the aircraft, Piero following, the first thing that caught his eye were the gold-plated seat-belt buckles hit by the shafts of sunlight coming through its oval windows. There were metal pegs where baseball caps had been hung, as if in a hallway, recent photos of his wife, and a toilet at the rear with the now usual gold-plated taps, marble sink and toilet bowl.

This time, when Piero looked out the window - Tern holding court behind him at the centre point of a semi-circle of business men - he seemed to see not the usual pareidolia puppies and cats, but an overweight, sneering dragon, a tyrannosaurus and the vague outline of a warship, briefly musing on whether its guns would have been covered in gold.

Around this time, Piero had moved into a colonial-style classic hall-and-parlour house he'd bought in Archer Heights with two large chimneys and lattice widows. He purchased it partly because he could now afford it and a perverse feeling of somehow getting his own back, at a more intimate level, on the physical environment of his childhood. It wasn't exactly Roman-classical, but here in America it represented much the same; it was old.

He tore out many original features: fireplaces, high skirting boards and small windows, got rid of cornices, coves and dado rails, removed the wall demarcating parlour from hall, re-plastered and painted virtually everything white. He created a large study in which his original watercolour sketches of his buildings he'd had framed and hung on its walls along with photos of the finished products. They gradually began occupying an increasing amount of wall space.

Tern then commissioned him to design a large shopping complex in North Rivermead. It was completed, from the start of his sketches to finished project, in three years, the mall having hundred and thirty stores, five and a half thousand parking spaces and a glass elevator. Lance had helped him maximise the functional, rather utilitarian space to Tern's satisfaction and also that of the town's consumers.

After a year, and another apartment block, this time in Bedford Park's square, a more interesting Tern project of flexible office and residential space came along which allowed him to experiment a little. Because of the site's limited space Tern had, presumably as a result of his aggressive, hard-dealing way, been allowed to go tall and Piero had completed the top with three separate, abruptly-curving floors. It had, apparently, received mixed reviews.

Lance, although aware that his employer wasn't that interested in what he called the 'parochial, insular opinions of the too-comfortable' had shown him media comments that praised the 'Sinuous, organic' work while another stated that it looked like 'a box with curved sticks of celery sticking out the top.'

And there were more: a tall building, though not quite a sky-scraper, to the south of the downtown business district, and two more malls, both departing from the conventional by high octagonal atriums, one in Wicker Park the other off Logan Square.

The taller construction was in a context decreed by the city's Planning Authority's need for it to look similar to buildings in relatively close proximity, three of which were Thirties creations, the other a postmodern loose imitation of them. He decided on a balanced hybrid of all of them, but with subtle curves and without reference to the surface ornamentation of the older buildings.

He still felt, however, somewhat hampered here, hemmed in, not really able to let himself loose, to create what he wanted; though it had been gratifying when Lance had said to him, 'You've designed part of the fabric of this city.'

Tern was now back in his hometown and Piero was with him, the latter having heard rumours months before he'd left Chicago, that he was returning to the well-heeled business circles of New York, the city where he'd begun to make his name and fortune. He had said nothing to Piero until a few weeks before he had come, requesting he follow him. There was little persuasion needed. Tern owned a few buildings in the city, though no major ones, but as he'd told his architect, he wanted another, a big one.

Piero was aware that Tern's chutzpah and ability to defy any setbacks had impressed many of Chicago's tough entrepreneurs who were the core of a city built on brash ambitions and a refusal to take other people's 'no' for an answer, and had little doubt he could also do it here in the mean streets of the New York property scene.

The architect had set up offices off Foley Square in Lower Manhattan, recruiting fresh specialist expertise and office staff. The premises were modest but unmistakably occupied by the architecture profession with hardly a square yard of wall area not covered by photos, blueprints, illustrations, impressions and copies of sketches of most of his buildings. He had found Lance an apartment a mile from his own.

After selling his mansion in DuPage County, Tern had been gutting and refurbishing another in Plymouth, Massachusetts and had, half-heartedly and as if he should by convention, asked Piero whether he was interested in contributing some ideas, knowing that period grandiloquence wasn't his thing; 'Period stuff' as he sometimes called it when not being vituperative about it. Piero had told him, partly truthfully, that his work on one of Tern's rare small projects, and his last in Chicago, were taking up nearly all of his time.

He had, however, visited the place. It was larger than the old one. Beyond the pillared entrance, marble floors met polished plaster walls in an entrance hall dominated by a swirling glass staircase leading to six plush bedrooms, and with a guest room, sitting room and drawing rooms with egg and arrow cornices, door frames and dado rails.

Piero wondered whether its owner had ever imagined his autocratic self strolling around a villa in ancient Rome wearing a toga, sandals and laurel wreath, with hair curled and brushed forward like a Hollywood movie-depicted Caesar. He'd been shown around with a barely-disguised gloating pride from his guide.

There were gilded basins in the ladies toilets, gold wall panels - possibly using up America's entire stock of gold leaf - and a library panelled with ancient English oak, its rare books, Piero suspected, as untouched as the day they were put there. He nodded in almost strained appreciation throughout the tour, which also included a walk-in wine room, manicured garden, a plunge pool and several garages.

He hadn't known who'd designed the staircase and other recent extensions to an obviously grand and ancient place, he'd heard that it was someone from the East Coast who'd known Tern from way back.

Tern seemed to have done it all so quickly. Piero wondered how many back-scratching deals would be made here - as long as he wasn't around; in earlier days when with Tern and his

fellow landowners and property barons he'd walked or sat behind them feeling like his master's pet dog.

He looked out of the deli's window again. It was becoming a
familiar sight once more: the traffic, yellow cabs, a trio of
trees, an awninged restaurant, hydrants, grill-steam, a fire-
escape; and the building directly opposite him with the gleaming, vertical steel struts rising, he knew, to its fifty-six storey,
six-hundred-and-fifty-foot height ending in a large, glistening
orb, even more familiar. It was Tern's latest, and designed by
Piero.

He'd read of controversies during its construction including
the destruction of historically important sculptures from the
small museum that originally occupied part of the site. There
were also rumours - Tern had sold his own Chicago construction company - of the underpaying of contractors. The residential section had been filled for a while and apparently its commercial and retail spaces had now been taken.

Piero, however, had little interest in any of this, what count-
ed was that it was another Piero Ronzi building and there were
more to come. But this time in Europe, perhaps England, not as
tall maybe, but since the Millenium things were changing in
that country.

Lance was coming, too, never having been there before and
rather surprised at himself for not having done so, and Piero
intended to raise his salary, only partly because he knew that a
lot of firms would want him. He had been approached before
but, gradually coming to share some of Piero's ideas; had
stayed. Piero had accidentally met someone connected to a developer in London and had submitted a design for a small project there.

But, perhaps more exciting, the economies in the Middle
East and Far East were growing quickly, they would, he
thought, be architecturally less hidebound, there'd be more
scope for innovation, perhaps a welcome for it. For him.

# CHAPTER 18

Before going to his Town Hall meeting, Liam had assisted a young surveyor in pricing a job; a small block of flats in Silvertown near Tate and Lyle. He knew the area only slightly now but had once known it well, often visiting a friend there as a teenager. It was a place where Victorian schools, old jobs and green grass had vanished and the Becton Gas Works, the People's Plan and Eleanor Marx would never be seen again, and no longer would Docklands dust swirl and settle or bittersweet smoke from the sugar factory and the stale ale smell of Unilever's wipe away the sun.

It was once Pollutown, where wheezing kids born with a Silvertown spoon in their mouths learnt to spit it out before choking on it, and stared at ferries dieseling across grey water perhaps wishing they were gliding into Rio while Albert Road crumbled under gas-farting trucks.

After it became Yuppietown and a floodlit St. Mark's guided screaming jets into the flight path of City Airport's second runway, it became a place where embattled locals sat in pubs wondering why nostalgia wasn't what it used to be and becoming increasingly surrounded by gangs of suits mouthing trivia into mobiles and scattering chicken burger cartons as 'No boots and overalls' signs were pinned to the doors, and Cundy's Café became a Pret a Manger.

The Town Hall was a run-of-the-mill Victorian building with not too many of the classical forms and details of Empire, the latter's frames of reference those of the 'glories' of Rome and ancient Greece. When you have an empire, he thought, there's money and time to show it off, parade its many manifestations in edifices of the ornate, of embellishments, scrolls, intricacies, whether it be the Spanish transverse arches and buttresses, the Ottoman's harmonious domes and articulated light or Chinese pagodas and pavilions.

America, he reflected, had a more modern empire, where lands, though invaded, hadn't been permanently owned, its propriety residing in its influence on the western world's - and beyond - speech, attitudes, eating habits, media, art and culture. There was no need for the expense of owning other countries; psychological ownership sufficed.

This seemed a more formal meeting than the church one, it was for a much larger project and with more council involvement - though the ecclesiastical background of the other had meant, perhaps, a more sedate audience - and there seemed a little more purposefulness here amongst the sixty or so people looking interestedly at a 3-D model of it in a pretentious glass case taking pride-of-place on a raised wooden dais in the foyer.

The online petition stated:

'We are appalled by the current application to develop the traditional and long-standing Plantation Market at 58-80 Harbinger Road and the erection of a tower over eighty metres tall, and the planning policies of the Executive. The proposed development is too tall, dense and obnoxious, and completely out of keeping with its surroundings. Please do not give planning approval for this monstrosity. '

There were a few print-outs of it on a central table which were outnumbered by illustrations of the offending construct. He wondered just how much significance for council members the petition really had

The developers' leaflets lying on a table inside the main door had small photos of three men, one again looking vaguely familiar. They were the same people who had been on the church brochure. This was a much larger project, however, than the one that had been intended for building on the site of a razed church. They had written:

'The building will comprise an exceptional design and take account of the existing form, character, appearance, and material palette of the local area… A transformational public realm will double the number of communal spaces with all the benefits of a village green and there will be a free viewing gallery. The old market will be retained on its lower floors and the narrow road which now leads to it will be widened to increase access.'

It was, he thought, like letting the Grosvenor Estate build a tower block in Belgrave Square if it repaired the sewer.

People had begun to wander into the main hall; Liam did so too, taking a seat at the front.

A woman dressed in a rather dated power-dressing suit came onto the stage and introduced 'one of the people responsible for this wonderful building,' the other she referred to as 'the chief planning officer.' After her own solitarily clapping as she left the stage, one of the men pictured on the brochure - not the one that had previously appeared at the church - came out from the wings with an obvious council official behind him.

He began with, 'London is facing a fast-growing population increase. We must prepare for it.'

Somebody asked him exactly how much of the proposed block was for residential use and how much for office space. 'It's pretty vague in the leaflets.'

The question was ignored.

'Tall buildings would minimise the need to build on green belt land. We predict more towns with rail connections, even those not connected as well as we are, will opt for skyscrapers. Tall buildings can breathe new life into town centres and are preferable to suburban sprawl.'

'Would you call Metroland, Ealing, Wanstead, etcetera a sprawl?' Liam asked. 'Wide pavements, green verges, trees; are you aware that there are nearly as many trees as people in this city?'

'I wasn't, no.'

'Trees are essential, a necessity. Put them against a period house or planted along a terraced street or in an urban square and they illuminate. They're our embodiment of nature. Is this what you call a 'suburban sprawl?''

'Not exactly, but - '

'What would you call *your* construction? Some sort of glittering citadel reaching for the heavens? The beauty of this city is in its flatness, trophy towers wreck that.'

The chief planning officer, who had been standing silently behind the developer, stepped forward and said to the rest of the hall, not looking at Liam, 'Don't forget that the present consultation is designed to elicit views, not to predetermine them. However, we cannot ignore London's growth, in less than a decade there will be ten million of us.'

Liam marked the 'us,' just like his previous 'we,' as an attempt to make his listeners feel that he, too, was part of the community and, perhaps, be friendlier towards him.

'We must ensure that this project has a positive outcome for residents, workers and visitors alike.'

'Another empty, impossible-to-achieve soundbite,' someone near Liam said, followed by 'They don't just affect people living near them, you know, they ruin streetscapes, views from parks - '

'We must have these buildings if London wishes to maintain its status as a world-class city.'

'That's one of the most superficial and desperate phrases ever coined,' said the same man. 'Does the world look at us with favour and admiration because of our skyline?'

'Have you all seen the model of this proposal?' the developer asked rhetorically, looking around at his listeners as if there was no obligation for him to answer their questions.

'It is elegant, it will provide over four hundred jobs during construction; it will enhance the local economy. We are committed to revitalising this area; it will transform it, helping create a Twenty-First Century High Street as well as enhancing the area's cultural offer.'

Before Liam could take the man to task for using the euphemistic catch-all of 'the economy,' someone behind him said, 'These plans are offensive. It's a disgrace to its location, the area, its planers and the architects involved. And it's too high, far too high, and don't try the old trick of saying you're going to reduce the height if there's enough of us against it so we'll think 'Well, it could have been worse.''

More people were making noises now.

'That's the oldest trick in the developers' book, mate,' someone else said, followed by a chorus of 'Yeahs.'

'St. Paul's will look like a pudding basin amongst chair legs the way this city's being built on,' a voice from the back of the hall shouted.

A fellow disbeliever calmly stated: 'It s all up for grabs. Any developer will tell you that tower permits depend on who lobbies hardest. The skyline's being disfigured by who gives the best lunch.'

Though experiencing a rather rare feeling of something like belonging, Liam was becoming annoyed, like he had in the church meeting, this time having a brief fantasy of smashing through the glass case and pummelling the model into all the shapes known to geometry.

For a crazy second he also felt like doing an American-Indian dance around an imaginary tepee chanting 'White Man speak with forked tongue.' A tongue full of developers and construction permit givers' clichés; though neither of the speakers had used 'regeneration,' as yet.

The councillor then said with a hint of pride, as if not only was it a good thing but that he was partly responsible:

'There are now twenty new tall buildings proposed for east London.'

His eyes quickly scanned the audience, then, emphasising each word, said, with an almost pumping fist as if it was or would soon become an absolute maxim, 'Appropriate buildings in appropriate places.'

He repeated the phrase.

Liam stood. 'Who decides what counts as 'appropriate'? What criteria, *whose* criteria are going to be used? Would it be for providing homes or, again, is the bottom line the inescapable expectational norm of profit? Don't bother to attempt an answer, it doesn't need one. This area will eventually be full of towers; the city is being trashed by them. What it needs, what the city needs are planners with a trace of visual awareness and developers not blinded by cash.'

There was clapping around and behind him.

'And you haven't mentioned the petition yet,' said a large man on the next seat. 'There's a lot of signatures on it, it shows the depth of feeling, or weren't you aware of it?'

'I think you are now.' somebody else shouted.

'Yes, of course, but this is a 'good' for you all, economically, culturally and, don't forget, the developer here is putting a three-million-pound contribution to affordable housing and three hundred thousand into our carbon offset fund.'

'That's legal blackmail,' said the large man. 'And what about the look of it? Is that a 'good'? Don't the aesthetics count?' Just because we can't measure what something looks like, this thing will have a deleterious effect emotionally; it will depress a lot of people. Or are we supposed to get used to it? Seeing it every day; going to and from work, or taking the kids over the park, or cleaning the car, always there in our peripheral vision, like a lump of grit in the corner of your eye.'

Liam was thinking how wondrously flexible aesthetics were when brought face-to-face with huge amounts of money. He was also surprised at the articulacy on display, and pleased at the genuinely felt dislike of this scheme propounded by people with money and wanting more of it and unquestionably thinking it was somehow a 'natural' urge, and their institutionalized response of justifying it in terms of being for the good of all.

He thought of psychology, which adduces mental characteristics of individuals to explain social forms when, he would argue, these characteristics were themselves the *result* of the very social forms to be explained. 'Society makes man, society makes greed,' he whispered to himself as he waited for an answer from the stage or another adverse opinion from the hall.

The council official then moved towards the front, held his hands up, palms outwards, and said:

'Alright then, you've had your say, made some good points, and these will be taken on board at our next discussion.'

'Who with?' asked someone.

'We, the committee and developers will go through the plan again; the matters raised, details, all of your comments, and come to a satisfactory decision.'

'Satisfactory for who?' the same person asked, a little louder.

'And, as explained,' said the official, ignoring the query, 'it will be based on what has been said this evening.'

The developer then said emphatically:

'And remember, this is progress. Think about it. Don't try to stop it.'

They both rather quickly left the stage.

Liam wanted to yell, 'What a fuckin' value judgement.' 'Progress.' What did it mean, and for whom?

He felt internally inarticulate. He thought of the old Concorde airliner when breaking the sound barrier over Bristol and its sonic boom cracking the windows of several houses. Was that progress for the people whose windows were smashed? He knew it was an inapt analogy but nevertheless...

He stood looking at the empty stage in front of him for a while then turned to leave, noticing that most of the others had already gone. He would have liked to have spoken to some of them, continue the discussion over coffee or something. Instead, he found a nearby cafe and, in a desire to settle himself, thought of the trees that had been mentioned, and of their being virtually wasted in the country.

There they were everywhere, sprouting from fields, hedges, hills, a tedious canvas of green, leaves mulching into tractor'd mud, of Disney horror branches against a moon. In the city they were magic: a frame for Georgian windows set in London bricks, overhanging park lakes, arching, touching, above an Edwardian street, bright fans behind Victorian chimneys.

They were sentries guarding a Palladian villa, a canopy for toppled tombstones, lightly resting on the head of a Christ, their curled leaves matching a lintel's Art Nouveau scrolling, emerald waves at the base of a Bauhaus tower, an Art Deco liner riding a tide.

Smiling to himself, he thought of Mary, seeing himself in a city where she had magicked him with her blossomed cheeks and green eyes. 'Don't leave,' he quietly said to the picture of her inside his head. 'You'd be wasted in the country.'

# CHAPTER 19

On the Tube from Heathrow Piero was surprised at the number of ethnic people travelling with him. There had been few when he last lived here. He looked around at the other passengers, they weren't looking askance or even curiously at them as he almost automatically expected, he wondered why.

Was it the famed English diffidence, their aversion to being considered 'rude,' or maybe being used to them? He guessed it was mostly the latter. He wasn't quite sure what he felt. As an Italian he was a foreigner himself, but at least he was European. But it wasn't really important. His buildings were.

Tern had been rather dualist in his reaction to his leaving. On the one hand he wanted him to stay, almost hinting at paying him a fee increase for any projects he may ask him to undertake, although knowing he hadn't anything big currently on his books, on the other he appeared to be genuine in wishing him luck in 'Europe or wherever yer gonna go.' The way he'd said 'Europe' implied it was some sort of feudal colony.

'Remember,' he'd added, 'you make yer own luck.'

Piero had asked him that if anything large came up to let him know. He could - along with a few trips - do most of the work from wherever he was, really, but an increasingly confident part of him wasn't really bothered, he felt near enough certain now that he'd make a success away from Tern and the U.S.

He'd let his house in New York, his sketches and watercolours were in storage and would come later, as would Lance when Piero had set up an office. A temporary one was his room at a hotel in west London he'd booked into while continuing work on a commission he'd negotiated before coming: a block of flats a few miles westward - realising they weren't called apartments here - that the developers wanted a spin on.

As it was in a conservation area and the height limited, he'd done away with vertical windows and made the whole of the long, sloping roof with flat windows. Feeling it a mildly interesting introduction to the practising of his profession in the UK, he briefly wondered how many of the students who had been at university with him in London had gone into the field, and what, if anything, they had achieved. He'd heard of none of them.

As he descended towards Fiumicino Airport, with aircraft gathered around its flat- pack central building like piglets around a sow, it looked unfamiliar. The last time he had been here was his migration to London some thirty years previously. He caught a taxi to his hotel, a sparse but clean place containing a sort of neutrality; he didn't want to wake up to any classical oppressiveness.

When he did wake next morning he tried, for the sake of it, to adopt the role of 'tourist.' He caught a bus to Barberini Metro and looked up at the Trevi Fountain as he alighted. He looked at its Baroque grandness, the statues in its walls, its formality and granite hardness; if they removed the water it would look rather menacing, he thought. He went back into the station then to Termini where his ticket inspector father had worked.

The great lobby hall was fronted by full-height glass walls covered by a concrete roof of a segmented arch; it was a modernist version of a vault from a Roman bath and which was integrated with a cantilevered canopy over the entrance which also recalled a similar achievement of Roman architecture, though he couldn't quite remember which one. Postmodernism; a few days ago he felt surrounded by it in London, now, here it was in Rome.

He caught the Metro to Testaccio where his parental home was - or used to be. Leaving the station, he saw the haphazard waste dump of Monte Testaccio where he used to play as a kid.

He wasn't that far from the Aurelian walls of Ponta San Paola nor the Ponticus Aemilia, but he wasn't a tourist, they were almost as familiar to him as his local cinema had been, part of his only known world, one he had escaped from.

Instead of getting a train to Piramide, his once neighbour-hood station, he decided to walk and was soon in an area of low, concrete post-war buildings with small, sparse courtyard gardens which seemed to be full of dogs. He walked through it towards his old home, wondering if it was still there. It proba-bly wasn't,' but then if it wasn't, perhaps it didn't really mat-ter; he didn't live here anymore.

He thought of the narrow ugliness of the house he was raised in with its black stove, dark spindle struts of the banister rail, brass stair rods, bronzes of Fortuna and Mars on the man-telshelf and his parents' bedroom with the mahogany wardrobe and chest, the whole holding a heavy, claustrophobic grimness for him.

It had been partly alleviated by the half-hearted use of bits and pieces of the Razionalismo interior style and later with wallpaper in his room with tiny Fiat cars, and in the living room the paper with greyhounds and flowers. In the kitchen had been an ever-working moka pot. Everywhere there seemed to have been framed pieces of fabric with religious motifs stitched on, often by his mother, at least three saying 'Looking Unto Jesus.'

When he arrived at where he thought the house should be, he was still in the estate. His old home had been swamped by concrete.

Perhaps feeing slightly lost because an old familiarity had been taken away from him, he took the Metro to Cornelia sta-tion and the Botanical Gardens. As he ambled around this mini piece of untidy countryside he dismissed the idea that public gardens should exist within an ethos of strict maintenance.

There were few visitors as he strolled through wild cacti and bamboo, under wide palms and yuccas, climbed a sloping terrace of gravelly paths, and found a dusty olive grove and heard birdsong for the first time since he'd been in the city. He smiled in a quiet triumph when he heard an English tourist complain to her companion that the nearby roses hadn't been dead-headed for years.

He then, against his aesthetic tastes, caught a jolting, swaying bus crowded with builders, nuns and children to St. Andrea Della Valle. He did so simply because it had been his mother's favourite church. Craftsmanship, yes, but the Baroque façade, apse, the Domenicheno-frescoed vault above the nave and the gold leaf was too rich for him, too ancient.

He took a short Metro ride to Piazza Venetia then walked through Via del Corso avoiding its meandering alleys - seeing London's Dickensian alleyways as an equivalent - then glanced at the fashion shop windows before going into one and buying himself two jackets and a neck scarf.

On the flight back the day after, he attempted to rationalise his experiences, his childhood: the tenseness, discordance, grim familial rituals, the feel of the time, the *fascismo,* which he could hear his father say with some vexation and sadness, had now gone.

But there had still been a hardness; an almost solid political pungency in the air, and certainly inside of his father who behaved, sometimes, when with his friends in the taverna, like a kind of honorary, unofficial soldier, shouting out his political beliefs. His mother would say little about any of it. 'She's *apolitico,*' he would sneer.

Piero remembered him taking him to the old airport where cab drivers shouted and pushed each other as they waited for fares that never seemed to come, and in the city, once, an aeroplane came droning over them with a *Vota Forza Da Liberta* banner fishtailing above the Teatro Dell' Opera where, his father had told him, the bourgeoisie clapped themselves for being there.

He had said it as if by rote, but his son knew now that he would like to have been a member of that class. He also wondered what would have happened had Mussolini won the day; his father's regret that he hadn't was, he now saw, always with him.

Walking through Heathrow, wondering if the airport's worn carpets would ever be replaced with marble, he decided that when he had completed the west London project he would neither fish for work nor accept any more commissions in England, unless they were out of the ordinary or he had a freer rein than he had, generally, been used to.

He would leave; already he had been in touch with an architect he had known slightly in New York and who was now working in Dubai. He would like Lance to come with him. He wasn't sure whether he would. But Piero would certainly go.

# CHAPTER 20

He used a Saudi Arabian company to navigate his request for a residence visa, which, pleasingly, was helped along its way by his name being known by the people he spoke to.

Dubai's International Airport, he knew, was the busiest in the world by international passenger traffic and, once completed, would be the largest building by floor space. He liked immediately the three terminal buildings' gleaming structures like aeroplane wings which covered half a million square metres, he also remembered from somewhere that it had nine kilometres of conveyer belts. He walked with his bags under wide, arched, windowed ceilings with chrome and leather seats everywhere and a large, fern-filled pool.

Not fancying the food on the flight and rarely enjoying airport cuisine, he walked along Al Khawaneej Street looking for a restaurant, noticing the streets off it were numbered, similar to New York. He saw one, guessing its culinary contents would be partly a legacy of, or at least resemble, a culture of mass-trading in spices and herbs. It was. There was sesame, saffron, black pepper, cumin, cinnamon and spice mixtures like baharat and harissa. Looking around at the diners' plates, he saw these edibles surrounding portions of lamb and chicken; goat and beef were also on the menu.

It was hot, fortunately dry heat, and the restaurant was air-conditioned. He hadn't really looked at the skyline. Sitting down trying to find his piece of chicken under the morass of green stuff, he did. He gazed through the window towards Al Mamzar beach and the Marina and there they were, in the clear air against an unblemished blue sky, the skyscrapers.

At first glance they appeared almost in a line: the height of them, their shapes, the spirals, convexes, the glass, those that curved, one that looked like a very tall medieval church adjacent to the sheer concrete side of another. Next to three that were like skinny, slightly concave cylinders, was one with a top like a sharpened 'V' and another with a traditional Arabian cupola made of concrete ribs. There were pointed and sloping apices, spires, inverted cones... He felt excited.

He took a red-roof taxi to his hotel a mile or so away - another brand new construction of concrete, glimmering steel and glass. His room was a large, modern one with little touches of Middle East tradition: the Arabian jasmine in an arabesque vase, a small Persian carpet and ceramic wall panel, even a faded print of a belly dancer.

He wanted to use his energy. As work on the proposed Metro had yet to begin, he took a taxi downtown, wishing to see what had been built there, glimpsing only bits of it from the restaurant. Here, the buildings were more similar to downtown Chicago or New York - though a  plus for him was the almost-absence of the international style - but only a couple as far as he could tell having Thirties-mode set-backs and masts, and they were generally more innovative anyway; there were no zoning resolutions, no  Gothic revival  here.

Walking in the midst of them, they seemed so fresh, a new city, beholden, despite being created by architectural firms from Europe, America and Asia, only to itself, its own style, almost its own symbolic universe.

After returning to the hotel he rang his architect acquaintance - still not sure where he'd first met him, probably at a poorly-attended architects convention somewhere - who he was to share an office with, at least temporarily. The man explained that whilst he would have liked to have met him at the airport, work commitments hadn't allowed it.

Piero saw him the next day in yet another just-completed tower office block, this one a little more conventional than most of the others he'd seen, with its curved concrete and uniformly-windowed sides. He had a commission for him that had recently come in which, having heard even more good things about Piero's work and having obtained a copious number of photos of it and needing to fully trust him - his own practice becoming increasingly busy - offered it to him as, theoretically, a joint venture.

It was for an important client, sheik Addulazaaz, a benefactor and patron of the arts and Head of the newly created General Entertainment Authority. He was, apparently, particularly interested in the circus. There was a long history and a growing interest in it in Arabia, specifically focused on equine acts and events; a Spanish circus and Cirque du Soleil had become popular features in recent years.

The commission was for a new building in a neglected area of the city to be called The Circus Conservatory, which would house Saudi Arabia's first accredited degree programme in the circus arts: 'A vibrant artistic centre with performance events and recreational facilities.'

Given some basic information, importantly the building's ground space and contact to its proposed builder, he went away to think about it, ideas already forming, an immediate one being to utilise the historic circus shape, a circle with a radial audience. He went back to the hotel, finished unpacking his bags including his sketch pad and watercolour squares still in their original tin box from his student days - a kind of creative security blanket - and began his usually successful process.

Almost habitually he worked into the night, wondering for just a few seconds if his ability to work, to produce shapes and flights of fruitful and utilitarian fancy would ever be slowed or marred. He grinned to himself. Of course it wouldn't.

In the afternoon, still working, and eating at the hotel, his new architect colleague serendipitously rang him to tell him that an office, though rather small, had become available on the third floor of his block. Piero rang its agent and secured it after only a little haggling over the price, knowing that it was the traditional norm in this country's culture to do so.

He was to move their in eight days, during which time he finalised some basic layouts and structures to the enthusiastic approval of his professional ally, rented himself a flat in Karama, a less affluent area to where he was staying, and heard that Lance would be joining him relatively soon. He relaxed and began looking for some Italian restaurants.

Though the Sheraton Grand near the Trade Centre had been recommended, not wanting to eat at a hotel, he went to Mas simo's at the Marina. With its rich mixture of Arabic and qua- si-Roman décor it wasn't the ideal ambience for him to enjoy food, but sitting on the terrace in the warm evening sun looking across to the man-made Palm Jumeirah Island made up for the cloying interior.

The home-made gnocci was the best he'd had for years, as was the biscuit tortoni he consumed while watching the towers light up as the sun sank and the muezzin in the nearby mosque called the locals to prayer.

While he ordered coffee, an African woman seated herself in the corner of the terrace a few yards from him. She looked a little familiar. As an immaculately dressed, waist-coated waiter, looking as if he was competing in a 'quintessential waiter' competition came out to serve her, Piero, listening to her order a meal, remembered where they'd met before.

She was one of only three women and the only black on his course in London. She was younger than him and, on the lit terrace, didn't look much older than when he'd first known her. She had, he'd heard, failed her exams. He looked away, trying to remember her name. Of course: Betty Begombe. He would, when she'd finished her meal, say *Ciao* to see if she recognised him.

When he did so, if was almost as if there had been only a few months since their last meeting. She didn't appear that surprised to see him. She was here on holiday alone, staying at the Holiday Express in Bur Dubai. After telling her, at her request, what he'd been doing in the intervening years, she said she was pleased for him, though had heard nothing about him after university. She herself had spent most of her time living in London and working sporadically as an actress.

She had, she told him, recently been back to Uganda because she was converting a building in Kampala into a guest house and holiday home.

Her voice, a little more modulated than the African accent he remembered, was rather quiet and precise as she continued with:

'It was horrible in Kampala; I stayed at my old house that my parents owned. It is really run down and I was woken one night by what I thought were the rats. I got up to chase them away and there was a man in the doorway. He hit me with a hammer on my shoulders and arms and then suddenly stopped and ran away. I think he wanted to steal my things. I think he thought I was rich. There is so much poverty there.'

Though feeling sorry for her, she was obviously okay now and having had little sleep and wishing to return to his room and rest, he suggested that if she wanted to talk more perhaps it would be better for them to arrange to meet. He did so more as some sort of obligation because he had once known her long ago. With a quiet enthusiasm she agreed to.

They met the next afternoon at the Caribou cafe downtown. He walked in and saw the back of her; she was the only customer. He went around her table and sat opposite her.

'Your hair's longer,' he said.

'Yes, I let it down.'

Her slow, gentle smile was familiar to him now.

'You begin,' he said.

She placed her elbows neatly on the table.

'As you may remember, I couldn't draw very well, though I did have ideas, and the maths was a problem too and I knew I would fail.'

'A self-fulfilling prophecy?'

'Not really. So, after a friend asked me to go to one of those audition things for extras, I got a few bit parts. Don't ask me what the films were, nobody's seen them and it's hardly a living, but I still have a little money my father left me.

'I will tell you what happened after this man attacked me. I went to a clinic and they helped me. The next day I went to my mother's house and she told me that I couldn't stay there, and my brother also said that I was not wanted there. I went to my older brother's house and he came back with me and started fighting with his younger brother. My mother was laying there and had blood on her head so I got between them and stopped them. I went back with my brother and when he left for work next day two policemen came and told me I must come with them. They drove me through the town. When I asked where they were taking me they wouldn't tell me.

'They took me to a place where other women were. It had faeces on the floor. I knew it was the mental hospital. Some of the women told me that their families had put them there. I was lucky because some people who I had grown up with had spotted me in a supermarket some days before and wanted to find me. They traced me. So I went back to the guest house for a while and then returned to London.'

She related this in a flat, almost matter-of-fact manner as if it was about quite mundane, everyday happenings. She looked briefly around her.

'Now I am here to be peaceful and to rest.' She then said, 'I'm sorry,' and picked up her cup. 'I need to go. I'm expecting a call from a company who just might have some work for me, and it's rude to talk on the phone if I'm with someone.'

She scribbled a number on a piece of paper she took from her bag.

'Ring me.'

She carried her cup to the counter and went to the door. After a measured walk towards it on her long, almost thin legs and a quick look back at him, the door swung shut behind her.

She'd hardly touched her coffee. He stayed, thinking of the fading bruise he'd noticed on her upper arm, a memento, he assumed, of the attack.

He tried to remember her from the past. All he could picture was her smile, the quiet way of expressing herself and the way she'd moved. As she'd walked out the café he'd noticed again the easy, casual manner in which she held herself.

After discussing ideas and fees with his office-sharing colleague, he rang her the next day and they met the day after in the same café.

She seemed a little more animated. He thought she looked, with her elliptical eyes and her black hair curling inwards at the nape of her neck, rather like an American-Indian. Childhood names and images popped into his mind: Hiawatha, Minnie Ha-Ha, and a Hanna-Barbera animated cartoon of Big Chief Rain In Face with a grey raincloud constantly floating above his head.

She asked him what he was smiling about. He told her. She laughed; it was a deep, almost husky sound.

He realised she attracted him.

'Why did your mother and brother not want you?'

'Oh, money reasons I suppose,' she said, dismissively flicking her long fingers.

He glanced at her prominent cheek bones and the long, slender neck; reminding him of old sepia photos of tribal women with metal rings round their necks to elongate them.

'She glanced at him questioningly. 'You *do* remember me, don't you?'

'Of course. You were the quiet one.'

He recalled then that she'd had a brief career on Ugandan TV and that her father had been the CEO of the African Division of United States Tobacco. She'd also told him that she used to be taken to her infants school in a limousine.

She looked at him steadily then said, 'I will tell you about my father. I was raised on a three-thousand-acre estate north of

Kampala near the Sudanese border where my father grew maize, tomatoes and red peppers as well as tobacco, which he would send to the local market for export to Kenya. He also had cows and a business which imported tyres. My mother ran an agency that sold the tobacco to other agents. He was assassinated.' There was no change in her tone.

'He had just picked up a new Land Rover when he was stopped by three men. They wore no uniforms, but had pistols. They were from the Secret Service. He was a big man so there was a struggle to get him out of his car into theirs. My mother was with him. She was beaten around the head with a pistol. The night before, his brother, who ran Central African Airlines and was a minister in Amin's government and a personal adviser to him, came to the house and talked with my father all night. I heard them. Their voices kept waking me.

'My uncle left the country for Kenya next day. The rumour was that Amin was going crazy and was charging around with a hand grenade. He'd gone to my uncle's house who'd called some men to help get the grenade away. I'm not sure why he hated my uncle. Another rumour was that Amin went to the barracks where my father had been taken and interviewed him, and when he found out who his brother was, shot him himself.'

Piero was about to use the line beloved of screenwriters, 'Why are you telling me all this?' but quelled the impulse. As tragic and gruesome as it was, he was strangely glad she was telling him, though relating it with a resigned sense of inevitability, as if this was just the sort of thing that happened in Uganda, in, perhaps, all of Africa.

Their meals came. They ate mostly in silence.

'There are other things to tell you, but not at the moment,' she said as they finished their dessert. Wiping her lips with a napkin she asked him what he knew of Africa.

'Perhaps the first thing that comes to mind is infibulation. Does a woman really have to lie back and think of the washing up?'

She smiled. 'It's not just about genital mutilation. The Loh tribe, who have a clan in Kampala, practice the opposite; they try to enhance a woman's pleasure. They start when a girl is twelve. They stretch her over a stool and spread the petals of her vagina between finger and thumb.' She rolled hers together in demonstration. 'And they also can make it long; it looks like a cow's teats. Mine's not long,' she said as a smiling after-thought. 'The muscles are somehow strengthened so a man cannot penetrate if he tries to rape her.'

She rose from her seat. 'I am tired, I need to go.'

'Again?'

'Yes. But there's a dance on at the hotel the day after tomor-row, It's only a small ballroom. I was thinking of going. Do you want to come with me?'

Piero said yes, paid for their meals and they went out into the evening to a taxi rank. Before climbing into one of the pink-roofed taxis that were solely for women passengers, she squeezed his hand and had gone. Before his own taxi had dropped him at his hotel, he received a text from her: 'Thanks for seeing me today; it means a great deal to me.'

Lance arrived the next day, looking enthusiastic as Piero brought him up-to-date in the taxi from the airport on what had been happening professionally. Before unpacking in his host's flat - he was happy, he said, to use the settee for a night or two - he was shown Piero's current work and, as well as discussing that and some ideas he'd had soon after Piero had sent him his first, rough drawings, Lance talked of new finishes he'd come across; such as nanogalvanic and slintered stone.

Piero told him it was good to have him here. They went to bed late. Switching his phone on, Piero listened to a voice message from Betty. She was speaking in her level, rather self-absorbed manner.

'I wanted to tell you. I have been left the three thousand acres. I wasn't sure I would get it, but I now have it. I was thinking of maybe starting a little school there because nothing's growing there now. I think that would be good. Maybe you could come with me and reconnoiter. I think that's the word. You could tell me what you think. It would be fun. Thanks. I will see you tomorrow. Goodnight.'

He listened to it again. He thought of the continent she had come from. He saw Africa, he supposed, through the words of Ali Mazrui: 'You are not a country, Africa. You are a concept... a glimpse of the infinite.'

His first image of Africa wasn't really of female circumcision, an act born of the insecurity of the African male and the fear of his woman enjoying sexual pleasure with other men, but almost mystical names that came crowding into him: Mogadishu, Burkina Faso, Djibouti, Mauritania, though he knew little about them nor where they actually were. And the events of unquestioned British colonial grandeur, glory and adventure: the Boer War, Rourke's Drift, the discovery of Victoria Falls - once being reminded by a Zimbabwean student in London that Africans really had been there for centuries before it was 'discovered' by a white man.

The following day he and Lance walked around Downtown before they went to a house agent's in Kamara where Lance found a place to rent and which he could move into in a couple Of days. When they got back, Piero changed into a suit, gave his temporary flat mate a spare key and, telling him he was seeing the architect he was working with and who he would introduce to him soon, went, at Betty's texted request, to her hotel room.

When she answered his knock she was in a dressing gown holding wet hair high above her head.

'Sorry,' she smiled. 'I won't be long, make yourself at home.'

She gestured towards the room behind her.

He sat on a sofa looking at two small, Giacometti-like sculptures and a painting of palm trees ringing a white beach.

From the bathroom she said, 'Those sculptures, as you probably know, are African. I carry them around with me for luck.'

He made himself comfortable then went to the window and looked out to the sea. He didn't hear her enter the room. She wore a long, tight, pale blue and turquoise dress and red, high-heeled shoes. She raised an eyebrow in approval at his appreciative gaze, opened the door and pointed along the corridor. They went downstairs in the lift. There was a bar; he ordered drinks. Her dress was a shining contrast to her dark, almost glistening skin.

'Why are you looking at me like that?'

He didn't answer.

There were covert glances towards her from several men and, to give himself a little time to adjust to what he was feeling, he offered her a piece of deflective disinterest.

'Did you know that Nigerians are genetically nearer to Norwegians than they are to Kenyans? I suppose people outside of Africa think that the whole place is a kind of state inhabited by a homogenous whole; which is understandable at a superficial level because of skin colour and… '

He stopped. She was looking at him with a smile like an African Mona Lisa.

'I remember, I don't know why, you saying a long time ago that we were programmed to react warily to people and things that are obviously different from ourselves. But do you think opposites might attract?'

This time there was a slightly teasing shape to her lips. He looked at her dress, the top low enough to show the hint of small breasts which, for James, had a subtle sexuality that was infinitely preferable to those that made their owner look like a galleon in full sail.

'Perhaps we should dance,' she said.

She hadn't, as yet, mentioned the request she'd made in her phone call.

Inside the hall, above the shiny parquet floor, were deep red walls with forty or so people seated or standing around and a six-piece band at the far end beginning their warm-up.

She looked around her and said, 'Come with me.'

She grasped his hand and led him across the floor to a door by the side of the stage which opened into a kind of changing room. She pointed to a bench. She seemed different, almost authoritative. Sitting next to him, but rarely looking at him, she began.

'Five years ago I brought a man back from Uganda who I lived with for two years. At least he came through the door and not the window,' she said with a smile. 'My parents knew his. We are bound by family, that's what it's like in Africa; family, family. But they are useful sometimes; aunties teach you how to roll around in bed with a man.' She smiled again.

'He left, but we kept in touch. He is now in England again. He wants to come back to me, to live with me. My mother keeps calling, telling me to have him back.'

She turned her head towards him.

'Please come with me to Uganda. I'll show you my old school, the guest house and the house I grew up in, you could meet my brothers. Just see the land, get the feel of it. It would be fun.' She stopped. He could see the excited glint in her eyes.

'Do you remember at the end of our fourth year at university when you stood up in the seminar when the lecturer went out for a while and you gave us a lesson on what architecture could accomplish in the future? You were so enthusiastic about it. Do you recall doing that? You were so interesting, almost mesmerising. You could have been a teacher. I know you have your work, your designs and so forth, but wouldn't you, just for a while, like to teach children? You'd be good at it, I know. Couldn't you take some time off, a rest from constructing things? Get someone else to finish whatever it is you're doing?'

He was silent.

'She looked at him with narrowed eyes.

'You know, the other women students were attracted to you, and one told me that the reason was the same one that stopped heer approaching you - your detachment.'

There was a lull in the music and then a female voice not far from the door was saying, 'Betty. Where's Betty? Someone said she was here.'

She turned her head.

'I know that voice. It is a woman who is staying here, she has become my friend. I want to see her.'

She went to the door, opened it and looked quickly around. A large woman with a huge grin and wearing a jilbab suddenly embraced her. Betty turned to Piero.

'I won't be long. Wait for me.'

She pushed the door shut with her foot as if to keep him there till she chose to release him. He sat there, beginning to feel used; a man she'd known infrequently, hardly at all in fact, being utilised to escape from another she'd lived with for two years and had known for at least five. Then a sudden, hard conviction: that she knew if this man came back to her she would forgive him - as, Piero suspected, she already had.

He could smell her faint, sweet, earthy odour; a strange scent, but having a kind of primitive familiarity. If he went to Uganda with her he would be the 'evidence' for her family to believe that she'd found someone else and ease the pressure from them for her to return to her lover - a lover he was convinced she wanted to be with anyway. It was contradictory... messy.

He felt he wanted to be with this woman, but not if she was split between the desire to escape from something and the need to run towards it. And there was his profession. To do is to be.

He felt restless, stood up, paced around. There were two sports shirts hanging on wall hooks, and a pair of trainers; the hall was probably used for various sporting activities.

How apt it was, he thought, for her to lead him to a changing room; she returning home, he invited to push himself away from an emotionally fenced-in life of non-relationships into what could be an adventure, perhaps helping to create something else other than... No. He had no interest in filling little heads with either facts or inspiration.

He opened the door. Music, voices, laughter sliced into him. He could see her at the far side of the hall laughing with a woman of similar age, someone she was obviously pleased to see. A man tapped her on the shoulder, she turned and, wide-eyed, hugged him. As he held her he guided her into the dancers and started dancing with her, she seemed to be taller than any woman in the hall.

She moved away from him and began swaying, slowly, relaxed, occasionally looking at her partner, grinning, widening her eyes, almost fluttering her lashes, bending her body, subtly, sensually.

He went back inside, feeling ridiculously alone. He could smell grass, see himself kicking a ball; hear his father shouting at him to 'Get rid of it. Cross it!' *'attraversalo.'* He went out again, started walking around the edge of the hall in her direction. She saw him, said something to her dance partner and moved towards him, weaving through the dancing couples. He stopped by the double entrance doors. She stood in front of him. Angrily baring her teeth, she said:

'Were you going to leave, then? Just walk away?'

'No. I... '

She pushed through the door then opened one a few yards from it which he could see led to the back of the hotel. He hesitated then followed her.

'I will tell you something. When everybody had finished the course in London we went to that club place, it was our last day there. Do you remember?'

It was too long ago. He couldn't recall it.

'I'm sorry, no. But I think you lent me a video of Acholi tribal dancers in - '

'And you and I were sitting on our own and you weren't really listening to me, you were looking at the legs of one of the students. If you had *really* been with me I would have asked you home with me. I would have pounced on you. I would have given you my body.'

Her eyes were narrowed. She flicked her long fingers dismissively away from her again.

He tried to joke. 'So I blew it then?'

He did remember; she'd walked out and gone back to the student hostel. And he probably had, absently-minded, watched a woman's legs, walking, sitting, whatever.

'Were you going to leave because I was dancing with someone? Couldn't you have waited a few minutes for me, or is it that you don't want to come to Uganda with me. Are you frightened?'

He took a deep breath, stretched a little so he was taller than she.

'This man; are you sure you're not using me to - '

'Using you? Using you?' She was shouting. 'What for? I asked you, suggested, you come back with me to look... and what *about* him? I lived with him, and even when he left I was faithful for three years.'

She made an effort to calm herself. 'I've had men friends since, but... '

That flippant shake of her hand again.

'*Is* he coming back to you?'

She glared at him, bent forward; beat her fists on her thighs.

'I... Oh, why do you ask?'

She looked anguished, turned her head away from him. She was motionless for a while then faced him. She seemed lost, smaller, as if she'd shrivelled inside her dress.

'I only asked you to... '

There were tears in her eyes. He could read a silent 'I don't know,' see the tears now running down her face.

Suddenly spinning around, she ran falteringly back inside. He saw her turn towards the hall.

He wasn't sure what to do, wasn't even sure of what he felt. He could faintly hear the music. It seemed to have happened so quickly: from a voice message two days before to an emotional confusion and a sense of some sort of loss - though he had never owned her, and had done so little with her except sit in a café, a hotel bar and a changing room.

Turning his back on the building he walked away. He didn't want to go to his room, didn't want to see Lance. He found a bar and sat there, agitated. He looked at a patch of soft, evening sunlight falling on the opposite wall; the shadow of the window's central strut and a hanging spider plant looking like a giant splash on a thick, dark horizon. He tried to imagine African light. Saw it blazing across vast spaces of cracked, red earth, across a splintered, inimical terrain.

He wondered about her, trying to grasp her personality. To him, now, it seemed elusive, like a slowly-moving quicksilver. There was a depth to her; she was shallow, attractive, ordinary, self-sufficient, dependent, a good fairy, a wicked witch.

He could feel himself getting angry. He strode across the road, hardly aware he was doing so. A car stopped a few feet short of him with a shrill of brakes. He was tempted to put a finger up to the driver, but couldn't bring himself to - his expression of rage was learned in the days of a different sign, his early conditioning loyal to that. Raising a fist and slapping his bicep, he gave the driver a *gesto dell' ombrello*.

He carried on walking. Another woman that had got away. Never mind, *non importa,* he would be in his new office in a few days. He would complete the first stages of his new commission then see what he could achieve in this ancient, new world.

# CHAPTER 21

He enjoyed his circus building. He visited the site weekly and more often when, after nearly a year, second fixings were virtually completed and the whole shape as well as its interior could be seen and appreciated, especially the ring itself and the spectator seats he'd had made from flexible glass. Between visits, as well as visiting the Marina where the very rich moored their boats and their sons indulged in offshore power boat racing, he looked at and inside some of the higher buildings. A few impressed him, certainly not all. But their seemingly unrestricted height did.

He passed the site downtown for the future Opera House. He'd been shown the CGI visualisations; it would look, utterly inappropriate, like a ship beached between two towers. He went to the Wild Wadi Water Theme Park, the long, swagged curve of the modern Beach Hotel which overlooked it having more interest for him than the water rides: the Faluj Fury, Wadi Twister, Falcon Fury, though he did indulge himself in a would-be relaxing ride along a blue water river in a shallow, inflatable plastic ring feeling a little self-conscious and his peace interrupted by the squeals and screams of energetic children.

He walked along Jumeirah Beach, seeing its buildings as maybe not quite so new now, even having a certain uniformity about their concrete finishes and shapes. He ate at Burj Al Arab Aquarium and watched the fish and other underwater creatures while sitting alone by the reinforced glass at a table for two. He thought of Rose for a brief second. He would have liked a woman's company; a meaningful one.

He visited large and rather grand restaurants, including the rest of the Italian ones, some movie theatres - he'd missed the international Film Festival - and went to a few museums and art exhibitions.

The UAEs' President, Khalifa bin Zayed Al Nahyan, had recently declared that he wanted Dubai to become the top tourist destination in the world. With what was there already and that which was coming including an already begun Downtown shopping mall with its twelve hundred shops which he hoped to become the most visited building on the planet, it could well happen.

By the time the circus was completed, just over a year after it had begun, he had moved to a larger suite of offices in the same block and increased his staff, leaving the choice of engineering-related employees to Lance again.

The topping-out ceremony was composed of a rather different demography to those he'd attended in Chicago and New York. Here, hijabs and burqas were seen but outnumbered by men's keftiyehs. Addulazaz couldn't himself attend, but it was pleasing for Piero that so many of the man's friends and associates did. He was glad Lance was there, especially in the restaurant afterwards, Lance more adept at socializing than himself.

The day after the ceremony he was introduced by the chief engineer of a firm that had done some work for Lance on the circus project to Sheik Hamad bin Rashid, a cousin to the crown prince of Dubai.

He was a large man, younger than Piero, and wearing the traditional ankle-length robe and headscarf. Led by the engineer, he came into the office and briefly shook Piero's hand before taking a quick glance around the interior with its usual wall-prints, photos and sketches of the architect's buildings, before telling him that he had been recommended to him by his friend, Addulaazaz.

'Incidentally, he apologises again for not being there yesterday to thank you personally but he is a most busy man, as am I. He is, as you are aware, pleased with the project.'

He gave an almost smirking smile and said, 'I also may have a job for you. It's rather a large one. Good day.'

Piero felt himself bending slightly forward from the waist as the man went out.

He hadn't heard of this person. He looked him up. He was forty and having a long career within the UAE government. He'd been to Cambridge where he'd read maths, then back to Dubai, eventually sharing with a brother the responsibility for controlling Dubai's state-owned ports. He also owned thoroughbred horses.

Piero wasn't really interested in the man's background. If he wanted a building designed, then depending on what was wanted, his ideas, the fee, the constraints - the less the better - he would create one for him.

He was, he supposed, thinking of images from an illustrated 'Arabian Nights' or the film of 'Lawrence of Arabia' when he accepted an invite to see Hamad Bin Rashid at his house in the Old Town, but it looked very different from those arched, ornate, pillared confections.

It was built in the traditional way around a courtyard with wooden cooling towers with not a plant in sight. It was bare inside too, with its greyish white walls and neither traditional furniture nor carpets. The wall photos added texture and interest, though not showing an Arabian past but skyscrapers, some in New York, mostly in Dubai.

This was all very different from Tern's overblown domestic scenery. Briefly thinking of him, his jokes and his often brash and loud company, Piero didn't miss him much.

The sheik was a rather light-coloured Arabian who, with his designer glasses and not wearing robes but a tailored, pale-grey suit, could have passed for someone born and raised in the West.

Piero accepted his offer of tea, thinking it was probably perceived here as ill-mannered amongst royalty, or near-royalty, to refuse a host's offerings. He was led through to an adjoining and equally bare room to be served by a girl wearing a long dress but just a light scarf, as if her boss was using her to show a compromise between the culture he was born into and the one he'd chosen.

Across a simple teak table, he told his guest that he had purchased a site and gained planning approval - his listener assuming that perhaps he'd meant 'bought' - for a project containing office and residential space and a hotel, the latter he wanted to be 'one of the highest in the world.'

'Can you handle this, Mister Ronzi?' he asked when he'd finished his summarised request.

Piero didn't wish to show his immediate enthusiasm, but it revealed itself when he replied rather loudly, 'Of course, of course.'

'Indeed, indeed,' said Rashid, smiling. 'I will take you to the site now.'

He asked Piero to follow him through the courtyard and out to a side street where a Bentley with a chauffeur standing almost to attention at its side awaited.

The drive was relatively silent except for the sheik mentioning his companion's New York building that he'd done for Tern and one in Chicago that he referred to, much to Piero's satisfaction, as 'The Lip.' Piero described, as best he could, his motivation for both designs. At one point, as he was about to answer a question, his hesitation was interrupted by the sheik saying, 'You are wondering if you should call me 'Your Sheikness' or something aren't you.'

Piero laughed. 'Yes, I was.'

'Call me Rashid. That is my name.'

The site was in a flat, derelict area but he could imagine the views it would afford over Business Bay Creek where he knew a large development plan was being prepared by UAE's Vice-President. He could, at a glance, see at least six high-rise buildings under construction. He conveyed this predictable observation to Rashid who, with a faraway look in his eyes, nodded sagely.

'I acquired this site rather cheaply, Mister Ronzi, and although Safa Park adjoins it, it will be neither in the Bay development nor Downtown, thus my building, which could well stand alone for a few years, will be more of a landmark, especially for those staying in the hotel. As you say, the views, eh?'

He told Piero he would send him his plans and ideas for the project as soon as he'd finalised a few things with an engineering firm who had, amongst half a dozen others, tendered a bid for the primary ground-working. Piero sensed that he would be working with a hands-on owner, which, though often meaning problems and a few tensions during construction, he felt would be a relatively smooth business.

It was. Rashid seemed happy from the beginning, when, after the designs, contractors and contracts had been arranged and signed, he stood with Piero at the edge of the site and watched as work on the shoring and piling began. This, using state-of-the-art structural techniques, would consume nearly fifty thousand cubic metres of concrete and almost five thousand tons of steel and take about hundred and forty thousand man hours to complete.

With a little help from Lance and a PR man he had hired part-time, Piero finalised the idea by showing Rashid the literature for the development.

'Designed by the architect Piero Ronzi, This 470-metre-tall edifice is strategically aligned to accentuate the view of Business Bay Creek on the south and the towers on the north. It will be an eye-catching (in retrospect he wished he hadn't used the cliché) hyperboloid skyscraper that flares out at the top and slightly resembles a crystal flower inspired by the Arabian rose.'

The latter was really motivated by Piero's rather reluctant pandering to his commissioner's sentimentalised wish, as if he felt guilty at his building's almost arrogant demarcation from its heritage.

'The graceful façade is clad in reflective glass... its 200-room hotel will be one of the highest hotels in the world. It will afford spectacular views and be one of the Emirate's defining landmarks and an iconic addition to the skyline.'

The two things Rashid wanted changing was the positioning of Piero's name, which he wanted to appear later in the text, and he'd noticed also that it had omitted mention that at its foot were fountains with jets and lights choreographed to music. He had also come up with a name for it: 'The Zenith.' Piero was expecting a name that was a little more Arabic.

The building took three and a half years from piling to pinnacle, a time in which the architect had begun and in some instances completed several smaller commissions: the almost inevitable blocks of low-rise apartments - two for Rashid - a frustratingly small shopping mall and, just outside the city's perimeters, a factory. He thought of a Rationalist's maxim, unsure who it was from: 'There is no beauty in architecture, only that which is formed for its function. The only beautiful building is a factory.'

He didn't try to incorporate the ideology of those words into this workshop, merely wanting it to be as light, both visually and in weight, as he could, which, because of the restraints of the specification, he annoyingly couldn't.

He wasn't told about the machines or their operatives, assuming they would be of the exploited variety. He thought of the subjective experience of the concept; if someone liked their job, even the person or group of people they were working for, how could they be 'exploited'?

Being unwell for a few days - some sort of 'Arab gyp' Lance had guessed - meant he couldn't be present at the topping-out ceremony. He was vomiting frequently on the day. He would have liked to have been there; feted and thanked. He did, however, read some reviews of The Zenith from architectural magazines. The Dubai Archdaily had stated:

'His strong conceptual awareness of nature's shapes appear as a source of inspiration... an attention to physical contexts and landscapes resulting in layered structures or powerful moving lines. Architecture as a seamless flow of energy and matter.'

This was more like it. Maybe he would, as Lance often suggested, read more of them. He had also brought to his attention that he could now use a virtual reality technology allowing him to 'walk around' a new building prior to its construction, an immersive experience to be used with headsets to enable a grasp of scale and to spot any problems with the structure, thus helping to avoid costly post-build alterations.

He arranged to see the device working and bought one to use for his next project. It brought up the increasing professional debate on 'hand-versus-computer.' For him it was, as he'd heard Americans say, a 'no brainer; his drawings every time, though he had, after presenting original sketches, ceded to the idea of CGI visualizations to show clients.

His next job, again offered by Rashid, was a mixed-use design in Business Bay and less tall than most of its existing and under-construction towers. He designed a hundred-metre atrium using an exoskeleton, or diagrid as Lance called it, uniting its two twisting sections containing ninety thousand square metres of office and residential space. There would be a faceted glass shopping centre in a podium at ground level straddling a newly-built subway tunnel.

Lance had solved the problems of building over the tunnel, and by this time had set himself up as an independent engineering firm, had his own office in the same block as Piero and although working steadfastly as ever for him, gained a rapidly increasing workload from other architect's practices. Piero was pleased for him.

He wasn't pleased, however, with a much-needed but tentative foray into transactional sex in a hot, sweaty un-air-conditioned out-of-town brothel whose address he'd got from a taxi driver; Piero still having little interest in learning to drive. Knowing that prostitution was illegal here, he was a little surprised when told of the rapidly increasing number of brothels in the current surge of sex tourism.

When ushered into a room in a nondescript, part-derelict building on the edge of industrial wasteland by a burqa-clad madam, undoubtedly wearing the garment not for religious reasons but to hide her identity, he was introduced to a girl in a black bikini who was Malaysian or Indonesian and who spoke immediately and quickly in a fragmented English he could barely understand.

He began undressing. When, at her request, he told her what his profession was, she responded with, 'You know Johnny the builder? He work in Business Bay. He my boyfriend. He big, strong man. He have lovely blond hair. He big man, very big man.'

Rapidly reversing the undressing, he gave her some money and left. As he did so, he heard her raised voice saying, 'Why you go? You come back. You no like Johnny?'

A few yards further on, he heard a window open and her again asking, 'Why you go, eh?'

He would stick to what he did best: his creations, ideas; his work.


The Business Bay job took almost three years from beginning to its end ceremony - a celebratory one where, present this time, he was duly feted, especially by Rashid who referred to him as 'The man who is helping to create this city's skyline.'

As satisfying as this was, Piero was beginning to feel unsettled. Although his office was fine, he was still renting his home, having not bothered to purchase one.

Maybe it was a need for changes of seasons, for a blossomed, fresh-green spring, for russet and gold autumnal leaves, a desire to sit in a comfortable atmosphere in a restaurant and for somewhere to sketch, colour, create in natural air rather than be immersed in a necessary but constant hum of air-conditioning that propelled him on his way to a return to England and its capital city.

Another factor was a building boom, assisted, it would seem, by a new and accommodating London mayor.

Rashid was disappointed when his architect informed him of what he was going to do but insisted he hold a farewell party for him. Piero told him that he wanted no fuss this time, merely a quiet drink with the man who'd helped him make a name for himself in this conspicuously thriving, heat-soaked tourist mecca.

They went to Massimo's - apparently it was one of Rashid's favourite eating places - where thoughts of Betty and their unsatisfactory promptings were dispelled when Piero was presented with a gift basket of exotic fruit, cheeses and a bottle of wine. Under its plastic bow-tied wrapper and lying on the fruit, was a limited edition Rolex. It was generous. The sheik was appropriately thanked.

Lance also was disappointed, but his own company was doing well, he felt more settled in the Middle East than his colleague and both of them knew that if either had a professional need for the other it would be satisfied.

Piero had been in Dubai for almost six years, rarely venturing far from it, though there had been visits to Abu Dhabi and Sharjah, even to Al Ain to look at a site for a small developer which had come to nothing. And although he had had ideas about working in Singapore which, he'd recently read, was the most open economy in the world, and Beijing, which was also currently in the midst of a building boom, he wished to return to London.

He had been in London for three weeks, staying at a west end hotel while looking around Richmond and Putney for a house, when he was asked to design a building in Newcastle. He knew little of the place except that it was the most populous city in the North East, was known for its shipbuilding, coal mines, the wool trade, and had two universities.

Whilst travelling to the site, not far from a large quay, though predictably not interested in the Georgian buildings on it, he quite enjoyed the Tyne Salmon cubes and, from a distance, the Millenium Bridge, though the former was rather small-time. The CEO of the development company was young and wanted something noticeable, something that stood out from the skyline.

Piero created an almost thirty-degree-leaning circular shape with purple-finished steel with each curved storey slightly smaller than its counterpart immediately beneath. The whole thing was supported by deep piles of finished steel struts. Apparently it had been nicknamed by the locals 'The Flying Saucer Building.'

He suggested to the developers that, because they had the same initials as himself - Pearson Rogers - that he brick them into the steel on the upper level. They were pleased for him to do so, especially when he slightly reduced his fee. He never intended for the letters to be clear cut, but able to be seen as other things; the ambiguity appealed to him. He'd even gone to the top floor himself and for a while watched a bricklayer working on it.

Having no desire for living in this area, he leased some offices in London's west end soon after purchasing a house by the Thames on the edge of Richmond. It had been left to run down and he intended to build a glass and steel extension into its rear garden, at the end of which he toyed with the idea of mooring a boat.

Before the Newcastle job had been completed, a young, keen development company had eagerly discussed with him a project in Kings Cross. He had hired someone to help with the visualisations from his usual watercolour drawings which were received enthusiastically.

Using a little self-plagiarising and the usual distant help from Lance in Dubai, he took the basic shape of the 'fat air-craft' building he'd designed in Chicago, narrowing the tips of the 'wings' slightly but this time raising them off the ground and making more and smaller windows which, he supposed, could be said to look like a bird's beak. For the exterior he had used two colours fused into each other.

He had begun sketching ideas for a project he'd been asked to do at the edge of a cemetery a little to the north of the City. It would, he determined, be tall, cylindrical and smooth, almost pole -like.

On the top floor would be a large, curved dome; a kind of atrium, and again another piece of exoskeleton engineering from Lance who he'd been in touch with regularly. He liked to see it as life arising from death. He toyed with the idea of call-ing it 'The Phoenix.'

# CHAPTER 22

They had been thinking of getting married, she a little more so perhaps. Liam had looked up a concise definition. He quoted it to her and said, ''wedlock' is in the definition and if you look up 'wedlock' you'll find 'marriage.' All definitions are tautologies.'

It was typical of him. So was his interest in the city and their walks around it. They'd spent most Sundays for the last few months doing it; passed Georgian houses, magnolia gardens and magic mews, gazed at steepled skylines, laughed and occasionally playfully argued around Hampstead and Highbury, Pimlico and Putney, and strolled the Thames to Henley and the Lea Navigation from Limehouse Cut to Ware.

He would point out the glint of sun on a London canal, forsythia hanging over a Victorian window in Hampstead, the curved Art Deco windows of a Chelsea apartment block, a steeple rising above chestnut trees and a teenage Sloane guiding her horse gently over Kensington cobbles. She told him that he had brought her into his world. He was glad.

Soon after they'd first met, she remembered him remarking on her grey-blue eyes, wide cheekbones and dark brown hair, telling her that he hadn't recognised her accent, then noting the slight stress on penultimate syllables and the not quite trilling 'r', he'd taken a chance and said, ' I think you maybe from northern Italy. It's the eyes, really. *Non ho capito, no parla Italiana, mi dispiace,'* he'd said, impressing her a little, until he'd confessed, 'Sorry, that's all l know. I just mimic.'

They had decided that perhaps living together may be better, though both were aware that her mother would rather frown on the idea. Liam had told Mary that most couples who lived together eventually wed anyway and she'd happily agreed to cohabit. She wasn't sure whether he would want her to live with him at his place or if he'd sell up and find somewhere new for them. The decision could wait.

As it was the beginning of her last year she had a long assignment to write and decided it would be on the effect of certain aspects of the man-made environment on individuals and families. She'd had a discussion with Liam which she thought would be brief but went on for a while, especially his explanation of its deterministic links with social class.

The course tutor was keen on students speaking to the people involved, the methodological weaknesses of anecdotal evidence he tended to ignore. But instead of focusing on those that were directly affected she wanted to ask questions of the creators. Liam had suggested she talked to people at the RIBA offices. She'd arranged to do so.

The person she was to interview a week later told her, as he invited her into his office, that he could spare only a few minutes because a 'top architect' would be there shortly and that the man's time was precious.

'Maybe,' he smiled, 'if he takes a liking to you he may even speak to you.'

As he said this there was a sharp knock on the door. It opened. A man entered. He was tall and tanned with rather long grey hair waved at the back. The man behind the desk stood and walked towards him, hand outstretched.

'Afraid I'm rather new here, that's why I haven't met you before. I'm so pleased to do so now. This lady,' he gestured towards her, 'has come to ask questions about the impact on people of what we do. Rather broad-ranging I'm afraid, but perhaps if you have time later today and she narrows the context, you could answer some things for her?'

The incomer glanced at her briefly without interest, nodded, forced the tiniest of smiles and said, 'Maybe.'

She began to feel uncomfortable. She wasn't cognisant immediately that it was something other than feeling a little shy in the presence of men she hadn't met before. The person she'd come to see suggested that they may see her in the restaurant later.

'Around one o'clock perhaps. Bye.'

The architect stepped away to allow her to pass him then closed the door behind her.

She found the eating place on the ground floor, sat and tried to go through her prepared questions, to narrow them down, elicit more contained answers. She found it difficult, she kept thinking of the man with the long grey hair. Eventually she finished her editing.

There was a noise, the restaurant door swung open and the tall, grey-haired man, with a bevy of people around him, entered. They were laughing, their voices loud. He was laughing too, his white teeth contrasting with the colour of his skin, his accent more discernibly Italian. They sat at a table, a waiter immediately coming across to them with a mock bow and saying, 'Good afternoon, Mister Ronzi. Welcome.'

Food was ordered.

She watched them eat. She'd never really enjoyed watching people consuming food, she felt they should either eat or talk, not both at once. In his open-necked linen shirt and tailored jacket he was the centre of attraction; sometimes the others appeared to be clamouring for his attention alone. She sat there, giving her questionnaire a last, brief appraisal.

She heard someone say his first name. Then it came back to her, almost overwhelmingly at first. She steadied herself and attempted to recall exactly when she had first heard it.

It had been referred to by a relative, an aunt from the old country when she had visited her and her mother in London. She'd been a young teenager then and had dressed up in her room with a new skirt and had come downstairs to show them and stopped outside the parlour to adjust it.

She had heard her aunt say, 'I thought you may have been over it by now, it was along time ago. But you will in time. The man was bad, Chiara. I never liked that side of the family.'

She'd spoken in Italian, but Mary had understood; her mother had made sure that her daughter would speak her own language as well as English.

Looking through the gap between door and frame, she'd seen her mother's face looking strained and apprehensive. Then it was hidden by her aunt as she went towards her.

'It will go, it will pass,' she was saying. 'He touched you, he ravished you, enjoyed you. It wasn't your fault. *Cristo,* you were fifteen, girl, how are you to blame? He was your cousin, you trusted him; he was family. You will be completely strong again, *ancora forte.'*

She couldn't understand it then, but gradually, sporadically began to, promising herself that she would one day tell her mother about the overheard words and ask what they had meant. The day after her eighteenth birthday, she had, standing inside the same door she had been outside of when first hearing them.

Her mother, sitting and looking across the room at her, told her that she had never wanted her to know, but would tell her now.

'I was, I don't know what it's called these days, 'despoiled' is it? No, that's a silly word. I don't want to use the real word. But I was very young and... ' She hesitated for a while then continued.

'It was my cousin, your uncle. He was older than me and we were friends. We were just...' She looked down. 'I didn't know what was happening really, till it was too late. I thought we were friends. We...' She looked up again. 'It wasn't my fault, Maria.' She rarely used her Italian name, except at home.

She stood and went to her daughter and hugged her.

'It's alright now. It was a long while ago. I try to forget it and almost succeed, and I want you to as well. We will speak no more of it. Yes?'

Mary had whispered *'Si'* in her ear and left to see her friends.

The subject being closed hadn't stopped her thinking of it. She imagined a fifteen-year old girl in her cousin's home, perhaps listening to a record with him, maybe laughing together and continuing their merriment as he asked her to come upstairs to his room to show her something.

She didn't wish to think in details. Her mother had once told her, and only once, that when coming to this country she had changed her name from Jiordano to Jordan to make them appear more English.

Mary knew that they didn't have to come here, all this way from home, but her grandparents had been offered jobs in England in a west London hotel, he as a *maitre d'*, she in charge of the cleaners, and had accepted. Her mother had married a Londoner who had left her a month before Mary had been born.

Her daughter had been unconvinced by the 'appearing more English' version as she knew how fiercely proud of being Italian her parent was, so much so that she had refrained from giving her daughter her father's name and had reverted to her maiden one.

She had known the real reason then. It was shame, a shame that had been forced onto her, on the innocent. Her mother had mentioned the cousin's name, but she hadn't remembered it, nor had she after hearing it from her aunt for the first time. She recognised now that a protective part of her hadn't wanted to. Her mother's face had twisted into a moment of bitterness when she'd spoken it.

She had often wondered whether her father had left because he'd found out what had happened. It seemed that everyone else had, though she wasn't sure whether the *polizia* had. Perhaps people had shunned her mother, vilified her, as if she was the wrongdoer, not the victim. There was so much she didn't know.

She looked across to the table again. The man's companions got up, shook his hand, enthusiastically wished him well and left.

He finished his coffee, wiped his lips with a napkin, stood and glanced at her. He frowned a little and walked away. Then he stopped and came over to her.

'Excuse me. You remind me of someone. I don't know who though, but there's a likeness.'

He made a quick gesture with an index finger touching his thumb in front of his face. *'Decisamente.* What's your name? Do you mind telling me?'

She didn't want him standing over her, or be near him. She said nothing.

'You do mind then. But there really is such a likeness. Are you going to tell me?'

She felt frightened. She reluctantly told him.

'It's Mary Jordan.'

His face was without expression for a few seconds then he spoke slowly.

'You have an Italian accent, though you've obviously been here for some time.'

He looked at her with more intensity.

'Not Jiordano?'

She didn't want to answer him, but if it would make him go away, she would.

'Yes,' she said, hardly hearing herself.

He bent nearer to her. She moved her chair away.

'I'm sorry, I want to go now.'

With a peripheral awareness she realised that there was nobody in the restaurant. It was probably closing, or had closed. No staff were to be seen, not even putting chairs on tables. Perhaps they didn't do that here.

She stood, and as she did, recalled the name. She knew now why she didn't want his proximity. Liam had talked recently of a friend saying that the unconscious was a good thing, it senses, intuits, it warns us, protects us. It was doing so now. But it was consciously that she wished to scream.

She put her hands in front of her groin almost automatically then clenched them. She wanted to push them hard between her legs, her knuckles almost penetrating her.

'I know about you, you're the man who - '

She could hear herself screeching.

She wanted to run out of the building. She calmed herself. Nothing was going to harm her. She wasn't her mother, they weren't in Italy.

'Now you know I'm somebody to do with your family,' her voice was quavering a little before becoming firmer, 'what do you want to say then? 'Sorry,' perhaps? The man in the office said if you took a liking to me you would speak to me. Do you like me? Do you fancy me? Maybe you want to do what you did to my moth - '

'Shut up. *Sta zito!* he demanded loudly. 'Go away.'

In a more measured tone he said, 'I shouldn't have asked you.' Then louder again, 'I do not want to see you, ever. Ever. *Capisci?'*

He turned and strode away, flinging a hand backwards dismissively.

'Aren't you going to rape *me* now?' she shouted.

He slammed the door behind him.

She stood there looking at the closed door for a while then sat again. She was in conflict: shock, pain, anger. She wanted to weep and simultaneously smash something, preferably his head; cleave it, slice his testicles, do something.

After a short, emotional confusion, a kind of inert congealment of her feelings, she vowed she wouldn't tell her mother that this man was here in this city. Never. She left the building.

# CHAPTER 23

He was walking along a road somewhere north of the City - not sure of its name and not really caring - feeling pretty good as he looked back over his career while gazing around at Edwardian villas, which he found, with their red bricks and gables, trusses and scrolls, rather miserable and imposing. He didn't wish to sit down to do his thinking, just wanted to walk; he had the energy.

He'd had a few setbacks, some negative incidents, but mostly good happenings. He was aware that it was a contradiction in terms, but he had made his own luck. Tern had been right.

There had been a problem with a building he'd designed which had reached the first storey when it and the surrounding land was bought by a rival developer and had been demolished, a larger, higher structure taking its place.

More recently, a crane working on a construction of his that was almost completed, had damaged part of it resulting in a fatality on an adjacent site. Both contractor and crane operative were blamed in the eventual court case. The judge had, apparently, remarked in an aside that perhaps there was too much reliance on computers in designing, but confessed this was merely the view of 'an intelligent layman.'

Piero hadn't read much about the details of the case. It was unfortunate, but he knew it wasn't his design or the engineering. If the builder chose to cut corners on expertise or materials then that was regrettable, as long as it was clear to everyone that it couldn't possibly have been a design fault. *Non e colpa mia.* A minor blemish, really.

Another was a small venture as a developer himself along with two partners, one of whom had been a fellow student in London with him and had got in touch to ask if he would, for a fee, lend his name to a project involving the demolition of an east London church and replacing it with a residential leisure complex which they had designed themselves.

It was denied planning permission, partly due, they'd told him, to protests at a meeting in the church where an apparently deranged Marxist had had his persuasive say. He had also lent his illustriously growing nomenclature as well as his expertise - suggesting design changes, more curves, and an increased area of glass - to another high-rise east London development.

Apparently, there had been a large email petition and 'moans,' as he tended to call objections to any building he was associated with, at a planning permission meeting in the local Town Hall. The project had gone ahead.

A minor experience in Dubai with am African woman meant little now and wasn't related to his career anyway. Nor was an incident a few months ago, involving another crazy person dragging up a past relationship, anything to do with his chosen profession.

He was becoming rich. Not like Tern of course - who, he'd heard, was thinking of running for Governor of Illinois, a coincidence in that he'd helped to design the building he would govern from - but he now had his Thames-side boat, had spent a holiday in Nassau in a hotel on the golden sands of Cable Beach, done a little gambling at the Crystal Palace Casino, even won a little money, and had himself some fine dining. There hadn't been much Italian cuisine on offer.

The style of most of the buildings in the city centre was of European descent which hadn't interested him, or the obviously limited scope for development; there wasn't the feel of real money there.

He had also gone to Singapore, and after seeing the Tanjong Pagar Centre, Republic Plaza and Marina Bay buildings, many of them exempted from height restrictions, he'd wished he had gone there to create his own edifices. But it wasn't too late.

But all this was in the past. He was now on his way to receive the Pritzker Architecture Prize. His energy was coming from this. He'd always remembered its definition, effortlessly, word for word:

'Awarded annually to honour a living architect whose built work demonstrates a combination of those qualities of talent, vision and commitment which has produced significant contributions to humanity and the built environment through the art of architecture.'

This was worth more than the RIBA Gold, and it had finally happened, and he knew why he'd been awarded it. He saw it almost as a Dubai retrospective.

It was a rather formal letter informing him that he had won this year's prize. Twelve days previously he'd been told that he'd made it onto the short list and was wondering whether it would end there and he would fall short of the ultimate recognition, the hoped-for legacy. He had composed a speech, rehearsed it silently and remembered every word.

He would begin by saying good evening to any notables that were there - he would enquire beforehand who they were - then talk of his happiness, pride, humility and respect, the latter especially tor the Prizker family for so generously supporting and bringing attention to architecture. He had decided not to thank the jury members.

'I recognise,' he would say, 'that I love to dream and love to build. For me, architecture is the art of materializing dreams throughout a long journey, and on this journey I have tried to pursue architecture that contains the whole universe. It hasn't been easy but my ambition was to awaken emotions in the people who live in the spaces I create, to become conscious of their experience, to transcend the established, to arrive at new and unexpected results.'

He would continue: 'Architecture is like music, but less ephemeral, it is like poetry but more prosaic. All this because I want to feel and to make others feel. It is a huge part of my life and I offer it to others.'

He wondered if it was a little too much. No. It would do.

He had decided to leave some hours earlier than the time stated for the ceremony at the Haslett Hotel to look at his latest building, not, of course, as high as the Zenith, but still the sixth highest in London. It was the usual mix of office and residential contained in a six-hundred-and-forty-foot edifice, but with a dome-like atrium at the top engineered by Lance.

He had plenty of time. He was taking a detour. He hadn't been to it since the topping-out. He could see the top of it in the distance. He went into a café to finish off his retrospection and to enjoy a celebratory coffee.


Mary, having finished her last, rather unsatisfactory assignment, as well as her course and busy applying for social work jobs, wasn't with Liam when he went into a café in Highbury. In the two days between completing one sub-contract and beginning another. He had been wandering around bits of North London; had ventured into Hampstead and Keats Grove, Belsize Park and its Art Deco flats and now, feeling a need for caffeine, walked between tubs of miniature trees surrounding the entrance and into its pleasant green and white interior. He ordered at the counter and sat.

There was only one other customer. Having nothing to read, Liam looked at him: tanned, tall, slim and well-dressed, a cane resting against his chair. He thought he looked rather old, before wondering why he saw people with grey hair as aged when he was beginning to go grey himself. It was hot, everything seemed sticky: the table was, the sun on the pavements, the leaves on the plane tree outside.

Liam protruded his upper lip so he could blow his breath onto the front of his neck to cool it, while the man he was looking at hadn't removed his jacket nor used the neatly-folded breast pocket handkerchief to wipe any perspiration from his forehead.

He went to the counter again to ask where the toilets were and noticed that the man was looking at a copy of the Architectural Review.

When he returned from the toilet he casually said as he passed him, 'Like buildings do you?'

'Some of them,' the man answered without looking up.

'What sort?' Liam asked a little provocatively.

The man looked at his enquirer rather lazily.

'Those that gets reviews like, 'The lilting serenity of his best buildings can almost make you believe we live in a civilized world.''

'If included in that is the idea that a city is a test of civilization, maybe, but should a buildings be 'serene?''

'What should buildings be then?'

'There is no 'should' really is there, but I have a feeling that the buildings I like, you wouldn't. I'm assuming we have a different aesthetic.'

'If you are going to say that yours would be a better one, then what I'll say is that we don't know what we have to presuppose to settle an aesthetic matter. You can talk of craftsmanship, perhaps that's one of your chief criteria, intentionality, size and shape obviously, environmental impact, whatever, but they rest on opinion, culturally or subjectively, if they can be separated.'

'Would you mind if I joined you?' Liam asked.

The response was a rather slow, weary gesture of a hand towards a chair opposite. Liam went to the table he'd been occupying, brought his coffee over and sat.

'I could be wrong, but I assume you're a fan of modern architecture and you've heard criticisms before about the lack of feeling for its immediate surroundings, the lack of congruence. You defend them, though I haven't made them yet, with phrases I suspect you've often reiterated. Am I right?'

'Perceptive of you.'

'You're right in that there's no absolute here, I agree with what you say, but my likes and dislikes are part of *my* value system.'

The man seemed to smile a little patronisingly as he sipped his coffee, and said, 'And they are?'

As he waited for an answer he looked at his watch.

'I want to look at something, a building' - he glanced quickly at Liam - 'It's not that far. You can walk with me if you wish. I'm Piero.'

Liam shook his hand, told him his name, drained his cup and walked out with him.

He looked around him. The sun was bright, radiating from white stucco, gleaming from windows, filling them with light, sharpening slate roofs, reflecting from brass door knockers, lighting up confidently overgrown front gardens

'So, what sort of buildings do you like then? Period stuff?'

Liam told him. 'I call them Eddie, Georgie and Vicky. I think that - '

'You see them as your friends?'

'Guess so.'

'But they're old, the past. Spiky, blotty things with bits stuck on, over-designed, elaborated, not a whole thing, parts of different things in one thing.'

Liam felt annoyed. 'How can you say that? Look around you.'

He waved an arm around him as if offering the street to the man.

'Look at the shape of the houses, that palm, the monkey puzzle tree against the window, that veranda, the, the - '

'Are you going to mention a camomile lawn somewhere? 'Why do you want to live in the past? Is it some sort of fantasized picture of golden days? Ladies and gentlemen strolling in period costumes, dresses, suits... a soft-focus haze of sunlight, moonbeams, nostalgia, a time that never was? You're a purist, a perfectionist, aren't you. Why? Are you that insecure? Most perfectionists are. Do you wish to escape from reality *that* much?'

As his voice rose; the accent becoming more noticeable, it reminded Liam of Mary's.

'You probably hate old buildings being torn down, whatever condition they're in, to make way for new ones. It may bother you, but a city has no memory. I imagine you cannot tolerate asymmetrical buildings; you cannot tolerate asymmetry in any-thing really, can you. Perhaps,' he said, smiling, 'because *you* are not symmetrical, you're not balanced.'

Liam didn't answer.

'The periods, those arbitrarily defined bits of time you love so much, are the past. Comforting aren't they, eh? An imag-ined golden age of pure, untrammelled perfection, of days now gone. Why don't you write a fucking ode to them, eh?' *una poesia del passato.'*

It felt, for Liam, like being at the receiving end of an analy-sis by an amateur psychotherapist. He let him continue.

'You get all misty-eyed when you see some little detail you fancy, do you? A Roman swag or something, that little galleon in lead and glass in a front door, all that stucco. Into curved windows are we? I'm sorry if that's true, but... '

He shrugged; a sarcastic smile on his face.

'Maybe you're looking for a family, didn't like your own one, eh? Families are important are they not? The preference for familiarity is so universal that some think it must be written into our genetic code from back when our ancestors trawled the savannah. You're exposed to something, it becomes famil-iar; family. It's survival. If you recognise an animal or plant, then it hasn't killed you yet.'

'That's the historical residue argument, that a brief case is really a Neanderthal club.'

'You're digressing, perhaps we both are. You're wallowing in the familiarity of the past: Georgian, Edwardian, etcetera, so much so that anything different from the structures of those times you immediately dislike. Do you feel they're going to kill you: the different, the new; the revolutionary? Maybe the buildings of the past are your idealised family, a compensation perhaps for the one you had to live with; a 'new' one better than the old. Yes?'

'No, but I imagine that's what you prefer with buildings.'

'But to... stagnate, stay in that which was, is all rather tepid and regressive isn't it? Modern buildings breathe new life into a city.'

'They're just context-free digital shape-making. Surely you see that trophy buildings undermine the historic character of wherever they're built.'

''Historic character' I find a rather loathsome phrase. Without wanting something new, without drive, desire, greed if you like, we wouldn't have got, say, the 'Shard.''

'The Shard is financial capital's greatest achievement over the imagination. It persuades us that there is no alternative. It's no great strain to see it as a cathedral to the inescapable expectational norm of profit. It's saying, 'Fuck you, London.''

'I doubt whether New Yorkers in the Thirties thought the Empire State was saying that to their city; nor even Parisians about the Eiffel Tower.'

'It exists because of a lack of a strategic plan for the city. It's about the commodification of the property market, the steroid thrust of a chaotic skyline. It's about conspicuous consumption and extravagant spectacle. Governments now will only back something that can be seen from outer space.' Liam could feel himself becoming angry.

'It's a sugar rush of architecture based on bluster and the instant icon. An 'icon' was once a religious symbol. What d'you think of churches? Cluttering up the floor of your canyons, getting in the way of serious money? It's architects tosh isn't it. Vanity lives. What of squares and mansion blocks? And don't talk about towers providing high-density living; terraces can house more people than the space occupied by isolat-

ed slabs. London was the result of the conjoining of many villages, now it's turned into Dallas. It's an amorphic mass with a
skyline for sale to the highest bidder.'

He could see the man looking down as they were walking,
half smiling, shaking his head slightly.

Liam continued. 'You know, I can see a future for London
as a cyberpunk hellscape, a lurid, neon-lit skyscraper-infested
conglomeration framed from above by gigantic advertising
holograms and multi-level motorways.'

His listener, who again wasn't listening, had stopped.

He had seen it; a lot closer now, in between rows of link
houses. The sun was hitting one side of it. Liam halted too,
looking at him, frowning.

The man increased his pace the few yards to the end of the
street and said, 'Here it is. This is what I wanted to show you.
Look.' He pointed towards it.

Liam looked up to see a phallus-like building filling and
wasting the air in front of him, hanging, brooding and menacing, bullying the cemetery lying near its base. It was like a female Satan's masturbatory fantasy. The monstrosity had risen
and now, faceless and depressing, towered over terraced
streets, utterly dismissive of the beautiful and harmonious. He
thought of Cobbett's name for London: 'The Great Wen, a
pathological swelling on the face of the nation.'

This building was more than that. It was a hideous protru-
sion on the swelling. He felt a fear almost, like a childhood
dream of something about to attack him, destroy him, perhaps.
'Nearly everything we fear we would like to destroy to rid ourselves of,' Clive had once said to him. Liam wished to do so
with the awful edifice in front of him.

Instead, he said, 'Do architects ever look at what's adjacent
to their buildings, do you think? Is their narcissism so great
that the proximity becomes a fog, a blank space with nothing
there *but* their creation?'

The man turned to him.

'Let me guess what you would call it. Something like, 'An ugly proxy-penile tower overshadowing a cemetery.' Am I right? And what would it be saying then, 'Fuck the dead?''

Liam felt angry. It was the anger of seeing monstrous structures wherever he seemed to be, but it was more than that. It was about his father and the cramped, mean, treeless streets of his infancy and youth; the sterile nothingness, the estrangement, alienation. It was all so strong, filling him, he felt his insides clench.

He wanted revenge on all that, and thought of something Clive had told him about babies wanting to be taken over, ravished by their fathers.

'Of course babies can't think,' he'd said, 'they have pictures in their heads, but I think there's an early desire to be fucked by their fathers. Okay, it's contentious, but are you going to say that it's disgusting? It's a feeling and, if I'm right, an ontological fact, and you can't put a feeling into an evaluative sphere.'

It was ammunition against this man.

'It could be saying 'Fuck *you*.' He almost blurted it out. 'Is that why you like it? Do you want to be fucked by it?'

He felt instantly embarrassed. The man would take no notice, wouldn't understand him. It was on the emotional level of a child's 'na-na-nanana.'

'There's the sort of stuff you like over there,' his non-listener was saying, pointing with his cane this time.

'You can see it's fairly new, but it's obviously meant to look old. Why do they bother?'

It was a brick building with a life-size brick relief of two figures on the outside of the second floor mid-way between two windows.

'*Cristo,* it should never have been given building permission, especially that ridiculous religious-looking thing up there. The whole thing's a waste of time and space, too flat, too low. An opportunity missed; a step back into the past.'

He walked over and tapped on the bricks with his cane.

'Look at these awful colours, the texture, it seems so primitive. Bricks. Why? Okay if you have a fetishistic love of bricks I suppose.'

The building should have represented a little aesthetic relief for Liam, but it didn't. Spotting a rare public toilet some forty metres away, he excused himself, saying he wouldn't be long.


It was three years ago almost to the day, and he still missed him. Not just on the job, but at any time really: looking out of a bus window at a brick-built house - he'd left London soon after the accident and was now working locally - watching the telly, reading a newspaper, travelling to a Toon game, or even if he saw something that was approximately trowel-shaped. Con didn't mention him much, but he was aware that she thought of him with sadness. Her brother was now looking after their mother, which was something positive, he supposed.

When they made sporadic visits to the local theatre, he came away still having vague thoughts about writing a play. It would be set in his home town and be full of Geordies, and, of course, be an anti-capitalist show.

Maybe he could set it back in the town's shipbuilding days or even in the times of its wool or mining industries, or maybe bring it up-to-date and have the Great Northern Run as a background. Perhaps he could have a Polish brickie in it somewhere, maybe he could somehow eulogise him.

It was holiday time and Jim had suggested they go to London again and spend more time looking at some places they hadn't seen before: maybe go to The Eye, walk around the whispering gallery in St. Paul's; watch the changing of the guards at Buckingham Palace. Cliched, but might as well go to the places you're supposed to.

He'd like to see the Toon play the Gunners at the Emirates but doubted if he could get a ticket now, and he knew it wouldn't be fair on Con to leave her on her own, unless of course he gave her a wad of cash and let her loose on Oxford Street.

They came down and stayed at an Airbnb place in Stepney, Con still thinking organising trips via a computer was new-fangled. They saw the 'should' things, and a few that weren't, like having a look at the Battersea Power Station development - Con finding a cafe she enjoyed while he went round it as quickly as he could - and watched a rather old movie about bricklayers in the Sixties in London. They saw a romantic comedy in the same cinema the next day to please her, and went for a random walk along the side of an urban canal.

They walked under a grafitti'd bridge, saw ,surprisingly, someone fishing, and enjoyed looking at the narrow-boats and reading their names, there were even two Geordie ones: 'Aareet Bonny Lass' and 'Bumble Kite.'

Then the place began looking familiar to him, and he re-membered the job he'd worked on not long before. Thomasz had been with him. If his memory was accurate, they could walk there.

'I wan' yer to see summat,' he said to his wife. 'You'll have to bear wi' me, but I'm almost sure it's just along from these canal steps.'

They went up them, he sure that she wouldn't mind his in-dulgence; she'd often taken pleasure in his craftsmanship.

'Ah, it'll be there.'

He grabbed her hand and walked across a cobbled area and around the corner of a brick building towards another.

'This is the one. Look oop a bit. See 'em? They're the ones I told yer about, the statue things. I really enjoyed doin' 'em.'

'I know, I recognise 'em.'

They walked towards them, he was still feeling pleased about working on them.

Then he noticed two people on his left walking towards what he was looking at. One of them, he taller, older one, was pointing at the building with a cane and speaking about planning permission, and gesticulating and saying that it was a waste of time. He was saying something about a fetish with bricks and religious figures. He wasn't quite sure what it was about, what was going on, but they were *his*, his special bits. Then the other man said something and went off somewhere.

Perhaps he was some sort of modern artist or architect or something that didn't care for this 'ancient' stuff, couldn't understand why it was copied. He watched him move along the front of the building, occasionally tapping his stick on the brickwork.

Who did he think he was? Who was he to rubbish his work? Jim began to walk towards him. Con reached forward and grabbed his hand.

'Leave it, mun. I heard him too. He's a crazy old man, it's not worth it. Look, take a pic of it with yer phone. Just take it and we'll go. Quickly.'

He stood there, his hands clenched. She took the phone from his pocket, unclenched a fist and pushed the phone into it.

'I know we've already got a picture of it, but take it. Let's go.'

He hesitated then took a picture. Standing there still, he continued looking at the man. Just then the other person came back and joined him.

Pulling her husband towards her, she said, 'I want us to have a really good meal this evenin', somewhere posh-like, get this out o' yer system. We leave tomorrer and I want this to be a good memory. Alreet?'

He didn't answer.

'Alreet?'

'Yeh, sure lass. Let's go then.'

She put her arm familiarly in his and they went off to find a place which, hopefully, had haggerty and saveloy dip and perhaps, somehow, they could find some stotties. He could certainly do with a pint of broon.

Liam had been trying to remember a Le Corbousier saying. It began with: 'You employ stone, wood and concrete and with these materials … '

He couldn't recall the rest. He went back to the man. He was looking at his watch again.

'I've got time, and you have also. Forget what you think of the building, let's go to the top, you'll enjoy the view, look at London from a different angle.'

Liam looked up at the construction again. Despite himself he would go to the top and point out some more architectural atrocities to the man.

'It certainly isn't Le Corbusier is it,' he said aloud as they made their way towards it. 'What was his phrase? 'You employ stone, wood - '

'And you build houses and palaces; that's construction. Ingenuity is at work. But suddenly you touch my heart, you do me good. I am happy and I say: This is beautiful. This is architecture.'

'I'm surprised you know it.'

'It was drummed into us at architecture school. I try to forget it.'

They walked silently towards the building then through the featureless glass doors of its entrance, across a stark steel and glass foyer and into a lift with steel doors. There weren't many people about, the lift occupied by just the two of them. Piero pressed Floor 44. They said nothing on the upward journey.

They stepped out onto a white marble floor with the sun flooding it through the steel and glass dome above them. Piero led the way to a door which opened onto a circular, railed balcony and leaned over it.

'This atrium is not too far off the area of the dome of St. Paul's.'

He looked behind him at Liam.

'Come and look at the view.'

Liam stood behind him and looked at the city. They both started walking around the balcony, seeing more of the metropolis and the surrounding counties.

'Hardly territories of beauty,' more a storm of contextual coincidences. 'It's becoming another Lego town.'

Piero stopped and bent over the rail.

'The man who designed this building you seem to hate so much, is, as was once said, 'A lover of new forms of light,' and once designed a building described as a 'glass of translucent air riding above the city.'

'How come then that he manages the feat of being simaltaneously lavish, dull, and offensive? I'm sorry, Piero, but if there wasn't so much crap about it would be a disgrace to the skyline, It's - '

'I really don't think you should talk to Mister Ronzi like that.'

''To'? Don't you mean 'about.' Perhaps you should try harder with your English.'

'No. I mean 'to.' I am the architect. I am Piero Ronzi. And the quote I gave you earlier related to *my* work. And this building,' he held out a hand, palm upwards, 'is called The Phoenix.'

Liam couldn't quite understand what had just been said and looked around him again, imagining the towers he saw were on a plaque at a high vantage point somewhere where the tallest buildings in the city were numbered and a name guide etched below.

He looked at the man again and recalled where he'd seen him before, though he wasn't wearing spectacles then or carrying a cane, the latter, he guessed, an affectation.

It was at the Architectural Association, and his photo had been on the developers' brochure at the church he'd made his speech at and, of course, on the leaflets at the Town Hall meeting he'd attended.

'I know you. I've seen you before.'

Liam told him about the Association's offices, the church; the Town Hall.

'You weren't that crazy Marxist I heard about at the church, were you?'

It was said with an amused sneer.

And then Liam was filled with Mary, strained and angry, needing to tell someone about her mother, her words bludgeoning him. He thought of the meetings on the religious course they'd been to, the deep morality, *her* morality, and now... this. They'd been walking along a quiet suburban street in Ealng.

He deflected it, tried to intellectualize, academicize it and thought of Clive's comments on incest, though could it be such if there wasn't consent? He'd mentioned that, in some cultures, brother and sister marriages were permissible and that amongst ancient Egyptian royalty, marriages to cousins were allowed; but in most societies it was a taboo.

But Mary's tale - he'd felt while she was relating it that it was a kind of confession - had nothing to do with marriage. He thought of the simplicity of Shakespeare's, 'There is nothing neither good nor bad, but thinking makes it so.'

They had stopped outside a privet-hedged house.

'My name should have been Maria, Maria Jiordano; my mother's maiden name. She didn't want any connections with the past.' Then, quietly, 'Sometimes she calls me Maria, though.'

She'd looked at him, her voice rising.

'Am I more exotic now? Do you love me more? Am I more sexy?'

She'd then begun to cry.

'I shouldn't have told you, should I, but he was her cousin.'

'Well, it's not an absolute that blood relations - '

'Stop making it so academic,' she'd shouted. 'I it happed to my mother.'

He'd held her tightly and told her he was sorry. She had then told him the man's name and of her recent meeting with him.

Liam and Piero were both silent, the former now having more to understand, to process. This man in front of him who... He remembered seeing a photo in a newspaper of the man's car, a large black Mercedes with a chauffer beside it. There'd been a tiny figure dangling behind the windscreen which, to Liam, now seemed to turn into Mary, though it was probably just a swinging Barbie doll or even an air freshener. He had no idea why he'd remembered it.

He knew nether what to say or do.

Then he blurted, 'You not only want to fuck up skylines but your cousin as well.'

For a brief moment the imagined the words as a sword thrust into the man's sternum.

'Did you want her as a boy? You couldn't do it though, it wasn't right, was it. All around you your mates were getting away with all sorts of things; stealing, bunking in the pictures or whatever. But you couldn't have what *you* wanted, your cousin, you couldn't get away with it. But you did in the end, didn't you, eh?'

The man looked alarmed, bewildered. His face twisted as he pushed it into Liam's.

'You *are* the crazy man, you're *stupido,* you know nothing about anything. Get off my building. *Andare!'*

Liam was never quite sure whether he had pushed back at Piero Ronzi and had made physical contact with him. But it was unfortunate that the building's chief janitor and general handyman had, that morning, argued with his wife. It was, as so often with them, over a relative triviality. Again she had bought plain yoghurt when she knew he liked cherry-flavoured. He'd asked her why. She'd told him that if he wanted to do the shopping then he should go ahead and do so. Feeling annoyed and, allied with the indisputable fact that Tottenham had lost an evening match the day before, to which he'd been, it became frustration.

Whatever the emotion, and however it was defined, he felt little different when two hours afterwards he was fixing a section of the top rail of the upper balcony his building that had, he'd been informed, come out of its socket again. He tightened the appropriate screws hurriedly and impatiently, knowing as he walked away that he should have checked just how firmly the rail supporting the curved glass was seated in its socket.

Liam had watched Ronzi fall, coat splaying, billowing out from him like a cloak. Simaltaneously, a tiny, deflective part of him - the surreal hyperbole of escape - saw it as almost aesthetically pleasing and wondered if there was a large puddle down there where Mister Ronzi could see his reflection, and before he became it, perhaps have time to admire it.

In the brief vacuum of detachment he wished he'd known exactly how far from the ground the balcony was and had a stopwatch with him so he could  calculate precisely how long it would have taken him, at 32 feet per second per second, to arrive at the ground.

There was a lack of sound: the building was silent, the city was silent; the air was silent, as was the burning sky.

Talking to the police twenty minutes afterwards was an emotional kaleidoscope of guilt, justified or otherwise, a numbing shock along with a sense of disbelief, and a hollow feeling of regret.

Mary had been incredulous when he'd told her, he guessing that she was silently shouting to herself that there was, indeed, a God. He wasn't sure. Perhaps he was doing her a disservice.

She talked to him comfortingly about fate for days afterwards. He didn't bother to intellectualise the concept; it had no relevance for him.

He took two days off work then before returning decided to go to a tanning salon, not really for a tan he told himself, but to cover up, detract from the pale face, the lines around the mouth. He'd never been to one before. He went in.

'Waddya want, lie-down or stand-up, babe?' asked a walnut-coloured peroxide blonde.

Through a partially open door he could see a horizontal, glass-walled sarcophagus and felt a pre-claustrophobic apprehension. He went for the alternative.

Ten minutes was too long. He left, feeling like a baked piece of meat and, arriving home and looking in a mirror and realising he looked like one, decided it was all the remnants of his own adolescent narcissism. It was narcissism in the face of mortality, the equation being that if he looked fit and tanned then he wouldn't age, ergo, wouldn't die. It was a subject he'd never studied: the psychology of death.

# EPILOGUE

The verdict of Accidental Death was confirmed quite soon after Piero Ronzi's demise. Liam Brett told the truth at the official inquest, though omitted mentioning his uncertainty about the final seconds before the fall.

There was, perhaps inevitably, short-lived speculation in the media that because it was the designer's own building it may, ironically, have been suicide. (There were rumours at the Daily Star newspaper that Ronzi had been the architect of a high-rise residential block in North Kensington that had caught fire resulting in more than eighty fatalities. Their headline article of 'Inferno Architect's Death Fall' was withdrawn before publication). A minority verdict found the caretaker was not to blame.

Various people were upset and saddened by the architect's passing, among them his colleague and friend Lance, as well as Tommy and Henry who had been with him in Chicago.

David Tern, narrowly winning the election for Illinois' Governor and increasingly adamant that he wished to run for the Presidency one day, was determined to show how upset he was by attending the Catholic burial that had been arranged for Ronzi in Dubai by Sheik Hamad bin Rashid assisted by Sheik Addulazaaz. He had intended to go to that city soon, anyway, to invest in some real estate; he also wanted another 'Tern' tower. It was a pity about Piero, but there were other architects.

The cremation in St. Mary's Church - said to be the world's largest parish - was a bizarre affair, with guests in kandura, gutha and the occasional burqa; as in Islam, Asian religions and Judaism, there is a belief in death as a transition to a more glorious place. The unthinking equation for the two sheiks had been 'Italian equals Catholic' and they had wanted to honour him. His ashes were scattered at the foot of The Zenith.

The incident affected Liam more than Mary had expected it to. He became depressed. It was almost a constant, there were no manic depressive mood swings - she would rather have had those - just the silence as he spoke less and less to her. She tried to get him to go out to the cinema, a pub, or resume their London walks again. He wouldn't.

He continued working for a while then stopped. He rarely touched her. Living together was no longer mentioned. She became impatient. Soon after they parted, Mary met a divorced Italian café owner and married. Liam bizarrely, and perhaps seeking some sort of hopeless revenge, signed up for a course in architecture. The maths wasn't there, nor, he realised rather late, was the creativity; the well-documented link between depression and the creative urge seemed to be absent.

Jim and Con Salmon no longer visit the capital. The former eventually wrote his play, entering it in a competition run by a large housing developer in Manchester. He didn't receive a reply.

Lance stayed in Dubai, his engineering firm now on the way to becoming one of the biggest in the UAE. He converted to Islam and recently married a Muslim woman.

Clive Jelien is still trying to understand, and meddle in, the arbitrary mess of compromise between an encultured self and an instinctual one in the egoistic battle between superego and id, whilst trying consciously not to play God.

Russell continues living at the Green Park apartments where he has now been made official janitor, though, just for the theatricality of it, occasionally tries to conjure some petty cash on public transport.

Betty Begombe lives in Kampala with her old boy friend, while Beryl has now had over a hundred poems published. Bill Bunden did appear on TV, just the once, in a stand-up comedy show. Bethaan recently died from malaria.

Returning to his subcontracting work, Liam now attempts to battle his melancholy by attending as many protest meetings against proposed tower developments as he can. There were, he knew, four hundred and forty planned high-rises in London currently awaiting planning permission. Judging by the record of its two previous mayors, he was also aware that the overwhelming majority would be granted it.

#0417 - 301017 - C0 - 229/152/16 - PB - DID2008003